# Faraday's Popcorn Factory

# Faraday's Popcorn Factory

## Sandra Lee Gould

St. Martin's Press

New York

*Design by Jennifer Ann Daddio*

ISBN 0-312-18578-2

*Dedicated*
*to those who love*
*and*
*to those who heal*

*And we all got out alive, did we not, my love?*

*We all survived.*

— CLEMENT

# Faraday's Popcorn Factory

# 1

## Willow

## Wednesday, December 27, 1978

## Moon: Balsamic

I pulled the pink chenille robe from Mrs. Faraday tighter and snuggled my toes into the thick yellow slippers from Amos Akkadian. Ruby's house was still quiet. As I scuffed down the dark hallway, I could smell the Christmas tree, sugar cookies, gingerbread and steam shushing through the radiators.

The streetlight glowed through my front window. Leaning near the glass, I saw that a thick snow had fallen. I yawned and wiped away the misty circle my breath made. My eyes got big as I gazed at how the roofs, window ledges, tree limbs, even the telephone wires on Evergreen Way, they all seemed coated in crystal and marshmallow cream.

I shut my eyes. I let the good feelings from my first truly happy Christmas in ten years tingle through me. I looked up and saw foamy black clouds opening. Pale oranges, yellows and blues shone through. Dawn looked like a magical shore along a dream ocean that stretched out into space.

Suddenly, brilliant streamers sparkled across the sky. They were blue like the Calliope River on a sunny day. They flashed above and through and then below the clouds. Just as quick as the lights appeared, they were gone. I rubbed my eyes and searched for more. I wished that I could fly like that. Glittering.

# 2

# Clement

## Wednesday, December 27, 1978

## Moon: Balsamic

I'd left so long ago that in Earth's precession of the spring equinoxes, our Sun then crossed the equator at Aries' western end. Earth had experienced a brief and slight cooling. Tsunamis plagued the Lebanon coasts. Volcanoes had erupted everywhere from Tongariro and Ngauruhoe in New Zealand to Krafla in Iceland, Fuji in Japan, Monte Albano in Italy, Ranier in North America and Pelee in the West Indies. Outbound, I'd passed the jet-black and ten-mile-wide Halley's Comet at aphelion. Light had just burst from the star Naos in the ancient constellation Argo. Although I'd traveled through asteroid fields and busy meteor swarms, most of the time, I'd sailed through sparkling solitude. Centuries passed without a meaningful encounter. And despite promising myself never to return, there I was, nearly home again.

Riding waves that swelled and rolled, I wondered what could pull from that far. The suction was like supernovas whose remnants had drawn so far back, they not only disappeared into themselves, they sucked in everything within their long reaches. Light could not fly fast enough to escape.

Nearing the Kuiper Belt, I could finally feel my Sun. Unlike the more spectacular stars that blazed bright and blew out quickly, I admired how my small, yellow Sun burned steadily, even if modestly, and would sustain its little solar family for billions of years. Quickly, I crossed the orbits of Pluto, deep-sea-blue Neptune and then Uranus. I felt welcomed by the honey-gold Saturn with the most glorious belts and the garnet-and-pearl Jupiter. After passing the asteroid fields, strengthening solar winds helped slow my approach. When I could finally see Earth, I realized perihelion was near. At a bit beyond one hundred forty-seven million kilometers, home would be closest to its star.

As a thin rim of scarlet and diamond white arced over Earth, dawn split the sparkling black. Earth's soft and shifting wrapper looked like a glistening veneer. Emerging from boundless and sparkling dark, the outermost edges were gossamer.

Above a billowing thunderstorm, I watched red and blue flashes shoot toward space and flare over hundreds of miles. Getting closer, the clouds were like frames opening sometimes broad and sometimes pinhole views of my variously more solid Earth. I loved reexperiencing the grace, power and pride I'd always felt in Mother's vapor ships.

In childhood, I'd loved riding the jet streams, skimming the cloud tops and zooming through sunlit chasms. Depending on Mother's mood, I'd either be looking for or running from her thunder ships, where the up- and downdrafts really surged and ice crystals tickled as they pinged, popped and bloomed into raindrops and hail.

When ocean currents, air patterns and heat were just right, I especially liked sneaking near Mother's merging squall lines and supercells. Fearing that I'd either be smashed or blasted apart, Mother strictly forbid funnel rides. Though her punishments could be severe (sometimes I couldn't visit Grandmother Beah), I occasionally risked a tornado plunge. I'd let the vortex snatch and swirl me down until I dropped from the cloud bases. Screaming, I'd plummet toward an Earth that was wet, wide open and nowhere near as developed as the towering structures, huge bridges, paved roadways and flying apparatus that had been invented while I was gone.

I was amazed to find so many man-made lights visible at such great distances. As night's indigo lace slipped from a cluster of large, icy lakes, I decided to explore buildings beside a river. Many produced their own clouds. One larger construction gushed voluptuous columns. Getting closer, I found the emissions repugnant, which was odd because on other worlds, sulfurous gases had delighted.

Pale golds glowed through mists that grazed the gray-white landscape like sheep. I sailed just above the river, then paused by an old stone wall. I listened and let the water's song soothe worries about the family issues that had forced me to leave millennia ago. I let the ruby and platinum sky absorb fears about the monster that chased me. If, across the light years, The Afreete did get near Earth, by that time I planned to backtrack and pull Its horrors away.

Looking up, distant Uranus traveled with pastel yellow Venus, which had risen like the Moon at last quarter. Jupiter shone high in the sky. Saturn glowed in the southern part of Leo with Pluto even lower. Closest to the rising Sun, hot, little pink Mercury twinkled as Neptune neared conjunction. I watched, feeling bedazzled and joyful as, one by one, those star worlds flickered and disappeared.

When all were gone, I drifted up a crooked, cobblestone byway, floating just above the cottony snow. Ice-coated oak and elm trees extended their branches over habitats built shoulder-to-shoulder, straight up. Icicles crowded the eaves, downspouts and ledges. Strings of garnet, pearl, turquoise and emerald lights blinked inside frosted windows. Then I saw an extraordinary tree. Its thick graceful limbs rose from a trunk patterned in flax and soft browns. The distant branch tips were as tall as the buildings and dangled small, ice-brightened seed spheres.

I was so intrigued that a female child surprised me. How had I missed hearing her footsteps in the crusty snow or the rustling as she pulled newspapers from her canvas sack and thumped them into doorways? Snow flecked her pink and yellow cap, her eyelashes and her brown cheeks. Her bright black eyes looked up, as though at my face, and she smiled. I felt so warmed, I could have melted. I could have grown as large and effulgent as one of the biggest stars. After all, my kind had been human once. And human remained the easiest and, for many of us, the preferred physical form.

I stood in front of a house clearly long abandoned. I was hoping for more human contact when an adult female exited the building across the street. Her shoulders were back. Her head high. Her gait was brisk. Snow fluffed up and swirled around her.

Bundled in burgundy and gray, her assertive posture captivated me. When she coughed, spearmint vapors puffed from her mouth. Maneuvering to see her face, I discovered lustrous and decidedly vigilant eyes. That's when I knew I must meet her. I must take some form, even though briefly.

After a few steps, the woman glanced back. I froze, mortified that she might actually see me. She merely frowned, shook her head and moved on.

I hung in the air, replaying her glance one million times. An eon compressed into one second as my developing heart thumped larger and larger.

# 3

# Willow

## Saturday, February 3, 1979

## Moon: First Quarter

In April 1969, during a bad rainstorm, Daddy and Momma's car slid into a ravine. Probably if Daddy hadn't been handy, that rusted-out Cadillac wouldn't have been on the road. Sections had been welded and bolted with sheet metal. Windows were cracked. Springs came through the seats. The state trooper said that Momma and Daddy died before the ambulance came. They had no insurance.

Our place back in Creame, Ohio, was rented. We never locked the doors. We had a windmill that pumped well water and a picnic table in the kitchen. Momma made curtains out of old sheets. She even hung one in the outhouse. And Momma braided strips cut from old clothes into rugs.

We had a fireplace, an old woodstove and grates in the first-floor ceilings to let the heat rise. The sofa and two chairs in our living room were old and heavy. They had nubby, dark green fabric and were stuffed real thick. Until I was eleven, we had no electricity. We used kerosene lamps.

We had a porch bordered with tall hedges. Out front were some evergreens that Momma and Daddy planted. There was a rope swing with a slightly tilted wood seat that Momma said was hanging from the old elm when we moved in. When we were little, Otto Melkpath, Terry Allister and I played there a lot.

After my parents were buried, all I carried out of our home was some pictures, Daddy's pool stick, a quilt, a thimble, Momma's emerald earrings and some clothes. Whatever fit in two suitcases and a bag, I carried to Homestead where I lived with my grandmother Lucille. Until then, I had only known Creame, Ohio's wide blue skies and flat land. After growing up with smells like dew on corn silk, plowed earth after rain, lilacs just before summer and Momma's butternut pies, how was I supposed to accept Homestead's smoke? I gagged on fumes from more cars and buses and trucks than I could count.

In Creame, Ohio, I had hens clucking and bees buzzing and cricket songs. So how could I handle hundreds of voices rising from Homestead's side streets? What could I do with the boomings inside dirty gray buildings that seemed as high and long as mountain ridges? How could I settle down with people who lived life so different? When I got my heart broken there, I caught the Greyhound to my only other known relative, Aunt True in Akron. Didn't know I was heading for more sadness.

The MileMaster Train and Bus Depot in Good Sky, Ohio, was a one-story, dark brown building with a pitched tan roof and dormers. The gutters and downspouts were the same bright red as the platform. Huge lanterns hung beside the doors. Inside, colored prints of locomotives and diesel engines hung beside old-time photos of buses with drivers smiling by the doors. A dark wood pedestal with a silvery ball about a foot in diameter stood in the middle of the station and reflected the room and skylight, which was stained glass stars forming a railroad track to a smiling moon.

When I came out of the MileMaster during that passenger and mail stop, I smelled popcorn. I wanted it even more than the pizza that was right next door. After passing the Elm Bowling Lanes, Hampton Plumbing and May Belle's Antiques & Collectibles that hot afternoon, I knew the bus would leave in twenty minutes. But the air under the maple trees looked green like Momma's earrings. Marigolds were everywhere. They bobbed in the grasses along the railroad tracks and grew in windowboxes and wooden tubs down the main street. The town's red and yellow brick buildings had leaded glass doors that sparkled. They made me feel hugged. Like Momma and Daddy were near. Most of the shop windows were pictures made of colored glasses just like the MileMaster's skylight, and I felt like Frau Edda was peeking through those scenes of flower gardens, sailing ships, birds flying over mountains and the windows showing what was in the stores, like stained glass cupcakes and pies, stained glass shoes and stained glass books.

Passing the little war memorial with red and white petunias growing around the bronze soldier statue and Goldberg's Jewelry and Watch Repair, Chang's Tea Garden and the Big Star Picture Show, most of the people sitting on the redwood and wrought iron benches looked up from their newspapers, books and baby strollers and smiled.

I couldn't resist the fudge and chocolate smells at Singer's Confectionery & Ice Cream. When I opened the door, tin ornaments clinked overhead. Jelly beans and jujubes, gumdrops and butter mints, the yellow and pink, purple, orange and green candies glowed like jewels around folks sipping root beer and orange soda floats.

Standing just beyond the white, wrought-iron tables covered with candy-striped cloths was Ruby Graham. She was creamy brown like Sugar Babies and her brown hair had red highlights. Ruby was stocky, with gold-flecked, brown eyes and stood a couple inches taller than me.

Rose Singer was a perky, little woman with a crisp, white apron over her flowery dress. Her auburn-tinted hair arched in pouffy, starch-stiff curls. With thick, blue eyeshadow over piercing brown eyes, she said to Ruby, "Why don't you put cards in shops and in the church bulletins? Run an ad in the *Gazette*?"

I gazed at the fancy, old-fashioned cash register. Swedish ivy hung in front of the windows. Cuckoo clocks ticked on the walls as Ruby said, "That's a good idea, Rose, but kind of slow. I'd sure like to get a new boarder settled in before I start traveling."

"Don't worry," Rose Singer said. "Everyone knows how lucky someone would be to get rooms so reasonable, especially with such good cooking. Word will spread fast."

Even though little bells had rung when I came in, they both looked up then as though surprised to see me. I said, "I'd like to get some popcorn."

"Oh, you want Faraday's," Rose Singer said. "It's just up the street. Redbrick building with a big sign."

"Thank you."

"You can't miss it," Ruby added.

I thanked them again.

"Such a nice girl," Ruby said.

"Yes," Rose smiled. "You must come back sometime. Here." She put pink and yellow bonbons in a white paper bag and said, "Free samples."

I knew I had to hurry. After all, Aunt True or my cousins Eddie and Jeffie would be waiting. But the farther I went, the lighter my heart got. I felt relaxed like the rest of those people sitting in front of Watson's Bakery, the Good Sky Bank and Trust and Schwartz's Flowers with the buckets of carnations, dahlias, hollyhocks and daisies.

After I passed Morton's Lumber & Hardware, Akkadian's Junkyard and the Longacre Grain Distributor, there, right across from Crawford Custom & Commercial Draperies, I found the big, golden-lettered, carnival-type sign that said, FARADAY'S POPCORN FACTORY, REFRESHMENTS & SUPPLIES BY THE BAG OR BOXCAR.

Mrs. Faraday was as round as the laughing Buddha statue I could see inside the doorway. Her black hair with white strands was cut even at ear level, and her skin glowed. She was a little taller than me. Laugh lines crinkled around her eyes. Mrs. Faraday must have been leaving and started when she saw me. She smiled quickly and bright, then bowed a little and said, "*Nǐ hǎo*. Welcome to my shop, pretty girl. How can I help you?"

"I came for—"

"Oh, I see. Well, you're the first one to apply. Amazing you heard about it so fast. We can't pay much, of course, but the job's easy, and it's a nice place to work. Usually my manager handles the hiring, but he's off on an errand so come in, young lady. Friends call me Mei-Yeh. You look like you're new to Good Sky. Tell me about yourself."

Mei-Yeh led me between tall shelves with tubs and boxes for popcorn, cups, straws, napkins and candies. When she noticed me watching her limp, she pouted playfully and said, "Darned stubbed toe. Now I feel storms two days before."

Mei-Yeh served me tea and fortune cookies in her cozy office filled with ferns, bamboo, spider plants and all kinds of glass and jade and ebony laughing Buddha statues and playful dragons. As she moved, I smelled her lilac dusting powder. Crystal suncatchers hung from lamps and by the window. Red and green tomatoes caught sunlight on the window ledge. She even let me call long-distance and ask Aunt True to send back my luggage.

Frank Singer, Rose's husband, showed me how to start the coconut oil melting on an old gas hot plate. Then he helped me roll in buckets of raw seed from sacks in the storage room. After that, we got the measuring cups. They were whopping, quart-size versions of the tin ones Momma used with dents for the ounces and quarter cups.

Hard to believe that for ten years I'd got up, walked down Evergreen Way and strolled past the Calliope River, no matter what the weather. Then I'd head past Birch Street and Laurel and turn on Pine to get to Faraday's. After I climbed the loading dock steps, opened the wooden door with a big window and passed the cartons of paper cups and napkins, tubs for popcorn and boxes of Tootsie Rolls, Now and Laters, Bit-O'-Honeys, Milky Ways, Mars bars and penny candies, I turned and opened the door to the popping room. It wasn't much wider than Ruby's kitchen but a couple times longer.

Running down the middle of the room were the stoves and other contraptions that popped and sorted the corn. Once the seeds and oil were in place, I felt like a symphony conductor ready to start the orchestra. I'd walk to the first burner and tilt up its kettle, which was the size and shape of Momma's hat box. Then I'd turn on the gas and strike a match. After a sky-blue ring of flames snapped up, I lit the next one. When all five fires were started, I'd lower the kettles, pour in an eighth cup of salt and seasonings, usually butter flavored, and a quart of popcorn seeds.

The morning I was to start by myself, Mrs. Faraday came in. Bright purple silk embroidered with frolicking yellow dragons rolled over her plump body. After the oil and buckets of corn were rolled out and everything was just right, Mei-Yeh scooped up a handful of kernels. As her black eyes sparkled, she said, "Believe it or not, sweet child, there's a science to all of this. It's been found that corn is best when dried to appoximately fourteen percent moisture. With more than that, the corn pops chewier and smaller until nothing happens. Going the other way, as the seeds get drier, they don't have enough moisture to expand the starches and get themselves out of the shell. Sometimes, the heat helps them crack it open, but they can't bloom."

Mrs. Faraday pressed one kernel real hard. "But the key to all of this working is the shell. It's got to contain all the heat and pressure that'll build inside and then break at the right moment. If all goes well, this dead-looking little thing bursts into something new and, if we've done our work right, it's at least forty times bigger." Mrs. Faraday paused as though she wanted to say more. Eyes sparkling, she shrugged her shoulders, then poured the kernels back in the bucket. "I think there's a lesson in that stuff. My husband, he would have had wonderful words for it. Until he died about five years ago, he had the sweet shop." Mrs. Faraday's face brightened even more. "You'll find me there a lot."

Maybe there was a lesson in the popcorn. I knew that the kernels weren't hand picked—and certainly never machine harvested—until the stalks were withered, and the corn was so hard the kernels couldn't be dented, not even with a fingernail. And I knew that after adding a cup of oil, the corn popped in a minute and gushed itself out of each pot's little latch door.

From there, a conveyor belt tumbled the snowy puffs into a big barrel strainer. It rolled like a Ferris wheel, sifting the unpopped kernels and shells into a tub underneath. The corn that popped big enough bounced into huge yellow plastic bags. When the bags got full, I twirled them and twisted a little band around the top.

As Mei-Yeh said, it was easy enough work. Sometimes I felt like a clock pendulum walking back and forth filling the kettles. Overflows were embarrassing, especially because I had to mark how much seed, oil and salt I used and how many bags got filled. But sometimes I did get distracted or daydreamed.

After a few years, the popping room was remodeled and got a miniature escalator that lifted the corn into a hopper with a trapdoor. That way, I could accumulate a lot more before bagging. When I had help, especially during school breaks and over the summer, I could do fifty or sixty bags in an hour.

Around lunchtime, I'd scrub the kettles mirror bright, sweep the wood floor that was covered with flowery linoleum and wipe everything. Then I'd help in the office until time to go home.

I was glad I stayed in Good Sky. There were so many who helped, like May Belle. I don't think anyone knew her last name, just like no one was sure where she went every spring. May Belle always kept her travels to find new old merchandise a secret. May Belle's skin was brown like a fawn. Her voice was light. She had the bubbliest laugh and the warmest eyes. Even in winter, May Belle wore pastel pinks and yellows and flouncy, bright green skirts.

Silvery bells tinkled above May Belle's door. Small, Persian carpets padded her polished, light pine floor. She had plain and fancy-carved wood tables, some so small, a dinner plate barely fit. Others were big as my bed. She had paperweights, jewelry boxes, saltcellars, little ornate picture frames and lovely lamps on beautiful, Oriental-print runners. While lots of the stuff in May Belle's Antiques & Collectibles moved real fast, there was a chess set that stayed. It had creamy tan and black marble squares and a jade border set in a mahogany frame. The silver and gold pieces were mounted on thin slices of jade over mahogany bases. They looked like Africans in flowing robes and wraps. The pawns all had drums of different types. The bishops wore turbans.

Just like I'd ask about the Japanese, Mexican and Indian dolls and the rose crystal glasses and the amethyst vases, all of which eventually sold, May Belle said, "The one who will receive this has not yet inquired." Her playful eyes winked.

Over the years, while I waited to see just who that might be, the oak and elm trees on Evergreen Way kept rumpling the redbrick sidewalks. Each of the four cobblestone blocks curved a bit, so Evergreen Way zigzagged from Cedar Avenue to the Calliope. That gave the street a kind of mystery. I didn't know what to expect beyond the next bend.

My rooms were on Ruby's second floor. All opened onto the hall. My kitchen was in front. My bath was in the middle. My bedroom overlooked Ruby's bricked yard. There, she had a small garden for collard greens, mustards, tomatoes and hot peppers along the pine wood fence. On the other side was the Watsons' yard. They ran the bakery. Looking southwest, there were hundreds of clustered housetops, the Birch Street Elementary School and Laurel Street Methodist Church steeple. Then there was flat land, the curl of the Calliope River and Crane Island. Beyond all that was the world.

Most nights, I watched television with Ruby and Amos. Ruby especially liked "Laverne and Shirley" and "Soap." Amos never missed "Happy Days" and "All in the Family," although he wasn't too happy when the woman who played Edith left the show. I liked "Three's Company," and all of us gathered for "Mork and Mindy." After that, up in my room, I'd read the *Good Sky Gazette* or one of those Victoria Holt or Mary Stewart romance books.

Sunday evenings, sometimes I'd go to Ruby's quilt group at Corinthian Baptist Church. It was white wood with a brown roof. There were windows of stained glass squares beside the arched doorway and a little tower with a bell that Pastor Martin rang on Sunday mornings. I liked how Corinthian Baptist always smelled like bayberries. I liked the church's dark red carpet, the bright oak, the raised altar with the lush green (even though plastic) ferns, the purple altar cloths with crosses like gold mirrors and the small choir stand with the red slipcovers and cushions that The Flying Needles made for the chairs.

Tuesdays, I usually went with Ruby and Amos or Mei-Yeh to the Applegate Mall. One Saturday a month, I caught the Greyhound to Aunt True's and gambled nickels at Po-Ke-No. Thursdays, I put away books at the library. It was a two-story, brown brick building with juniper hedges along the walls, terra-cotta roof tiles and leaded glass windows that made rainbows on the cherrywood tables and tall book shelves. I'd stamp library cards, do some filing and alphabetize things in the card catalogue. Mainly, I worked in the children's room.

I liked picking books for tabletop displays, especially around Christmas, Easter and Black History Month. I liked cutting the turkey, teddy bear, umbrella and snowflake activity announcements that were photocopied on bright-colored paper. I also cut out paper favors, little crowns or feathers or moons and stars, things the children could wear during the stories. Sometimes I'd show cartoons, but mostly I read to the children and watched them grow up. That's where I first really noticed Clement.

# 4

## Clement

## Thursday, February 22, 1979

## Moon: Last Quarter

An atom was a very small thing. Quite a few million play on a pin's head. And the nucleic center, the protons and neutrons, were one hundred thousand times smaller than their electron shells. So between the proton and neutron core and the electron cover was vast space, rather like marbles centered in a large stadium. Thus, anything built from atoms, anything that could be called matter, magnolia trees, roosters, rivers, human beings, these things were essentially and spectacularly nothing.

My earliest tactile sensations were of fission. As atomic particles coalesced, molecules grew and developing cells jelled. Varying with the entity being structured, I generally saw a cacophony of brilliant colors. Becoming human, I tasted salt but smelled cardamom and heard a sound like blossoms rustling. After my mass was generated, I could rest. I just dreamed and let my Self transform.

Shifting moods and curiosities sometimes required that I again be physically unhindered. When I wanted to be my ethereal Self, I merely shed or dissolved the carnal form. That didn't take long. And subsequent resumptions always got quicker.

I began each new manifestation with an inventory. When I checked my freshly human fluid levels, motor and fuel capacity, minerals, salts, surface integrity, defensive systems, hemoglobin, serotonin, bone structure and phenylethylamine, all were adequate. It was odd seeing by reflection again. So many other senses were either crimped or missing.

I'd nearly forgotten what a charge the hormonal and enzyme activity was and how awareness skittered on little electric impulses. I marveled at how complicated, time consuming and distracting functioning inside a small universe was. But I adjusted. I always did.

Wearing clothes was peculiar. I wondered how humans tolerated those constricting and cumbersome addendums, especially when building up layers sufficient to ward off cold. Sometimes so much got piled on that I scarcely recognized myself when it all, piece by piece, came off.

In taking human form, I most easily assumed Father's regal height. I had a long and graceful stride that must have been Father's when he was young. From Mother, I inherited creamy skin and black, catlike eyes. The textured hair was a mix from both parents.

At first, I just listened and watched. As people smiled and said things like "Good morning" and "Nice weather, isn't it?" I learned and interacted more boldly. The two most encouraging people, in fact the two who suggested that I came from overseas, were named Ruby Graham and Mei-Yeh Faraday. I often encountered them at the Five and Dime, the bakery, at Gerelli's Fruit & Vegetable and, of course, the sweet shop. They also told me about the library.

I started with picture books and worked my way up through children, preteen, adolescent and finally adult. Reading so enlightened and fascinated me, as with books by Gwendolyn Brooks, Alexander Dumas, Emile Zola, that I often expedited the process, as I did one Thursday when I arrived at the library just ahead of Willow. I started *A Tale of Two Cities* the human way.

*It was the best of times, it was the worst of times. . . .*

Wanting to finish quickly, I moved to an isolated area, picked up the book again at 5:56:32 and, although the process literally took days, I reached,

*It is a far, far better thing that I do, than I have ever done; it is a far, far better rest that I go to, than I have ever known.*

at 5:57:08. Of course, there was the middle section that slowed me. The part about a world's "greatnesses and littlenesses" lying in a star . . .

*And as mere human knowledge can split a ray of light and analyse the manner of its composition, so sublimer intelligences may read in the feeble shining of this Earth of ours, every thought and act, every vice and virtue, of every responsible creature on it.*

Had Mr. Dickens somehow known Father? When I was last on Earth, humans had redeveloped civilizations on all of the habitable continents. Back then, they bickered and had diseases, crime and poverty. But while humans continued damaging everything, including themselves, they had also advanced their artistry and ability to heal. Best of all, the wonderful memorials built into the stars survived. Most of the constellations had hardly changed. I spent whole nights staring into skies and replaying the stories.

How exhilarating to think of Orion, so tall he could walk across the sea floors with his head above the water. Orion, lover of a goddess, who as hero and victim shone so brightly. He whose constellation's rising at different hours heralded the changing seasons. Whose enemy, the Scorpion, would forever chase him across the heavens. Why, I wondered, did the warrior flee rather than attack?

And to think that humans developed calculations like Hubble's Constant suggesting that the universe's billions of starships spread away from Earth at one hundred or so kilometers per second per million parsecs. What an astounding notion. Especially in that parsecs measured interstellar space by figuring the distance from Earth at which stellar parallax was one second of arc or one hundred ninety-one trillion, eight hundred billion miles, or how far light beams traveled in three and one quarter Earth years. Which only served to remind that light was always moving. Even if only a few feet in some part of a second. Which also meant that physical observation could never be concurrent with the event.

Thus, watching Willow's lips as she spoke would always be nanoseconds after the word formed. I wondered if a simultaneously generated and received experience was possible. Especially because Willow diverted, bent and ricocheted light around herself. She didn't even know. No one did. Just me.

I'd felt the energy that first morning. There was a glow in how Willow's fingers lifted her hood and the spirit with which she braved the sharp winds. Willow was only chest high to me. The first blush of youth had already visited, leaving a strength of character suggested mostly by her posture. Willow's skin reminded me of dark sands when moonlit. And there was her alluring mouth, so full and pillowy. Finally, seeing Willow from my window and at the library just wasn't enough.

Still, I had to leave. The Afreete's obsessive pursuit made confrontation inevitable. When It attacked me again, I'd need a place where timing and space were much more elastic because perceiving its pounce at light speed would be far too slow. Worse, if that fearsome thing found this world, It would destroy more than me. Knowing It like I did, I doubted that Mother or Auntie Carmelita or even Uncle Winter and the rest of Grandmother Beah's brood could subdue It. Which left the decidedly unanswerable question of what I would be able to do. But I had time. I had space. That's what I thought. And after celebrating New Year's Eve, I did want to experience more such festivities.

Granny Mei-Yeh (that's what my heart called her) tried to help. One blustery afternoon, I found her inside the sweet shop where the decor then included red and pink heart-shaped lollipops and cinnamon heart-filled tubes topped with red heart propellers, foil windmills and flags. Mrs. Singer had gone into her storage room to get more red heart gift boxes. As Granny Mei-Yeh stood beside the magnificent brass scale, a shining construction with a removable bowl on one arm and on the other a fan-shaped brass case with a glass window enclosing the wand for indicating weight, as I inhaled chocolate, taffy and licorice aromas, I described how I'd tried smiling at Willow while shoveling snow and sweeping my sidewalk. Shoveling was a vexing nuisance. Sweeping I rather liked. At any rate, I'd waved and called out pleasant greetings. At the library, I'd been as gracious as possible. Nothing I did held Willow's attention.

Following Granny Mei-Yeh's advice, I put a rose in Willow's mailbox before sunrise on February 14. With it was a fragrant parchment on which I'd written,

*For the lovely young woman*
*Who lives cross the way,*
*I hope for the chance*
*To meet you someday.*
      *Your neighbor,*
      *Clement*

I watched from my window scarcely breathing as Willow discovered the rose. My heart pounded as she read the note. Then Willow moved out onto the stoop and into the feeble sunlight where she crumpled the paper and stared—no, she actually glared—at my window.

Instantly, sweat coated me. All blood plummeted to my feet. My brain spun like a pulsar. It took days before I left the house and then considerable prompting from Granny Mei-Yeh before I dared approach Willow again.

*"Bú yaô pà,"* she said after catching me slumping along Cedar Avenue. "Don't be afraid. Try again." Finally, I constructed enough new backbone to put a little box wrapped with buttercup patterns and tied with a gold and yellow ribbon beside Willow's morning paper. Granny Mei-Yeh assured me that inside were Willow's favorites, brightly colored and minted gumballs. I wrote,

> *Lovely and good neighbor,*
> *Let me dine with you one evening,*
> *Just to enjoy your smile.*
> *I'll bring my own fresh baked bread,*
> *And wine. We'll dine in style.*
> *Most respectfully,*
> *Clement*

Willow stopped coming and going by the front door.

After a week pacing my creaky floors, doing deep inhalations and exhausting myself with sixteen thousand two hundred ninety-four push-ups, I decided to meet Willow. Not like the brief recognitions we had exchanged on Evergreen Way and at the library. No. I would really speak to Willow.

The appointed morning, snow fell like iridescent ticker tape. Hoots from boats mingled with faint train whistles. Willow yawned as she stepped from Mrs. Graham's back door, a portal where Willow may have noticed the crocus shoots starting up in the snow.

As Willow gazed across Mrs. Graham's iced-over tomato cages, the wilted collard plants and slush, she no doubt questioned why she'd let my small gestures send her along this route. I allowed that Willow did have cause to consider me, well, different. I still had a lot to assimilate.

But surely Willow could tell from the way I greeted everyone—cheerfully but with restraint—that I was a gentleman.

I sneezed lightly so that my form materializing in the mists wouldn't frighten and said, "Good morning."

Willow's thin brows arched gracefully over her brown-black eyes. Falling snow shimmered in her short, natural hair. Willow blinked, pulled up her hood and mumbled, "Morning."

"Yes!" I beamed, "It certainly is!"

Willow coughed, quick and rhapsodic. She measured whether she'd pass easier to my left or right. Before she actually moved, I said, "I'm Clement. I sent the rose. I hope you liked it."

"I, well, yes, it was okay. I never got gift-wrapped gum before."

"'Twas my pleasure." The sun suddenly shone in great circles. The way Willow stamped her booted feet and how her spearmint breath puffed into the air as she said, "Excuse me, I'm on my way to work," left me flushed and bubbly. With perhaps a tad too much joy, I gushed, "Of course you're on your way to work!" Then I paused, cleared my throat and said, "Please permit me to walk with you."

Willow shoved her mittened hands deep into square pockets. She shrugged and trudged toward the sidewalk. Bouncing behind her, I asked if she would tell me her name. Without a word, in fact raising her shoulders like little walls, Willow kept going.

That's when Granny Mei-Yeh glowed in my thoughts. I imagined that plump, red-cheeked woman smiling, nodding, prodding me forward. I heard Granny Mei-Yeh saying, *"Rú Yî."*

We had been in Watson's Bakery when she said, *"Rú Yî* is good luck. For the Chinese, at least as I remember my grandfather showing me, good luck is from two symbols. One means 'as' or 'according to.' The other is for 'whatever you wish.' When combined, the desire is that things will go as you hope or intend. For Chinese, that is Good Luck. *Rú Yî."* Granny Mei-Yeh opened her arms wide, as though awaiting a shower of gold.

I whispered, *"Rú Yî,"* then answered my own question. I said, "Willow. Ah, yes. Those angels of the riverside. What a nice, oh, tone your name has. Rare and special. Magical. Did you know that willow trees can be grown from the smallest branch? Their roots are great for holding the soil together. The tree is thought to be a protector, a healer. Many believe that blessings come through your namesake. Perhaps that's why there was a place once, my Grandmother Beah told me that willows were the only—"

Willow muttered, "What did you say your name was?"

"Clement."

"Well, CLEment, I can—"

"Please, call me CleMENT. Accent the last syllable. That's how my mother named me. It rhymes with 'cement' or 'element.' "

The scent of coconut cream pies saturated the chill air. But so did dank concrete and mud as Willow said, "Well, CleMENT, as I was about to say—"

My heart stopped. Willow was ready to walk past as though I were a twig, sodden tissue or a crushed soda can. "Listen," I whispered and raised my hand.

Willow frowned. She tightened one corner of her lovely mouth and said, "I can go on my own from here. And don't—"

Desperate yet trying to retain some dignity, I said, "No. Please wait. For just one moment. Listen."

Except for patting her boot, Willow did stand still. At first, I'm sure the only sounds Willow noticed were cars and boats, rubbish being dumped, doors closing, a bird, the wind. Then, Willow heard. First, from a drainpipe and the streetlamp. Next from the roof behind the hardware store. Melting snow pattered everywhere. Willow's eyes were as large as Aurigan greder bubbles when she said, "How could it suddenly get so noisy out here?"

"It's spring serving notice on winter!" I inhaled deeply. "Ah, yes, most people think Auntie is quiet and delicately beautiful. They forget how rudely spring begins her season. The vixen throws us off with baby birds and pretty flowers, but first she numbs our eardrums and brains by dripping faucets everywhere."

"What are you saying?"

"What am I saying? Goodness!" Truly appalled at my indiscretion, I sputtered, "I'm just having fun. Please excuse me." I bowed.

"You're strange." With Willow's sharpness softening a degree, a star-blind wonder filled me. I couldn't tell if Willow smirked, but her melodic voice lightened as she said, "I've got to go."

"Do have a wonderful day. And . . . and, if you'll share an evening with me, this evening perhaps, I . . . I'll bake bread and bring wine, a light Beaujolais, or maybe, yes, even better, an effervescent."

Willow blinked, and her perfect oval face went blank.

Easing myself off the hooks of hope and anticipation, I asked, "Is seven o'clock all right?"

## Mother

*In late January, gale-force winds and tornadoes wrecked Florida's Gulf Coast. No lives were lost. That month, Florida recorded twelve twisters in all, and Mother brewed three in California.*

*February was fairly quiet. And I could tell, thanking every good luck charm I knew, that Mother might suspect, but wasn't certain that I'd returned.*

# 5

# Willow

## Thursday, February 22, 1979

## Moon: Last Quarter

Sitting at Ruby's table the evening that tall, thin, nougat-colored—well, maybe more like buttermilk—that Clement man stopped me on my way to work, I stared into the steam rising from my kale and, for a moment, everything got misty. Inside that shimmery fog, seemed like I smelled more than Ruby's greens and ham. There was a sweet incense.

I shook my head. Ruby's kitchen was hot, but I wrapped my arms around me. I remembered Otto Melkpath from back in Creame, Ohio. Otto was big boned, sturdy built and blond like his father. He had a round face like Frau Edda's and her gray eyes. Otto read more than Terry and me put together and was the dreamer, the thoughtful one in our trio. Otto loved tending cats and dogs, cows and horses. Even onery animals were calmed when Otto talked quiet and careful. When he touched gentle but purposeful.

And I'd never met anyone with hair as sunset red and eyes as summer blue as Terry's. His skin was milk white. He had freckles all over.

Small and delicate looking as Terry was, he whooped and hollered and ran without looking where he was going along the trails through Blue Meadow until I was amazed Terry didn't break more bones. Out there, we called him Terry the Terror.

Terry's brother Reece and sister Corrine were six and four years older. Then Terry's sister Maureen and brother Cade were just toddling. So age wise and like Otto and me, Terry was in the middle and all by himself.

Thinking of being alone, I remembered how, after Kinshasa, Tyrell Webster and especially Jimmy Anderson, I made up my mind that life ought to be much greener. Life ought to be like pool-table felt. Life ought to let me glide like one of Mr. Porky's billiard balls. That way, I could have a hard, bright veneer and try to roll without bumping . . . without being bumped.

Seemed like part of living was that everybody had sad times. Some more than others. And couldn't much be done about heartbreak and grief and staring out windows for folks who wouldn't come back except being amazed at the ice pieces that started like little crystals sticking and building into chunks around my heart.

Ruby told me once how her Ellington died. How a metal door blew off one of them big mill ovens where they baked coal into coke. And what parts of her Ellington the door didn't crush, the hot coal, two thousand degrees she said, it burned her Ellington. That left Ruby with four children to raise and that house nestled tight between Evergreen Way's other houses.

After her kids moved out, Ruby made her dining room a bedroom. She covered the walls and cherrywood dressers with family pictures. Then Ruby took in boarders and fixed their meals. Usually Amos Akkadian, a neighbor who also owned the junkyard, he came too. I admired how Ruby found ways to be happy and keep her life going. Only in the last year, it finally seemed like my life was rolling, even if the movement was more like a whiffle ball.

As Ruby sliced some ham, I sipped cherry soda and fiddled with threads in her crocheted tablecloth. I heard her chair creak. Then I noticed the biscuit pan inch toward me.

"Have some, sugar," Ruby said.

When I nudged one of the big, fluffy biscuits free, Ruby said, "Mighty cold out, ain't it? Don't look like the weather'll break early this year."

I nodded while buttering the biscuit.

"You keeping warm enough upstairs?"

"I'm fine." I shrugged and glanced at Ruby.

Ruby's lip curled like when she'd find mold on a peach. She eyed me up and down and asked, "Are you sure?"

I looked around the room as though maybe Ruby was talking to someone else. "What do you mean, am I sure?"

"I just couldn't help noticing that rose in your mailbox, sugar. I also saw that cute little gift by the paper. But I ain't seen you going out with no one, and I ain't noticed you having no company in."

My face got hot as the biscuits while Ruby said, "Wouldn't it be nice if you had someone in your life again?"

At first, I couldn't answer for thinking how Ruby was my landlady. She was my best friend. But she wasn't Aunt True, my father's blood sister. And Ruby definitely wasn't "just" Lucille who saw spirits. "Just" Lucille who was my grandmother. So I answered Ruby. I said, "No."


The last guy I dated was Tyrell Webster. Tyrell was the color of plywood, freckled and balding with a nice trimmed beard and stood a bit taller than me. He worked at the post office and read things like *Make a Million in Mail Order, Fast Money in Real Estate* and *Be Rich by Forty.* Tyrell took me to dinner and the Big Star Picture Show a few times. We even went to Aunt True's twice. After Tyrell moved to Denver, I got one letter and one postcard since Thanksgiving 1977. In that Good Sky was a small town, there hadn't been anybody else and, just for one night, I decided not to be too choosy.

When that Clement man did come over, of all things, he had on a tuxedo topcoat with tails. His button-down collar and denim bellbottoms were clean but frayed. Through the opening in his shirt, against his smooth chest, a star, a chess knight and a crescent moon hung from thin, gold chains. Wrapped in a white towel with yellow pinstripes and resting on a chipped, silver-plated dish, he'd brought what smelled like cinnamon bread, and he had champagne.

Clement had a nice enough face. His mouth and nostrils were round. His almond-shaped eyes were bright like a starry night and so black I couldn't see the pupils. His hair made me think of rusted steel wool, and he wore a small diamond earring.

The man strode with surefooted grace, like maybe he'd been a dancer. He set his stuff on my table with such, well, finesse that I'd have thought that bottle and old dish were mother-of-pearl. Then he looked at me with eyes that for some reason seemed innocent as a baby's, and he said with a voice that could have been mellow wine, the kind that set fires in susceptible women, certainly not me, "I'm a bit embarrassed to present myself this way, but one can't stay isolated forever. My circumstances haven't always been this, well, reduced. They're bound to improve soon."

I shrugged.

"I'm fixing up the house across the street."

"You're fixing it up?"

"Indeed. Inside, great transformations are taking place. And it's not easy."

Clement had big, smooth hands and neat fingernails, so I asked, "How long's it going to take?"

"I've discovered that repairing fractured lath and fixing dead toilets is very uninspiring work. I suppose I'll be there until everything's magnificent, unless the landlady gets impatient. One day soon, I'd like to have you visit."

"No rush."

Clement looked around my kitchen and so did I. I liked how the floor was green and white squares. Two years ago, I'd put up white wallpaper that had yellow polka dots and daisies with bright green stems. Curtains with big, splashy pink and yellow flowers hung in the window. A vinyl tablecloth printed with marigolds covered my slightly wobbly table.

It was an old-fashioned kitchen that had been in the house when Ruby and her family moved there. Ruby's children had the third floor, and they used the second-floor kitchen for breakfast. "Guess I ain't the first one to have boarders here," Ruby said when she first showed me the house. "When my family was here, we liked not having to go all the way downstairs in the morning. Reckon of the two kitchens, we always liked this one better."

I reached up in my cupboard for plates and glasses. On top was a shoebox with old chess pieces. A rook and a pawn bounced onto the counter. That Clement man, he picked them up and smiled like they were jewels, saying, "I've been wanting to learn chess."

I handed him a bread knife and said, "Moving the pieces around isn't hard. It's the strategy that's tough."

"Really? Would you teach me?"

"I'd rather not. I mean, not tonight. I've got to . . ."

"How about tomorrow or even the day after?"

I watched Clement slice the bread. Considering how he talked, how every word flowed out so proper, like he was a newscaster, maybe Walter Cronkite or somebody, I didn't think I could stand having him around that much. But some company, even him, at least that'd be a change. And I could eat dinner with Ruby in peace.

When I looked up, Clement gave me a slice and asked, "Would you like to see magic?"

I chewed some bread and said, "You can't do magic."

"Let me amaze you."

He pulled out playing cards and shuffled awkwardly. Next he looked at me, eyes bright, and asked, "Are you comfortable that there's no opportunity here for prearrangement?"

"You could shuffle some more so I'll be sure."

"With pleasure." Clement shuffled again, with a lot more flare and flourish. Then he put eight cards face down and asked, "Did you realize your table wobbles?"

"Yes. I guess I've gotten used to it." For the life of me, though, I didn't remember that table having one leg too short until Jimmy left. So I grumbled. I said, "And while we're on 'did you realizes,' your bread is heavy as—"

"I thought it seemed oversubstantial. I'll do better next time. Now, my dear, please select one card."

I couldn't bear his sly smile. I pored over the cards, swallowed more champagne and tapped one.

"Oh my!" He sat back. "You may possibly have undone me!"

"Yeah?" I grinned and drank more.

"This is going to call for superpowers." Clement's elegant fingers slid my chosen card forward. Then he squinted, rubbed his temples and said, "It is done." He pushed back his sleeves and turned over my card. It was the three of diamonds. After Clement plunked the other seven on top of the deck, shuffled and waved his hand over everything, he said some mumbo jumbo and peeled off the three of clubs, three of spades and three of hearts.

My jaw dropped.

Clement blushed as he asked, "Were you pleased?"

I sauced around for a minute and finally said, "Maybe." And "maybe" seemed real generous because he really was, well, odd. Not odd as in dangerous. Not odd as in nutty. Just odd.

———

A month later, I woke up realizing I'd had ten chess sessions with Clement, and it seemed like they'd never end. I decided to find a way. A frosted branch tapped my window. A cardinal sang outside. I stretched, loving how the sun pushed bright warmth through the glass. After showering and dabbing my face dry and clearing steam from the mirror, I smoothed my eyebrows and hair. Then I had some rose hips tea and raisin toast. By seven-twenty, I had on my flowery cotton panties, no bra, blue jeans, gray sweatshirt and my parka.

When I reached the stoop, Ruby stopped sweeping and grumbled, "This is ridiculous. Who ever heard of lightning storms this time of year? Did all that commotion wake you?" Ruby picked up and examined some twigs, then looked up at the big sycamore and said, "Hope it didn't hurt the trees."

Surprised, I looked at the clear sky and said, "I didn't hear a thing, Ruby." I started softening up a bubblegum ball.

Ruby huffed, "Sugar, I do believe you'd sleep through Judgment Day."

I looked at Ruby's bright red window boxes and said, "Well, your daffodils look nice."

Ruby smiled at her flowers. "I reckon." Then she nodded across Evergreen and said, "Seems like a nice fella."

Clement's gray house with its empty first- and second-floor windows was shoulder to shoulder with the Valdezes' red house with bright green trim and cheerful, cotton print curtains and the Carpenters' yellow brick house with white trim and elegant sweeping sheers. As I glanced toward Clement's tired and lonely-looking building, a tiger-striped cat with white paws darted past his car.

It was a sooty, rusting, noisy little thing. When Clement started it, that turquoise rattletrap sputtered and sparks flew out the tailpipe. It always stalled halfway up Evergreen. Then Clement went through that whole startup racket again. The car only had two seats. Rocket cones stuck from the tarnished bumpers and the round rear lights. The hard top had portholes on each side. The hubcabs were pleated chrome. One grubby whitewall was flat, and I doubted that Clement could fix it.

"If you see him today—"

"I don't plan on it."

"Invite him for Amos' birthday dinner. The boy looks like he could use some good home cooking. And he needs to meet his neighbors proper."

"Ruby, I—"

"You're walking by the river, aren't you, sugar? Ought to be nice down there."

Faraday's Popcorn Factory was ten minutes away, twenty if I strolled along the Calliope. That morning, even though the winds blew down from the Great Lakes, there wasn't the slightest scent of gas from the Calliope River Coke Works. In fact, the air had that fresh, moving-water smell I sometimes wished would clean over the whole world. I waved good-bye to Ruby, blew a pink bubble and headed toward the river.

Along the Calliope, the railings and wrought-iron streetlamps had vines and heart-shaped leaf decorations. Big, gray stones were stacked up from the water. Little rainbows rose through mists. Underneath, the Calliope sparkled out where barges channeled through the ice.

I watched a dried leaf fall. It twirled, seeming to struggle skyward. The wind, as though offended, slammed the leaf into the railing, then tumbled it onto the Calliope's ice. The leaf somersaulted until a tip got stuck in slush. I watched the water build shining layers over the leaf until its brownness disappeared into the black depths. My heart sank with it.

From far across the Calliope River, I heard the faint whiz of cars and diesel trucks. A robin flew overhead. It chirped. Two mallards waddled by the railings. One splatted on the ground and then waggled its tail. A goose splashed and settled elegantly on the river. When I turned toward Birch Street, I saw Clement. He leaned on the railing and stared out over the water. When I walked up to him, he jumped. Clement's skin was pale. Crow's-feet hung under his eyes. Yet he looked so glad to see me, all I could think to say was, "Your car has a flat tire."

Clement blurted, "Cabrilla?"

"You named your car?"

"Why certainly." Clement looked over the Calliope. Even in his tiredness, he was graceful. "She rides, she has the feel of, of a Cabrilla."

"I never heard of such a thing." Feeling suddenly grumpy, I eyed Clement up and down and said, "Didn't get much sleep last night, did you?"

"That's expecting just a bit too much when Mother visits."

"Your mother came to Good Sky? Last night? Why didn't you let someone know?"

"Believe me, Willow, Mother caught me by complete surprise."

"Why didn't she—?"

"What big questions you have, my dear." Clement glanced at his wrist with no watch and said, "Goodness! You're going to be late. Here, let me walk with you."

"Well, why didn't she let you know?"

"Mother chanced into the area. I'm her only child, Willow. She hadn't seen me in a while."

To keep up with Clement, I took long steps. After thinking a minute, I said, "What's your family like?"

"There's not much to tell. Honest. Besides, I've never wanted to be a walking family album. I try to live in the moment. When it comes to old news, I need time to think."

"You mean make up a story."

"Oh, no. I wouldn't outright . . . lie. Not to you."

Seeing the color come back into Clement's face and his eyes sparkle, I got suspicious as he said, "But my family situation is . . . complicated. They're a peculiar bunch and frequently overbearing. I've learned that it's not good to dwell on them longer than, oh, say, ten seconds. One never knows what one's thoughts might conjure."

"Are they all as weird as you?"

"Well, they're all rather distinctive."

"What's your mother like?"

"Mother?"

"Yes."

"She's got a temper." Clement stopped as though that was the only description needed. When he saw that I expected more, he said, "Well, she's short. Matter of fact, she's about your height." Clement looked surprised by that realization. Then he looked down on me with eyes that mixed oldness with, I don't know, maybe worry. I'd seen that look when a person was fond of someone and knew that what they had to say would hurt the other person or maybe make them sad or angry.

"I want to be truthful with you, Willow. With all my heart. I'm not ashamed of my family or anything. In fact, I love them all very much. And I know that they love me. It's just that they're . . . we're not agreeing. Once things get settled, it'll be easier for me to say more."

"Okay, Clement. Alright."

"What else can we talk about?"

"Let's try this. Isn't it a nice day? Just look at the sky. Isn't it beautiful?"

"The sky begins at your feet, you know."

"There you go again."

"It's true, geophysically and physiologically."

"Sure."

"What you think of as sky is just sunlight sliced and reflected by dust. And yes, it is beautiful. Say!" Clement picked up a stone. "When you were young, did you ever make music on these railings?" He clanged the wrought iron.

"I didn't grow up around here. And how can you call that music?"

"Yes, this stone doesn't have quite the tone I'd hoped for." Clement pitched the rock into the Calliope. He listened with quiet pleasure to its plop, then said, "Have you got keys?"

"Don't you?"

"I never lock the . . ." Clement searched his pockets. "Ah, Cabrilla." He struck the railing.

"Isn't it a little early?"

Clement looked like a child. "That's the joy of it, my dear. The pure impetuosity." Clement breathed deep. "It's quite liberating. As a matter of fact, if ever something's troubling you, you must come down here and let your music ring out over the water and into this river. Rivers enjoy this kind of thing, you know. They will listen and try to help you. They may even lure away your demons."

I thought about my grandmother, my "just" Lucille. She was said to have a second sight. She claimed to see haunts and spirits and things not of our world. Even though I trusted "just" Lucille, still I had to tell Clement, "I don't believe in demons."

"You don't have to, my dear. They just have to believe in you." Clement's voice got further and further away. "Some just follow you around like a bad debt with a mean appetite. It rears up on you like a tsunami with claws." Clement blinked. "Goodness. Where was I? Well, what matters most is how we deal with them." Clement handed me the keys. "Here. You try."

"No way."

"I'm being foolish, aren't I?" Clement blushed.

The wind played with Clement's loosened hair. He smiled and said, "I'd better go. I'm delaying you."

"Okay."

"Can we play chess tonight?"

All I could answer was, "Clement, you're so str—"

"I know, strange."

"What else can I think?"

"Did I ever tell you how enchanting you look when you frown and chew gum?"

"Cut it out, Clement!"

"Can we play?"

I took my good old time before saying, "Mrs. Graham invited you to dinner Monday. It's Amos Akkadian's birthday."

"She's magnificent!" Clement kissed his fingertips and repeated happily, "Magnificent!"

Maybe so. All I knew was I managed to flood my workroom with popcorn for the first time in a long while.

# 6

## Clement

## Monday, March 19, 1979

## Moon: Disseminating

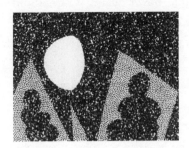

Infatuations were not unusual for me. I'd found joy in all kinds of shapes, sizes and molecular-cellular forms. Oh, the pleasures in variety! But none of my past experiences compared to or prepared me for Willow.

That evening, I gazed at Mrs. Graham's house from my third floor and then into the sky. I missed the Corona Australids. I'd just missed the moon's eclipse. If I didn't get going, I'd miss Mr. Akkadian's birthday.

I had asked Granny Mei-Yeh about a suitable gift, and she recommended May Belle's. Despite all the packing and final preparations to leave her shop for a while, May Belle made me tea. She had me sit down and, with a light, singing voice, asked who I had met in Good Sky. How did I like the town? Would I be staying long? Then, with a perky, spring-like step, May Belle presented her marvelous wares. What to choose? A crystal-handled letter opener? A small, bronze statue of Kuan Yin? A carved-ivory shoe horn?

Back in my rooms, I nervously glanced at a pan of Parkerhouse rolls and the small package wrapped in shiny sapphire paper. I thought about how, when Willow's birthday came, the Earth would have turned ten thousand, two hundred eighty-seven times and carried her on twenty-eight solar circuits, fourteen billion, seven hundred fifty million miles, not counting the rotations. While on a cosmic scale, that wasn't much, the real significance, as was occurring to me, were accomplishments during that time. That was a weighty contemplation, especially for one as old as I.

I had brushed my hair and teeth. I had even grown stubble so that I might shave, though never again. With gifts in hand, I reached the second floor before climbing back up and re-ironing my collar.

Finally, I got to the outside door. I looked at the sycamore's trunk, Cabrilla and Mrs. Carpenter unloading groceries. I saw shadows and crimson sunlight playing across the redbrick sidewalk and the cobblestone street. I watched a robin pick up a leaf stem and fly off. And what did I do? I slunk back to my rooms. I reshined my shoes and gargled. Then I stared past the horizon searching for shooting stars, the ignited dust of long-gone comets. The celestial footprints that, in time, blazed, then disappeared in Earth's atmosphere like my pawns and rooks into Willow's victorious palms.

I looked for Father's crown of cottony hair and long, fluffy beard. I sought his rugged face and wise but tired eyes in the constellations. I thought how Father was masterful at chess, or anything where quality and consideration counted more than the quantity. If I had let him teach me, perhaps the last year, or thousand, would have been different.

My travels had produced scintillating moments. I'd frolicked with the Bot in their bubble ponds. I'd swayed with the half-asleep and silvery Iket. I'd had an altogether fantastic time until something out there frightened me as badly as the afternoon Grandmother Beah called, "Boy, go out there and bring me the biggest, reddest tomato you can find."

I'd been sitting on the back porch where her spearmint and tea roses grew. Walking through Grandmother Beah's grape arbor, I passed her lilac bushes, baby cabbages, lettuces, butternut squash, pumpkins, string beans, peppers and cucumbers.

I spent some time looking for the best tomato and almost got it all by myself. Then, deep in the vines, a horrendous blue-green monster reared its hideous, beady-eyed, snapping head. Hundreds of horrible arms waggled at me. A maw opened that was bigger than me.

I could never recall screaming, but knew that was the first time there were two of me. One stood there, feet planted. The other me hightailed toward the house, but couldn't get far. Not while the physical me stayed frozen in the garden.

Grandmother Beah rushed to me in a violet satin slip and matching fuzzy slippers. Her crinkly white hair was loosed from its two braids and streamed across her shoulders. Grandmother Beah's pepper-black skin had even lost a shade or two of color, and her chest heaved.

Given that Grandmother Beah had titties so big that, if she turned too fast, she could knock down buildings, I actually toyed with the idea of staging more such crises when she was changing clothes. But that idea self-destructed when Grandmother Beah leaned over me, obstructing all daylight, and rumbled, "Boy! I thought you was dying out here. This better be good! My bunions are killing me."

Trembling, unable to even look at that dragon in the vines, I could only whimper and point. When Grandmother Beah spotted that bulbous terror, she frowned so fierce she could have fried the beast. She snapped, "Now listen up, Mr. Caterpillar. I done sent my precious grand-baby out here to fetch me a tomato. This here is his first trip by himself, and you've got a lot of nerve scaring him. Now you just back off this vine so my darling child can pick his fruit. Come to think of it, you might want to pack your bags and move cause I'll be back soon to clear your kind out of here." Then Grandmother Beah mumbled, "One thing bad feet'll teach you is to watch where you're stepping. With all them legs, he's got to have a few sore toes."

When I thought about that caterpillar, sometimes I couldn't move. The cryogenic fright never went away. The worm-initiated stasis. The larva-generated suspended animation. At least as time went by, I didn't wake as often with frigid sweats. The grub-induced shakes did subside.

I could feel the dusk gathering around me. I breathed deep. I raised my head and pulled back my shoulders. I opened my fists and let the past sift through. I shook myself, realizing that if I didn't get going, I'd miss the party. But even the constellations drifted. Weren't Alkaid and Dubhe sailing from the Big Dipper? Besides, I wasn't sure how to ease the hot and tingling tensions that sometimes surged in me. Thinking of Willow brought bursts of physical and soulful neediness that left me glowing and exhausted. When I was last home, I was so young that the very nature of closeness . . . the sensations that arose from feeling another body's warmth, inhaling her fragrance, tasting her emotions . . . all of that had changed.

I finally crossed Evergreen, handed Mrs. Graham the Parkerhouse rolls and hoped my nervousness didn't show. As she stood there with crisp curls in her hair, wearing tan and red-beaded moccasins and a pearl and tangerine-colored dress under a mauve ruffled apron, I nearly crumbled when she said, "Thank you, son. Come on in out of that cold. It's about time spring got started, don't you think? Three months of winter is long enough."

Mrs. G's living room was tufted and creamy French Provincial. Her bedroom was red velvet. Her kitchen muskmelon gold. Pink, yellow and red balloons and ribbons festooned the table and hung from the light fixture.

Mr. Akkadian was short and trim. He walked like a seaman. A few closely cropped ashen hairs rimmed his bald head. He had small, shrewd eyes, a large, hooked nose and a pencil-fine mustache over thin wrinkled lips.

Willow wore a grass-green sweatshirt that matched little emerald earrings set inside diamond chips. The gems twinkled like stars beside Willow's dark skin. When I said, "You look beautiful, my dear. Stunning," Willow frowned, cleared her throat and waggled her spoon against the knife.

I handed Mr. Akkadian his gift, a small but lovely astronomy book that May Belle said he'd been admiring. He said, "Thanks, son. Sit yourself on down. Pretty new around here, ain't ya?"

"You're right, sir. As a matter of fact, I'm from—"

Willow coughed and Mrs. G, holding the mashed potatoes, turned and asked, "Sugar, are you all right?"

"I'm fine. Go ahead, Clement. Tell them where you're from. This time, will it be Tulsa or Timbuktu?"

"Don't you think it possible that I've been to those places?"

"No."

I lifted a pitcher that had orange and yellow citrus sections painted on the glass. While pouring ice water for Mrs. G, I said, "I'm from Bagdad. Santa Rosa County, Florida."

Mr. Akkadian leaned forward. Squinting, he said, "Don't rightly know that I've ever heerd of that place, boy. What's it near?"

Willow smirked.

I replied, "It's on the Pensacola Bay."

Pouring Willow's water, I imagined beaches with soft sand that glittered like powdered diamonds farther along the Gulf. I heard palms and people and even the wind singing over the surf. I saw swimmers and fishing boats and smelled salt water, effervescent blue rippling out to an ever-bluer sky.

Amos Akkadian said, "Pensacola's durn near in Alabamee. Funny, you don't sound like you come from down thetaway. Musta been gone a long time, boy. I been to Florida. Always on the ocean side. Never on the Gulf. Nice there, too?"

"Very nice. If you like fishing, sir, there's lots of red snapper and flounder and the sweetest crabs you'll ever taste. They catch shrimp, too. The air carries hyacinth blossoms and Spanish moss, and the sky at night makes you think the door to the universe opened." I filled Mr. Akkadian's glass and said, "This dinner looks divine, Mrs. G. Thank you for inviting me."

"You're welcome, son. Come on over and help me out any time you like. This little group can't eat all I cook."

Mrs. G surveyed the pots, platters and bowls like a queen reviewing troops. Then she nodded, untied her apron and said, "Let's eat."

Mr. Akkadian said grace and, overwhelmed by Mrs. G's aromatic table, I added a hearty amen.

During the meal, Mrs. G told us about her children, her Betty and Ellington, Jr. and Clifford and Lena. Mr. Akkadian talked about his youth on Great Lakes freighters and divulged the intricacies of junkyard management. Then, as I suctioned salad, mashed potatoes and string beans, Mrs. G said, "Sugar, you're not one of those vegetable people, are you?"

I nodded.

"Well, no wonder you're so pale."

"Really?" I patted my cheeks and examined both arms wondering how much I should adjust that impression.

Mr. Akkadian chuckled, "You look fine, boy. Woman, everybody's world don't revolve around meat. Clement done made it this long on leaves and seeds, reckon he'll make it the rest of the way."

"Sugar, you got any brothers and sisters?"

"For heaven's sake, Ruby, call the boy by his name."

"Was I talking to you?"

"No, but—"

Quickly, I answered, "As a matter of fact, I am an only child."

Mrs. G nodded sadly, then looked at Willow and said, "This child didn't have brothers and sisters either."

"Oh, woman, being an only child ain't so bad. Cain't be," Mr. Akkadian said. "Momma dropped twelve of us, and with that many kids, there was something going all the time. Least being just one, you got peace and quiet. You get your way."

Mrs. G kicked him under the table, then looked from me to Willow and said, "For a good ten years, she's also been an orphan."

I felt myself drifting again. I thought of what it was like when the distances to those you loved were parsecs, when your loneliness was like starlight at the edge of the knowable.

"Your parents, sugar, I mean Clement, are they still in Florida?"

I looked into the ice water and then at the crumpled napkin. I answered, "My mother travels a lot. My father is . . . he's gone."

My response had, perhaps, been too melancholy. The room got so quiet that I heard the battery running the clock. I looked into Mrs. G's brown eyes and said, "I want to thank you for this wonderful meal. It's been a long time since I've had anything as good."

"We're not done yet, darling." Rising, Mrs. G said, "Isabella Watson outdid herself."

Willow helped clear the table and then set down four small plates as Mrs. G opened a white box and placed the birthday cake onto a stemmed, glass platter. The candle-lighting ceremony excited me. As Mrs. G sliced, she said to Mr. Akkadian, "If you don't mind, I'm going to cut a piece for the Singers and Mrs. Faraday."

"Fine with me."

"I'd save some for May Belle, but she's leaving soon. Reckon she'll want to travel light."

"She always does."

Willow asked, "Do you know where she's going, Ruby?"

Ruby twisted her lips and said, "My guess is debauching young men."

"Be nice, Ruby," Mr. Akkadian said.

"I am."

I offered to do magic.

"You can do that, sugar? Oh, how exciting!"

I made a quarter appear to drop into and then vanish from a glass of water. Although they heard a splash and saw the coin, it had always been under, not in the glass. I'd merely helped them see what they expected, and—in so doing—pleased them. The only difficult moment that evening came while I attempted pinochle. That's when Willow asked, "So, Clement, when's your birthday?"

"My birthday?"

"That's what I said."

"It's in December."

"December what?"

"At the end."

As I tried to remember what day I'd arrived, Mrs. G said, "Willow, sugar, we're waiting. It's your turn."

It was after eleven when I rose and hugged Mrs. G. She said, "Come again, anytime, sugar. You like rice, yams and collard greens, Creole dishes and that kind of stuff?"

"Mrs. Graham, I'll love anything you cook."

Walking home, my heart beat slow and my lungs filled with a broad and warm goodness. My shoes floated like helium. Climbing the stairs, I tried to decide whether it was soundless or so tremendous a concussion that it was unhearable. Out in the universe, it happened. Planets and stars, even galaxies collided. Sometimes there was a great shower with lots of sparks and fire and ice. Smoke and cinders polluted the cosmos. Most of the time, because the stars were so far apart, the process was like seeded dandelions mingling. A delicate and soft coming together. What was becoming what would be.

I stood at my window for a long while. Looking up into a starscape veiled by thin clouds, I thought about Willow's laughter, the way her eyes could shine, her earthiness and strength.

Way off, more felt than heard, was thunder. I checked the air's taste, the sky's color, the direction the birds swooped in. The trees stood so still that only the tiniest branches tingled. It could have been just an evening storm. But if Mother was heading my way again, I hoped that she would really listen and be patient because I had decided to risk staying home longer.

# Oull

*Before me, who had named myself Oull, Jayah was a world of*
*shimmering rocks and underground seas. There were no predators.*
*No prey. I would swim slowly toward the Larct, humming quietly but*

deep as they did. Then, when very close, I became myself. I
multiplied my bulk. Glowing talons burst through my skin.

The Larct, although their vermilion scales could see, never
escaped. Realizing my presence, a sweet fluid spurted through their
scales. Their bodies contracted, and they fled in curling paths.

Their panic aroused me. Soon enough, I recognized when the
Larct were exhausted and inciting more terror was useless. With
large, jagged teeth, I enjoyed crushing them, the pulverizing, the
grinding that other Larct could hear.

When I came upon My One, I was pleased with its Larct
disguise and delighted to have found it alone. When close enough
that the One should have sensed me. I slipped below and came up
several lengths ahead. My One paused as though seeking recognition.
As I prepared to annihilate My One, as I grew and closed in, the sea
foamed. My One rose, breaking through the rock. In showers of blue
light, My One then blazed across the sky.

Angered, I sated myself on Jayah, leaving just enough Larct to
reproduce themselves. I might return. While basking on glistening
rocks, I considered My One's course and nature. Then I leisurely
followed My One across the three large and four small star systems.

# Mother

*There would be tornadoes in Alabama, Arizona, California and
Colorado. Three in northwest Florida. More tore through
Georgia, Illinois, Iowa, Kansas. Kentucky got the year's first
killer. Mother's forces devastated parts of Louisiana, Missouri,
North Carolina, South Carolina, Oklahoma, Tennessee and
Texas. That March, there were nearly fifty tornadoes. In April,
Mother's busy season began.*

# 7

## Willow

### Monday, March 19, 1979

### Moon: Disseminating

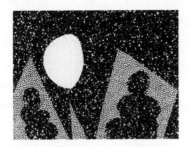

Once in a while, I'd wonder what made a thing destroy itself. I'd feel a flutter around my heart and remember when Aunt True and my cousins Eddie and Jeffie came to visit. The boys and I usually played Tonk on the porch after supper while the grownups listened to stories and music on Daddy's radio. Thick hedges around the railing blocked the wind. When darkness came, we could light a candle, and the flame held steady.

One evening, a moth circled our candle, then flew into the twilight. Once, it came back and flew so close, the fire jumped. We figured the moth learned its lesson. Ten minutes later, it thumped around the ceiling, then swooped so low, we ducked. After another big circle, it shot straight through the flame and came out the other side like a dive bomber on fire and trailing smoke.

Eddie and Jeffie's eyes bulged so far, I thought they'd fall out. Maybe mine did, too. Eddie was the first to joke about it being a kamikaze moth. After that, we relaxed a bit and finally got brave enough to see if anything was left. We looked under the glider and chairs. We even got a flashlight and never found a speck.

I used to wonder what made the moth do that. But what made anyone do anything that didn't make sense? In my mirror, I studied eyes that were just like my daddy's. I patted skin that was like my momma's, like her father's . . . like molasses. It was skin that I thought was one reason Jimmy's people didn't want me.

When I was younger, I always thought there was something I could fix that would make people be nicer. Momma would say, "Now, Willow, you keep your hair nice. Don't want white folks thinking you're fresh from the jungle." And, "Willow, make sure you wash up good. Don't have those folks saying we can't keep ourselves clean." And, "Willow, you know white folks think we're dumb. Study hard."

Sometimes the effort made me feel like I was drowning.

Like with Miss Dover. She was a small, brown-haired woman with a mole on her chin, a pale pink mouth and light gray eyes that got big and round when she was happy. She'd paste little stars on students' papers or draw them on the chalkboard beside kids' names. I tried hard to get Miss Dover to do that. But when Miss Dover looked at me, seemed like the effort was almost too much for her to bear.

After all, there were only a few colored kids in the school. I was the darkest. The one with the thickest lips. The widest nose. The one with the nappiest hair. The one truly chocolate chip in my school's vanilla cookie. On Miss Dover's last day, Alex Baker's mom had a party. Even the mayor came. Probably because of the important man Miss Dover was marrying. Everyone said how Miss Dover was such an inspiration and how her leaving would be a big loss.

The Saturday before the Fourth of July, Terry, Otto and me, we sat on the steps outside Creame Grocery & Hardware. We were by that red Coca-Cola cooler and the crates of empty green bottles and the barrel of nails.

Every store on Creame, Ohio's main street, had one or two American flags out front flapping on poles. Creame Grocery & Hardware had three. All those stars and stripes waving made the street real cheerful.

We were seeing who could flick pebbles the farthest. Nobody else was outside. Just one car stirred the dust a block away when Miss Dover strolled up. Her fiancé was a strapping man with blue eyes and white-blonde hair and a face like uncooked hamburger.

With their shadows falling over us, Miss Dover said, "Look who's here, Harrison." Miss Dover's eyes got that big roundness, and her dainty perfume wrapped around me when she bent down. Her taffy voice was soft as she said, "Here's some of my students that I won't be seeing anymore. The three musketeers I always called them. The little monkey girl and her nigger-loving friends." Miss Dover stood up. She smiled at each of us, then wiped her hands and straightened her skirt. It was gathered with big yellow and pink roses printed on a white background. Strolling away, Miss Dover's lily voice drifted back to us, "Bye-bye, children."

At first, I hardly heard Terry. Then he shouted, "You bitch! You bitch!"

That Fourth of July, when Otto, Terry and me were finishing paper plates of fried chicken and potato salad on the Melkpath's big front porch, Frau Edda brought a tray of cherry vanilla ice cream and apple pie. When Frau Edda went back inside, she stopped in the room where the mahogany end tables held glass candy dishes that rang. When Frau Edda opened them, we got peppermints, licorices and chocolates in paper cupcake liners. That time, we heard her open that tall bookcase with leaded glass doors. Inside were Frau Edda's gilded albums. Many of them were operas by a man named Wagner. After a record started playing on her phonograph with the morning glory horn, Frau Edda got the big leather book with the gold-edged pages and beautifully painted fairy tales. Then she sat under the green awnings near her lilac bushes. Her rocker was carved with flowers, leafy vines and birds. She called us close.

Frau Edda's skin made me think of fresh-baked biscuits, and her gray eyes were as bright behind her gold-wired glasses as the crystals around her reading lamps. She was tall and limped from being born with one leg shorter than the other. Frau Edda had tough, strong hands. Her long, silver braids were pinned in double-decker circles like a crown. That day, she told us of Siegfried and the stolen and cursed wealth, the lies and murder that brought down a kingdom of gods.

"Such a thing, it could not stand," Frau Edda said, "Like the Third Reich. It was supposed to bring such greatness. That's what the Nazis believed. And because of them, we had the *Kristallnacht*. A pretty-sounding name, *nicht wahr*? But what does it mean? The night of the broken glass. The night that was to begin the end of Jews. The night that made me and my Jacob and our little Erik come from Hamburg to here."

Frau Edda held up her hand. "We had to wear yellow stars. The Jewish star. Even me, a German woman, because my Jacob was Jewish. It was the same for the gypsies and communists and other people. We had to wear these on our arms or over our hearts or go to jail. This became law so that others who needed to think they were better could refuse to sell us things or buy from us. They could keep us out of places. But we saw that fall, *nicht wahr*? And all those who believed in it."

Frau Edda paused a long moment, then said, "I was a little girl. Much smaller than you. Maybe seven or eight. In Hamburg, I would sometimes watch ships from the North Sea come and go from our harbor. One day, I was very sad. My best friend, Karin, we had not spoken. I sat on Baumwall with sun shining on water and ships and, far off, warehouse cranes lifting and lowering the cargoes. Then I heard a man. He sounded like hearty singing when he say, '*Guten morgen*, pretty *fräulein*. Or, in the language of my homeland, *Tudo bem*.'

"When I looked up, the sun was behind his head. He was for a moment like Jesus. Such a Black man I had never seen. And such colors he wore. Like a parrot. When he smiled, two gold teeth I saw. He was surely on his way to the Reeperbahn, and he said to me, 'I am from Brazil, Rio de Janeiro. I have seen many wonders in this world, *fräulein*.

Casablanca, Havana. The Gold Coast. New York. But nowhere such a marvel as you.'

"He laugh so deep and pat my head. He give me licorice and say, '*Süsses für die Süsse.*' When I smile, his face gets very bright. 'Now the day, it truly shines,' he say, and he is gone. Such a compassion, he did not have to do. He could have walked past my sadness. But he stop. He make a little happiness. He never see me again. There is no difference and yet there is. And that is, I think, how it is better for us to feel about such people as Miss Dover. Keep happy."

The music was ending. I had liked it. Parts sounded triumphant and other sections were peaceful.

"Götterdämmerung," Frau Edda said. "Dawn and Siegfried's journey on the Rhine." She paused, "We may not see the downfall. Still, it comes. As surely as apple trees produce only apples and cows give milk, not beer. Like Siegfried crushed the power of the old. And how? By reforging their weapons. Then he went through the horrible fire and found the love that was there before his birth. A love that would follow him in death." Frau Edda picked up my hands, squeezed them softly and said, "In big ways and in little, we can do the same. We can be warriors and fight for happiness in our lives. And we do not need swords and spears. Siegfried's most powerful weapon was that he was not afraid. Remember that, *Meine kleiner Engel*, my little angel. *Er hatte keine Angst.*"

When I had my pajamas on and turned off the lights, I looked across Ruby's snow-covered garden and the building tops. Usually I read myself to sleep. That night, for a long time, I looked past Faraday's Popcorn Factory and the Calliope River and the low hills on the other side to where the land stopped. Beyond that, there was nothing but stars.

# 8

## Ruby

### Wednesday, March 21, 1979

### Moon: Last Quarter

### Spring Equinox 12:22 A.M. EST

Just like the sun sets and the moon rises, just like autumn puts life to sleep and spring wakes it up, there's seasons for everything. Can't always see the flow. That's why some folks wear themselves out, make themselves sick and pretty much ruin things fighting what's inevitable. But if they'd quiet down, they could sense how things are going. They'd know to carry umbrellas and wear galoshes when it's supposed to rain.

Some folks, you can advise. Some just got to get soaked. I raised four kids. Sure they worried me, but I give them room. They turned out fine. For entirely too long a time, I've been suggesting the same approach to this one sister-in-law. She just won't let my nephew be. Drove the poor child away with all her prodding and haranguing. On the one hand, it's a shame they didn't get to share some important years together. On the other hand, I'm right proud of the boy. I could go on, but I don't want to be putting all my family business in the street. Let me see who else I can talk about.

Take, for example, Mei-Yeh Faraday. She and I go back a lot further than anyone would imagine. Naturally we know things. Like how Claire O'Brien never made a dime of that money she's prissy-stepping around here with. Better hold onto it, cause her husband won't.

And I do believe that of those two spinsters living next door, Astrid Svenson may have opened her legs at least once. But that cranky Mia, I'm sure she always kept her knees locked tight. I can see that they were pretty once. Should of let themselves have some fun while their roses were blooming.

And Sunny Hall, now that woman should be ashamed of herself. Here it is 1979, and you'd think she was from Jim Crow Dixie. I swear she'd a voted for that racist George Wallace if she'd had the chance. It's pitiful to be so small-minded in such a big universe. As for Betsy Collins, she ought to go on and marry Sid Jones. For years, they been fooling around like nobody's supposed to know. Then there's May Belle down at that secondhand . . . well, she calls it an antique shop. And antique comes closer to describing May Belle than she lets on to them barely bearded boys whose eyes and other things she keeps opening.

Yep, Mrs. Faraday, May Belle and me, we been out there. We know what the world will and won't do. We move away when stuff stinks or acts like it'll break a back or a heart or a mind. When we sample something bitter, we refuse seconds. Maybe that's what makes living so nice. Just paying attention is rewarding. Having night eyes helps.

Night eyes is what I call seeing in the dark. 'Cause life's been planned out that in broad daylight, folks can only see a short ways. But at night, that's when they can see forever. That's what I be looking for. Like my friend Amos Akkadian, he's got those night eyes. But don't go getting ideas. Amos and I, we go back so far we're more like family. Just two old people helping each other through this here life.

No one can replace my Ellington. Not this time around. Ellington wasn't that tall. He wasn't what most folks'd call handsome. But Ellington was strong. That Anderson boy Willow liked so much, he coulda been like my Ellington. The parts was all there. In fact, when it came to book learning and handsomeness, that Anderson boy was deluxe.

Now, my Ellington, he could add, subtract, multiply, write his name and read the paper, but he wasn't what anyone would call bright. Still, my Ellington knew up from down. He could see at night enough to hold on to a good thing—me—when he had it. And it's a shame books couldn't teach the Anderson boy that. But then, if he was supposed to, I reckon he would have.

My little Willow, she's learning. She's getting her night vision. She's come a long way since she showed up looking like a spooked fawn. Then there's that boy who lives across the street. Sure, folks think he's strange. They don't know the half of it. If they did, well, maybe some like my Willow girl, maybe she wouldn't be so hard on him. But right in through here and for a little ways to come, I suspect strange is really the way it will be.

Everyone has feelings about that house he's in. Ain't nothing wrong with it, except for years whoever owns it, and I'm not naming no names, wouldn't fix the place up. That house was always a little, well, lonesome. But I'm surprised ain't nobody said nothing about the tree. First off, it's the only sycamore in Good Sky. And I don't think trees normally grow as fast as that one.

It sticks up so high it's a better landmark than the coke ovens. The tree sheds like crazy, and its trunk overruns the sidewalk and curb. What saves it despite those fat leaves clogging everyone's gutters is that it gives good shade and the squirrels sure love it. And, well, it is a mighty handsome tree. Some mornings and when the sun sets, if I catch the light just right, the leaves flutter like silver birds. The trunk and branches look absolutely gold.

I like trees. And I like tree people cause they want depth. Shallowness is hard on them. They need to rise and spread their branches into the wind and sun. For a bitty, delicate little sprout coming out of a hard, dry shell, trees do a lot of growing. Most of it no one ever sees. But what shows generally pleases the eye and the ear, the mind and the heart.

And since it's what a person pays attention to that determines the quality of their life and what happens in their shade, I'm particular about what I notice.

'Cause if all a person wants to do is make somebody else happy, I figure we ought to accept that. I get after my Willow cause I see the boy across Evergreen is trying. Who knows better than me that Willow ain't got nothing more going on.

Fortunately, those two are getting off to a good start, not that I'm nosy or eavesdrop. Now I reckon I can sit back, see what spring cooks up and enjoy, like I said, the natural flow of things. After all, I am who I am, and I certainly understand how things happen best in their own good season.

# 9

## Willow

## Thursday, April 12, 1979

## Moon: Full

When things I saw in the news and heard people saying got too depressing, I walked by the river. Some mornings, when the sky was peach colored and the Calliope sparkled, I'd look in the waters and imagine misted valleys and castles and dark forests. I'd see purple mountains rise to shining peaks. I'd search for the flirtatious nixies who teased Alberich until he got so mad he took their magical gold. Some still mornings, the Rhinegold's opening music came through clear as when I sat with Otto and Terry and Frau Edda.

Watching the water, I believed the Calliope did understand my feelings, though I knew it couldn't help like Clement said, even if I did make noise. Some places, the Calliope was nearly a mile wide, so that the river seemed more like a country. Like a place no one could mess with, least not like a brook or a stream. That's when I wouldn't think about how people hoarded gold. I wouldn't worry about inflation, job layoffs and oil shortages. I couldn't see how cars waiting at Price Is Right sometimes reached Hampton Plumbing, even the Big Star Picture Show. I could forget that people drove ten miles to Applegate Mall, then panicked and got back in line to fill up again. After waiting a half hour, all they could squeeze in the tank was, maybe, a gallon.

Instead of dealing with all that aggravation, I'd watch the Calliope moving and think about starting at Lake Erie and rolling south past Good Sky and then on to the Ohio. From there, I'd float to the Mississippi and the Gulf of Mexico. Maybe I'd go on and see the ocean where the sun would lift me up in mists. Then I'd be a cloud that sailed all over the world until one fine day, I'd rain back down.

Maybe if it had rained on that carnival years ago, I wouldn't have gotten in trouble. Terry and me, we met at the wishing well. We found Otto at the ring toss. The sun burned yellow white. The earth was stomped hard. Banners and flags, red and yellow, white and blue flapped over dirty canvas. I smelled dust and hay. People laughed and hollered. Loudspeakers squawked. Merry-go-round and Ferris wheel music jangled.

Otto was about to loan me some money for one of the big apples coated in thick red candy when the next table fell over. While a thin, scruffy guy picked up giant pretzels, Otto, Terry and me, we grinned and nodded. Then we each snatched apples. Terry's stuck, and it made the tray clatter.

That evening, watching the fairground lights shrink under the stars, hearing the carnival noises fade into the meadow sounds, I figured Daddy would have laughed if he hadn't had to pay five dollars for a ten-cent treat. Even with the manager ranting about Otto, Terry and me running and then lying, Daddy might have chuckled if the wind roaring through the window hadn't chilled as it passed Momma.

I couldn't go outside for anything but chores. In church, the minister preached on nothing but stealing and sparing the rod was spoiling the child. I thought my life was ruined. Then Otto's dad came by and said Frau Edda missed me and wanted to see her *Kind der Sonne*, her child of the sun.

The day Terry and I could visit again, Frau Edda took us into their kitchen. On the stove was a big steel pot with a lid made in two halves. Either half could be lifted with wooden knobs. Across the lid was a handle with gears and a tiller, just like on the ice-cream maker. That crank stirred the corn we popped.

After we got our Kool-Aid, Frau Edda sent us to sit on the old peach-colored carpets that covered their wide porch. Then she limped out to her rocker with that book full of pretty pictures and pages with gold at the edges. She rocked slowly while reading of the night-dark treasure ship with ghosts and bloodred sails.

Vanderdecken, that's what Frau Edda called the captain who'd been too proud of his skills to seek safe harbor. As Frau Edda read, I pictured towering clouds. They were purple, red and gold above boiling blackness. Lightning flashed against waves higher than the ship. The winds tore and shoved so hard that Vanderdecken should have cried for mercy. Instead, he cursed both God and the devil. "*Und der Teufel horte es,*" Frau Edda said. Then she whispered, "And the devil heard."

They were doomed to sail forever. No rocks would break the ship. No storms or battles would sink them. Thanks to an angel, Vanderdecken could land once every seven years, and seek a virgin bride who would be faithful. That way, their torment could end.

Rising, Frau Edda said, *"Hort! Musik aus meiner Heimat."* Her music of home. Frau Edda went inside. We heard her open the cabinet, pull a thick black record from one of the gilded boxes and place it on the gramophone. As *Der fliegende Holländer*'s opening music played, my skin tingled.

Rocking back and forth, Frau Edda whispered, " *'Ein heil'ger Balsam meinen Wunden.'* My wounds have found a holy balsam. *'Dem Schwur, dem hohen Wort entfliesst.'* Her oath, poured out in noble words. *'Hort es, mein Heil hab' ich gefunden.'* Hear it, I have found my cure. *Und* Senta, who loved Vanderdecken like he loved her, she says, *'Von macht'gem Zauber überwinden.'* What powerful magic overcame me and pulled me to his rescue? *'Reisst mich's zu seiner Rettung fort.' "*

By then, big dark clouds rose over the Creame, Ohio, horizon. The wind blew cold. Far off, lightning flashed. Thunder rumbled. Terry, Otto and me looked at each other a little spooked. Otto's father brought their car around and came up on the porch, saying, "Mama, I better get these youngsters home. Look at the sky. I don't like that green. I think a tornado's brewing."

To the south and west, sheets of rain fell. Frau Edda glanced at the dark thunderclouds and said, "*Ja. Ja. Nur eine Minute noch, mein Sohn.* The storm, I do not think . . ."

Frau Edda licked her finger and held it to the wind, then pursed her lips. She sniffed, then lifted her glasses and squinted. The flaring darkness swept more and more toward the north and east. Sunlit patches of blue flecked with gold and white were opening. Frau Edda settled back in her rocker and said, "I do not think the bad weather is for these lambs. Not today."

Shaking his head and walking inside, Otto's dad said, "Maybe so, Mama. But just to be safe, one minute more."

Frau Edda turned to Otto, Terry and me and said, "When you do a hurt to yourself, no matter how big my darlings, there is always a part that stays pure, stays *rein.* No matter how much mud covers, you must find it like a little light across big, dark *Ozean.* You must give that part your loyalty and your treasures." Frau Edda tapped her breast. "Your heart and your soul. Sometimes, you might think that the best parts in you are *kaputt.* But it is only, maybe, a little crushed. It is waiting to be found and cared for and given a chance to grow."

That evening, I showed the children, including Clement, a cartoon that started with zebras marching into a meadow playing flutes. Then an alligator cha-chaed through the bright, smiling flowers. Cows, foxes, cats and bears played fiddles, saxophones and drums. Mice and giraffes jitterbugged with so much energy, trees started bouncing. White clouds rumbaed and then dark ones came, all excited. Finally, a tornado boogie-woogied across the field, whirling the animals into the sky.

In the projector's flickering light, I saw Clement brooding. Even after the storm went away, and the animals parachuted back to Earth. Clement was quiet through the dinner Ruby left for us, and his chess game was so lousy, he even rocked my table and grumped, "This short leg's distracting as . . . as . . . ."

"As hell, Clement."

Clement looked like I'd just stated we breathe air and said, "I only paused in order to name the specific kind and depth of hell that this rocking suggests."

Setting up the next game, I said, "Don't go getting sour grapes, now. You promised you could take losing until you could win fair and square."

"Sour grapes? Isn't that the fable about a fox who disdained what he couldn't reach? That certainly doesn't apply here. Besides, Mrs. G prepared such a spectacular meal that I overstuffed myself again. We all know what that means."

"What does it mean?"

"Why, that the blood cells normally working in my brain have to go and help my stomach, leaving me temporarily impaired."

"And just exactly where did my brain cells go, Clement? We ate the same dinner. Anyway, I never heard of such a thing as blood leaving the brain because you eat. I never know when you're telling the truth and when you're trying to pull my leg."

Clement grinned, "Willow, dear, whenever I tell you that I want to pull your leg, please believe me. So listen carefully. Sweet Willow, I want to—"

"Pay attention. It's your move."

Clement jiggled a knight and then a pawn. Then he pointed to the little ridges under his nose and said, "If I tell you what this spot is called, and if I lose the next game, can we call this contest a stalemate?"

I twisted my lips and looked at Clement so he'd know that I didn't believe that space was called anything.

"My dear," Clement said, "what good is science if it doesn't divide things and then name the pieces?"

I counted ceiling cracks while Clement babbled on, saying, "I really thought I'd be doing better by now. You've quite blown me away, my dear. I won't ask this largess of you again."

Drumming the table, I said, "Make it good."

Clement beamed. "That general area has a number of names. But that special place, some very few of which are as lovely as yours, of which I believe only Makeba's may have been as beguiling—"

"What's it called, Clement?"

"Well, some call it the sniffle gutter. Technically, it's the philtrum. But my father told me that people have many lives and a special angel watches. So, after people die and before they are born again, they know everything. Hopefully, their peace and contentment outweighs their regret and anger.

"When they are about to return to adjust their celestial scorecards, so to speak, their angel presses a finger above the lip, leaving a distinctive imprint and sealing their past from their conscious mind. That's why my father said it's called the angel's touch."

"Cute, Clement."

"I hoped you'd like it."

Around ten, seemed like the world got quiet. Peacefulness settled like a wind-fresh quilt. I felt a sigh, a definite warmth. The past rose up like yeast dough in Momma's blue bowl. I was back down dusty roads where memories bobbed like lightning bugs deep in the woods. Dreamy like, I saw Clement move a pawn and watch me with one eyebrow raised. I moved a knight and remembered.

Momma's name was Verdell. She had big pretty eyes and the longest lashes I ever saw. Momma was slim, and I got to be about her same height. When the shirts and dresses she made wore out, Momma cut them and made quilts and placemats.

When I was ten, Momma started growing popping corn just for me. The kernels were dark and shiny, like rows of midnight and deep purple pearls. But she always grew marigolds, kiss-me-over-the-garden-gates, love-in-a-mists, calendulas, zinnias and petunias. She had cabbage and sweet peas, tomatoes, leaf lettuce, pole beans and field corn. Momma dried straw flowers, sea lavender, hydrangea, globe amaranth and oregano blossoms and sold all that right from our yard.

Sometimes Momma sold those things in Creame Grocery & Hardware and at the county fair. That's where Momma also sold her apple butter, strawberry preserves and pies. Through the summer and fall, Momma had a table at the Porrima Farmer's Market and a couple times a year, we drove to Cincinnati.

I was fifteen when Momma and I waded through Blue Meadow's slate-blue flowers and past the young willow trees. We both had tin buckets and Momma carried a basket for flowers. We had on big straw hats and white and pink calico dresses that looked pretty bouncing around our dark skin.

When we got to the willow grove, Momma said, "All those young trees, my goodness, they grew so fast. Aren't they beautiful?"

I still wasn't used to Blue Meadow without the cottonwood and crab apple, the locust and elm trees that were there before the big tornado. The only tree left was the willow that had a branch I could lie on like a bed. Momma said she went to that tree a lot before I was born and read to me. When I could go by myself, I lay on that branch reading mail-order paperbacks and books from Creame's tiny library. The library was just a side room off of Creame Grocery & Hardware that Terry's mother kept going. The books I remembered best were *Arabian Nights* and *The Story of King Arthur, Treasure Island, Pinocchio* and *Call of the Wild.*

Watching Clement lift a bishop, his fingers cautious yet graceful, I thought of the birds coasting over Corey Creek. In the springtime, the meandering stream swelled and made the land marshy. By late June, the waters settled in a pond, and by July, we had wild raspberries.

I thought about how, as Momma and I walked that day, she'd said,

"You're big enough now, Willow, I'm thinking I can tell you some hard things. 'Cause sometimes, if we don't understand our background, if we don't know what pieces is in us and what ain't, we can be limping through life and not even know it. I want you to grow up strong, so I figure sometimes even bitter truth is better than sweet not knowings."

Sunlight coming through the straw hat dappled Momma's face. Standing there stiff and a little stooped, Momma reminded me of Mariah. Mariah Thompkins was my great-grandmother. She lived most of her life in a big, two-story house near Bridge, Kentucky. That house sat like a black dot in some tobacco fields. Rain had run the paint off years before. Rose bushes along the front porch were wild and always more thorn than flower.

More than once when we pulled into Mariah's lane, Momma sighed, set her jaw and said, "Seems like no matter what time of day and what lights are on, those windows always look hungry."

Daddy said, "I think that house just took on her way. Meanness."

Long before I was born, Mariah became blind to her only child and started calling her "just" Lucille. That was because Mariah believed— and when Mariah believed a thing, she held to it strongly—that "just" Lucille couldn't really be my grandmother because she hadn't been a mother first.

When Momma was nine months old, "just" Lucille ran off. The leaving was like a hole dug in a garden that never got a seed. A place that couldn't bud and then bloom in Momma's heart and in Mariah's mind. But "just" Lucille sent me birthday cards with taped-down quarters. When I got bigger, "just" Lucille sent crisp, two-dollar bills. I had just finished ninth grade when I first met "just" Lucille. Small like a doll and the color of butterscotch, "just" Lucille held herself up so anyone'd think she was tall as Daddy.

"Just" Lucille wore a shiny, peacock-colored dress to Mariah's funeral. She held a cigarette with just two fingers and sucked it like a milkshake, glowing up a whole half inch at the tip. Then "just" Lucille shot a tight smoke stream toward the ceiling, tilted her hips and braced her legs straight and wide while women like Sarah Compton bit into their poppyseed cake and grumbled about proper dress and behavior at a funeral.

I moved a bishop and Clement, cautious, slid a pawn over and took one of mine.

I remembered how odd it was in Mariah's house without her cataract-clouded eyes watching and her arthritic hands laying mashed rutabaga on cracked china beside coarse cornbread. There was no rutabaga smell around "just" Lucille, whose sometimes green and sometimes gray and sometimes purple eyes could strike like fire, like when she tapped ashes into Sarah Compton's lemonade. Before "just" Lucille's bracelets stopped jingling, before her sweet fragrance settled like the red feather that floated from her black straw hat with that sequined veil, "just" Lucille had hugged Momma, Daddy and me, and she was gone.

Riding home from Mariah's funeral, Momma talked about Lucille's "other" vision.

Daddy had a slow way of talking, especially when he asked, "Do you really think she sees spirits?"

Momma hunched up her shoulders. I could hear her crinkling the bag of fried chicken and cake she'd packed. Finally, Momma said, "Union, I don't know what to think. I hardly know Lucille. The little bit I do came from Mariah."

After a pause that took so long I thought I'd bust, Daddy, he finally asked, "Well, what did Mariah tell you?"

"Just that Lucille's mind was always going places where it didn't belong and that she just plain got grown too fast."

Daddy's jaw moved like he was chewing. It took hitting a hole before he said, "Well, I've heard of people with a second sight, but Lucille don't seem the type."

The highway clicked by another mile before Momma said, "Lucille told me to sell the place. She said she'd always seen things in Mariah's house, and the lights shining in there now is bound to be unsettling."

"That so?"

"She's got nothing to gain. Anyway, I've always felt strange in that old house. Maybe Lucille could see what it was."

"You keep talking like that, and you're gonna scare Willow."

Momma turned and smiled. It was the same worried look she had when I was little and in bed with fever. "You didn't hear none of this, did you honey?" she asked. "If you did, don't pay it no mind. Ain't nothing but talk."

"Momma," I said, "I'm not a baby." Besides, that wasn't the first time I'd heard about "just" Lucille's vision. They did sell Mariah's place, and Momma had to move quick to pay off debts before Daddy gambled the money.

During a break from shooing flies and chiggers, Momma smiled just like she did in the car. She said, "You know, 'just' Lucille wasn't Mariah's only child."

I nearly dropped my raspberries as Momma said, "As best I understand, cause I never even knew their names until we buried Mariah, there was a girl born before my mother whose dress or nightgown or something caught a spark from the fireplace. She got burnt alive. I think Mariah saw it happen. Then there was a boy who got pneumonia. My grandfather, the records say his name was Samuel Thompkins, after he'd been missing about a week, Mariah found him hanging from a tree. That was in 1920."

Momma wiped the sweat that glistened on her forehead and nose and said, "I guess Mariah held Lucille in too tight."

Momma jiggled her bucket as though to make room for more berries. "I never knew my father. To hear Mariah tell it, Boston was a snake. He was shiny black, but a pretty man. Mariah said he charmed people out of their money so he hardly even needed the dice and cards. And he romanced innocent women into sin.

"But Daddy Boston was my father," Momma's voice got small. "In pictures, he's dressed fancy. He's handsome and has pretty teeth. When he got to Bridge, and when he left with my mother two years later, Boston was the only Black man who'd ever had a car. I suppose it's the one considerate thing Lucille and Boston did was leave me." Momma's voice trembled. I could see she was back in that dark house under all that sky repeating what Mariah must have said a thousand times.

Clement moved his queen. I wrapped my arms around me thinking how loneliness, it was an awful thing. When I finally pushed out a pawn, Clement tapped my hand gently and said, "You know, a rich and fulfilling inner life is one of the most satisfying blessings a person can have."

I rubbed my eyes and asked, "Well, what were you thinking all that time?"

"I was thinking what a splendid game you're playing, even in absentia."

"What were you really thinking?"

"I was thinking—" Clement glanced at a bare wrist. "Gracious! Look how late it is!"

"Clement!"

He sighed, "Willow, this is awkward. I'm still trying to become more at ease with how things are done here. I have thoughts and ideas, and I'm not sure how people will respond. If people laughed or snubbed them, it would hurt. Tell me, am I being too sensitive? Am I taking myself too seriously?"

I said, "Yes, Clement. You are too sensitive and taking yourself too serious. Now, if you want, speak up."

Clement paused. "Well, I was thinking about how babies, in those first special days, read nature far more accurately than they ever will again. Their brains interpret the visible world in a tactile way. True, the stereoscopic vision that allows us to see fine detail and perceive depth and notice things like holes in the sidewalk and the edges of cliffs, those skills do come in handy. But wouldn't it be better, safer, even healthier, if others could see us as we truly are, rather than as we seem, or what they think we should be?"

I felt like a great big bell had rung. My insides tingled.

Clement stood up, stretched and said, "Why don't we call it quits for tonight? I hope you had a pleasant journey. I feel about due for a deep, intracranial voyage myself."

Watching the way the light lit Clement's hair, the way his hair framed his face, his hands rubbing his arm, the gentle almost dreamy look in his eyes, a hotness flashed up in me.

Two months before, I didn't even want to know Clement. One month before, I allowed that, maybe, we might be friends. That night, I didn't want Clement to go. But I couldn't form the words. I just couldn't ask him to stay.

Sitting on my bed, looking out the window after Clement left, I wondered how to tell if I was moving toward the kind of loving that would be good. I heard the Rhinegold music again. Goose bumps tingled down my thighs and out my arms. Then my stomach, no, someplace way deeper in me opened, purple and golden centered like a morning glory. I gasped as pearly waves washed over what felt like dawn inside me.

# 10

## Clement

### Thursday, May 3, 1979

### Moon: Crescent

Mother's outstanding traits were her firm touch, her decisiveness and her temper. Of course, there was her fragrance, that honeysuckle and juniper. As Mother's Day approached, I mused over what to give a woman whose small, crisp voice cut through miles of squalling thunderheads. Amazing for one so petite.

Long before I was born, Mother had mastered the ways that mountains and plains, snow, ice and water channeled turbulent air. For her most spectacular displays, Mother had her assistants bring dry air over the Rockies and hold it at six to ten thousand feet. Underneath, Mother summoned tropical winds, topping them with cool, Canadian air while her stewards held a strong, polar jet stream in the upper atmosphere.

Mother knew that when the heavier, iced air sank, the warm winds would be upheaved. As those succulent, one-hundred-mile-per-hour updrafts corkscrewed into the chill upper atmosphere, their moisture mushroomed into clouds seventy thousand feet high and ten miles wide.

Inside, colliding ice crystals merged in the violent up- and downdrafts. When the droplets were heavy enough, Mother's supercells could release a million tons.

Her thunderclouds turned Earth's normally negative charge positive. That energy shadowed the cloud, reaching up trees, flagpoles, even people until the sky's negative impulses pierced the air's density and reached the ground's positive streamers. Then, mega-million-volt, fist-wide currents blasted skyward at four hundred twenty-two million feet per second. Surrounding air reached fifty thousand degrees Fahrenheit, reacting in thunderous compression waves.

There was always that pause, that second or ten minutes when all of Mother's approaching violence, the winds, rain, hail and lightning stopped. There was only far-off thunder and the deceptive calm of her main updraft feeding. And although mesocyclones could cover six miles, the faster they turned, the narrower they got. Their black clouds churned beneath supercells and were veiled above the wall clouds that spun them. The longer moisture rose, the easier it was for Mother to lower a vortex or send down the entire mesocyclone. By the time she launched a tornado, the updraft could raise moisture at one hundred fifty miles per hour while two- to three-hundred-mile-per-hour winds raged around her funnel.

To build mesocyclonic nurseries, Mother's officers merged multiple storm systems. They also drew surface winds at radically different trajectories and speeds from those directly above. When Mother forced this wind shear from the horizontal into the vertical plane and had a rear-flanking downdraft concentrate the updrafts, she created better spin. Then Mother could bring the downdraft closer than the normal several-mile span from the updraft, intensifying the rotation and cyclonic capacity.

At twenty miles an hour, wind was four times stronger than at ten. Eighty-mile-an-hour gusts packed sixty-four times more wallop. And while three-hundred-mile-per-hour winds were doldrums on Jupiter, on Earth they were deadly. Even though my Auntie Carmelita and her hurricanes were bigger, pound-for-pound, Mother's concentrated energy generated the most powerful storms on Earth.

Yet the most amazing woman I knew was Willow. Because of her, I actually contemplated commitment. Struggling to understand this change, I read that in many male mammals, awakening sexuality created a reckless bravado. Perhaps that was why, in unguarded moments, I believed I could divert rivers, bring Earth another Moon and settle down.

I loved thinking that Willow was the energy that had drawn me across light-years. That I had actually recognized Willow's evergreen and emerald bouquet, felt her tropical smile, seen her eyes in the skies a billion miles away. How had Willow pulled from such distance? How had I become like a planet circling her star?

For a long time, running away had been what I was. I rationalized my flights with the delusion that beyond, out there anywhere, farther and further, I could escape. Searching for any and everything different, I plowed into space's scintillating vastness. I bypassed places where formalized civilizations had developed, where too many refinements separated from what was naturally and simply intricate. I also avoided worlds with multi-legged, crawling green creatures. Otherwise, I dropped into one cosmic playpen after another.

Circling the red star Hokak was the white and violet planet Diire. There, the tiny, snowlike Soet sometimes clustered like mountains. Other times, they drifted alone, basking in their chartreuse days. The Soet radiated such joy in finding one another. Even strangers were only old friends who required reacquaintance. When Diire felt too much like home, I sailed the cold currents and hot tides, the maelstroms and calms, pursuing increasingly distant lights.

I could have wandered forever, but while meandering through a great and shimmering nebula, I felt my Self changing . . . involuntarily, like when teeth erupted and bones made one taller. I felt older and harder, the very things I ran from. Somehow, maturity was overtaking me.

Resisting and frustrated, I violated the first rule of travel. Not watching where I was going, I plowed into a blistering proto-star cloud mass.

Inside, stars gestated. How could I have missed a thing that huge? Clearly irrational, I refused to go around, as would have been polite. I charged in with such force that I crashed through an igniting star.

Along with a sense of being sheared, the spreading nuclear reactions created an excruciating dissolution. The blessing was that, after being disintegrated and reassembling myself, I felt lighter, freer and more ethereal than before. I would have been even happier if it weren't for The Afreete that started following.

After running from The Afreete on Jayah, I stopped on Pulai. I loved how the shallow mercury seas crested gently as seven moons minueted through the strawberry sky. What extraordinary tides as Pulai danced around its twin Ialup while revolving around their brilliant blue sun. Though just four times larger than Earth, one day took one hundred fifty Earth years.

The Pulaii looked like bamboo. Made of stone, their entire existence involved rising above the little mercury wavelets, soaking in their sun's heat and light, then contracting into coconut-sized pods to dream.

Light could have crossed the Milky Way in the time The Afreete took to manifest. After that escape, I suspected that, in all the universe, I was the only being who could give The Afreete what It craved. Thus, I stayed out of murky depths. Submarine worlds had too many unknowables. Even on Earth, where I'd played in the deeps as fish, porpoises, otters and penguins, I'd learned there was no telling what might come gliding through the dark and grab.

## Oull

*Suddenly, I was. Viscous. Thousands of claws glittering through an opalescent membrane. Needful. Lonely. No help, except the nothingness that wrapped and pressed in and gnawed, building a rage obsessed with finding the One whose essence had been there, close enough to grasp. When I* realized that the nebula was not all and burst from it, I easily followed the One's trail. Yes, Jayah was the first encounter. After the One fled, I did rest. In time, I did laugh. I understood. Of course, the One would retreat to a gentle world. That was the One's way. Of course, after a scare like Jayah.

After the slashing at Ue, the search became tedious. Te-Za-Teret was one of thirteen moons circling Ret. In the petroleum seas, the Te were bulbous, rainbow-striped entities that rolled and bounced across the bottoms. Za were needlelike beings that spurted through the oil. All were blind and sucked minerals from the gritty surface. As mindless creatures, they communicated no fear after increasingly vicious attacks. Worse, after only a few rotations on that world, I understood that the One had sensed my presence and fled.

I encountered other metamorphic and ethereal forms near many other worlds. They ran from me. It did not matter. My only interest had become the One.

Cautious. Yes, I would have to use much more care. After the strikes at Zoltat and Teoal, I reflected on how my Pursued One dodged, retreated, skipped and circled. And although the star systems were more numerous and the path incredibly vast, a clear and distinct knowing excited me. Dare I hope? Could my suspicions be true? Might my Pursued One have gone home?

# Mother

*April 10. Lawton, Oklahoma. A vortex dropped from pitch black skies. Hundreds were hurt. Three died, including a baby girl when the car she rode in was flicked from the highway.*

*The same day, fast-moving thunderstorms shot ten tornadoes through Texas. One killed in Lockett then whirled northeast to kill eleven more in Vernon before crossing the Red River into Oklahoma. Another landed near Halliday, leveling a path at times a full mile wide. A fierce updraft sucked people and merchandise from a Wichita Falls shopping mall, killing more than forty.*

*One hundred twenty tornadoes were recorded during seventeen days in April. Two thousand thirty-seven people were hurt. Fifty-eight perished. Mother in high season.*

*Mother.*

# 11

# Willow

## Wednesday, May 9, 1979

## Moon: Gibbous

Every year, storms from Kansas, Nebraska and Missouri kicked up tornadoes somewhere near Creame. Some didn't come clear down. The rest tore up little patches and didn't last long. They weren't bold columns like the one in the *Wizard of Oz* movie or in that children's cartoon I showed at the library. Ours usually had too much rain and hail to see unless they were close.

By the time the big one came, Terry'd gotten taller than Otto. Otto was more broad shouldered and muscular. His skin stayed clear as a fresh-cut apple while Terry was always sprouting pimples. Both their voices sounded funny, like they sometimes belonged to someone else. I noticed they had to wait for me when we ran the pathways through Blue Meadow, and tussling with them stopped when my breasts started. After my period came, Momma found even more ways to keep me home. That was probably good, because funny feelings were starting between me and Otto. It was getting as awkward to be with him as it was hard talking with Daddy. I was learning things at school and from my books that Daddy didn't know, and our fishing trips felt childish.

Riding home that Wednesday, the air was so muggy, no one wore their jackets. Terry and I watched little kids show Mother's Day cards they'd made by cutting hearts, flowers and butterflies from paper doilies and pasting them on construction paper.

"What are you giving your mom?" I asked Terry.

Terry's blue eyes sparkled as he said, "Pops drove us over to Hamilton last week. I got Mom the biggest card I could find. Cost sixty cents. Bought a nice ribbon, too. I'm going to tie up some lilacs from the Jenkins' place."

I thought Otto would tell Terry he could get lilacs from around their porch. Instead, real quiet, Otto said, "Dad got our gifts in Cincinnati. We agreed that I'd buy some bubble bath, and Dad got the perfume. It's my mother's favorite. Smells like roses." Otto stopped talking and stared at his hands. After a pause, he said, "But it doesn't feel right not getting anything for *Oma*."

My heart felt as heavy as it did the day of Frau Edda's funeral. My shoulders drooped. Terry didn't say anything. Neither did I. Bumping along, I remembered how Frau Edda used to soak her lilacs in oil that she wore. Frau Edda also used to make a little bottle for me and Momma. I was getting real gloomy when Otto said, "Hey! Let's go fishing. Just like old times."

I didn't have the heart to say I needed to let my parents know. Terry didn't say anything either. He passed his stop, and we got some old poles from the Melkpaths' shed. Down the road toward Corey Creek, chilly winds swayed tree branches and bent the grass. We all put our jackets back on.

"Oh, drat!" Terry said, sniffing the air. "It's going to storm."

"That's okay," Otto said. "We can build a fire under that big rock like we used to."

Clouds that looked like burnt biscuits prowled over us. Cows headed for trees. I couldn't swallow. The back of my neck tingled.

Boomers and lightning started and the prickly blue air made both Terry and Otto look fluorescent.

"Damn!" Terry said. "I ain't never seen that color before."

The wind stopped. All I heard was distant rumbling and my heart. It felt like we were in a giant bottle. Like if we could just get out of Blue Meadow, we'd be back in a real world.

The wind built fast. It sounded like women shrieking. Just when the siren started, rain beat us, then hail. Thunder blasted. Lightning sizzled. Otto, Terry and me really started running as deep-night-looking clouds churned in a big circle. Otto had grabbed my hand and was nearly dragging me. It was all I could do to keep from falling. Then, we heard the *BOOM*! The ground shook. We all lost our feet. By the time we got up again, drenched and muddy, the tornado was whirling right at us, wider than two barns and shimmering deep blue and silver, just like the air.

Maybe we all hollered. I couldn't even hear my self. Then truck lights flashed. Brakes screeched. Mr. Allister was driving so fast, he nearly ran us over. After Terry and Otto hauled me into the truckbed, I saw the lady's face. She was beautiful and right up at the clouds. Watching her, what I knew was that my tongue tasted too sweet. Somewhere, not in my nose but in the back of my head, I smelled juniper and honeysuckle.

Later, folks said I was overexcited. That my imagination got worked up. One thing was sure, we should have never got in that truck even though there wasn't no place low. Trees, fences, birds, parts of houses, dirt, a bathtub, a car fender, all kinds of stuff flew like bullets, but nothing hit. We got to the Melkpaths' storm cellar and just about jumped in. Then the men swung up and bolted the door. Shivering inside the towel Mrs. Melkpath gave me and huddled around the lantern, I tried not to hear the ripping and crashing.

Our shadows ran over the heavy wood slats to Frau Edda's glittering jars of tomatoes and corn and beets, her pickles and peach butter. Water dripped behind them and puddled under the floorboards. For the longest time, I couldn't take my eyes off the rhubarb standing as straight and pink as when Frau Edda won her ribbons. I always helped pick the rhubarb and washed it while Frau Edda cut the ruffly green tops. Frowning and pursing her lips, she'd grumble, "*Schon, aber Gift.* Pretty but poison."

Something shook the ground. I couldn't breathe watching Otto's dad search for a station on the transistor radio. "Betcha that twister blew the tower over," he said, calm as a Sunday supper.

That's when I remembered Frau Edda playing the record and heard the Valkyries. Louder and louder came, "Hiyoho! Hiyoho!" As the music grew, I heard Frau Edda saying, "*Wunderbar!* See Brunnhilde ride the mighty Grane. See lightning flash from the hooves. Brunnhilde and her sisters. Mighty women, like you one day."

Like me?

Like me?

Otto's mom stared up at the shaking and leaking storm doors and then at our faces. Real dry, she said, "Did I ever tell you how a tornado sucked one of my aunt's lace curtains under the sill of a closed window and not another thing in the house budged? That's what she said. Wasn't sure I believed her, but a dresser mirror did land in cousin Jordy's yard. Didn't it, Erik?"

"Yep. The glass blew a quarter mile. The owner's house and barn was flattened, but their mirror didn't have a crack."

I'd heard that Terry's dad once wanted to be a painter. An artist. He'd even planned on going to New York City. Then World War II came and he was blinded in one eye and sometimes his right arm went numb. He couldn't move it. So Terry's dad stayed in Creame and ran his family's farm machinery business. And just like summer weather, most of the time Mr. Allister was a big and blustery but nice man. Sometimes, though, he'd drink so hard that folks would find him on the road and take him home.

Mr. Allister breathed hard and fast. His good eye glittered. His red hair, even his beard stood out. He wiped his sweating face, pulled out a flask and nodded to Otto's mother, saying, "You don't mind, do you?" Without waiting, he gulped some down, then said, "I, ah . . . These damn things spook me. Did you know about the one that pitched a railroad tie straight through a station window? The railroad tie was balanced half in and half out, and the glass never shattered. Maybe the Indians were right. Maybe some kind of spirit is involved. Did you know one showed up the same place and day three years in a row?"

Even though she didn't have much time, Otto's mom had brought down a picnic basket. When she ripped open a bag of store-bought gingersnaps, everyone jumped. She smiled at us in her wry way and passed them around as Mr. Allister talked louder, saying, "A twister picked up a train engine, turned it around and set it on the track heading the other way. Explain that, why don't you? Then there was the couple having dinner when their house got picked up, and the roof and walls were sucked off before they were set back down still sitting at their dining room table as nice as the pie they were eating."

Otto's mom said, "Don't you think we've been real fortunate?"

But Mr. Allister cut her off, saying, "People don't know as much as they think. Everyone said they don't cross water. So how come one left Missouri, crossed the Mississippi and tore up some of Illinois?"

Otto's dad winked at Terry, Otto and me. He took a deep breath and said real loud, "Reckon you're right, Dave. I was always amazed at how one came through back in '46. Plucked my father's chickens. You should of seen that ornery rooster strutting around the yard stripped naked. Despite what those hens went through, we didn't lose a bird. Matter of fact, they laid more eggs that next week than they'd dropped the whole month before."

When we finally climbed out of the Melkpaths' storm cellar, the sun was low and red. Hail glistened everywhere. Mr. Allister's truck was twisted and upside down a few feet from the door. The roof and one side of the Melkpaths' barn was gone.

The tornado shaved a path over a half mile wide through Blue Meadow. The only thing left was my reading tree. And only willow trees grew along with fresh grass and flowers that actually made Blue Meadow more paisley and prettier.

At my home, drying our floors took days. Rain had gushed in from all directions and leaves got through or stuck partway in the tiniest cracks.

Mr. Allister found the Melkpaths' whole barn roof, but we never saw anything but bits of the barn walls. All summer, until the Melkpaths' barn finally got torn down, I marveled at the corn that grew in that loft.

# 12

## Jimmy

### Monday, May 28, 1979

### Moon: New

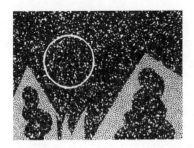

*Dear Jimmy,*

*I got your flowers. I was surprised. I did not expect to hear from you again.*

I'm James Anderson. A Certified Public Accountant. M.B.A. thirty-two. Dark brown. Square and muscular. Five-ten. Wide, full mouth. Small mustache under straight nose. Crinkly hair, black. Lately, there's been gray.

I make good money. Like gin on the rocks. Custom-blend cigarettes. Two weeks and two days ago, I had Mr. Burns, the florist, write: *Dear Willow, On this day, especially, I think of us. I'm divorced now. I'd like to see you.*

Mr. Burns is thin with white hair and mustache. He looks kindly through wire-rimmed glasses. Putting the blue pencil behind his ear, Mr.

Burns turns the yellow tablet. Asks, "Is this the way you want it, Mr. Anderson?"

I nod. Ask, "When will the flowers get there?"

Mr. Burns peers at a large wall clock. "Later today. If not, first thing tomorrow."

"Make sure it's got baby's breath. Lots of it."

"Yes sir."

I know that Willow's last name hasn't changed. She still lives on Evergreen Way. Works at Faraday's. If someone's involved, let the best man win.

I get long-stemmed American Beauties for Mom. Walk outside. My hand flinches. I trip. Something's gnawing at me. Feels like small rabbits. White.

*Just want to thank you and say I'm sorry your marriage did not work out. It took me a long time to be happy after you were gone, so I imagine divorce is even worse. I am okay now. I hope you are too.*

When I get to my parents' home, Mom is at the side door. I grin. Shake my head. This heavyset woman saw that Lonnie, Melinda and I were scrubbed, polished and pressed. We were deodorized and ash free. We had real silver. Leaded crystal. We spoke quietly and pronounced every syllable, especially final consonants.

I hand Mom her roses. Hug her. She says, "Thank you, son." With hard-red, manicured nails, she opens the box. Large, ivory teeth brighten Mom's dark face. Golden brown curls brush my cheek when she kisses me. Says, "They're beautiful." Then Mom leans against me in her tailored lavender suit. Whispers. "Try to get back for Father's Day. With his heart like it is, your being here will mean a lot."

I think about things that have made Mom happy. Her marriage. Children. Symphony tickets. Ballet. Dinners on time. Airy soufflés.

Honor Roll certificates. Becoming the first Blacks in this neighborhood. Keeping uncultivated kin away.

When I once followed lines on maps, I asked Mom about Hindsight and God's Eye. She'd said, "Those places? We don't bother. That's just where people stayed down South."

Of the photo albums in the attic, Mom rolled her eyes. Sighed like the subject bored her. Said, "Remember, James, they didn't even have indoor plumbing. Maybe they still don't. Then there's the chickens, dogs and pigs. Those people aren't ready for the twentieth century. We leave them alone."

I thought Mom was right. The proof was in our thick carpets. Real Oriental rugs. Classical music from nineteenth-century Europe. No honky-tonk, boogie-woogie, rhythm and blues, zydeco. No dusty roads. No patched-up clothes and crusty feet. No shacks where folks ate chicken with their fingers. Wiped lips on sleeves. Laughed with their mouths full and wide open.

Mom pats my arm. Says, "Come on in, son. Let me put these flowers in some water. Your father's waiting in the living room."

Dad rises awkwardly. We shake hands. I stare at my dark around his tan. Ask how he's doing.

Dad taps his chest. Says, "Like Doc Weaver said, if I eat right and keep moving, I should last another day or two."

Dad looks Spanish or maybe Greek. He could have walked away from his Black blood, but he too much loved the people who adopted him. Folks Black as Mom. As me.

I pause. Ask, "How are those accounts in Akron and Youngstown?"

"Treat people right, keep your business respectable, and people flock to you." Dad chuckles. "It's the best kind of mousetrap."

"Do you still have business in Good Sky?"

Dad nods. "Frank Singer and Mrs. Faraday are fine." Gently, he adds, "Nothing has changed there."

I look down. Mumble, "Thanks." After a few moments, I walk into the dining room. Study pictures on the wall. My parents' wedding. Dad at his first garage. Lonnie in his white waramba. Me, Melinda and Lonnie at our proms. Our graduations. My children Wendy and Jason with a fat white man in a red and white suit. With Easter baskets and a white rabbit.

There is the holy Madonna, white arms outstretched. The Last Supper of white men. Beneath all that, Willow wore a pink and green minidress. Black patent-leather shoes with low heels. Pink pantyhose. Jade green love beads. On the table, Mom's best china. Crystal. Silver. For appetizers, we nibbled pedigrees. What Willow didn't realize was that, like earthenware, some honesty never reached our damask. Truths like Dad being delivered to the Andersons' house by some white family's colored maid.

We also didn't discuss how Mom's people weren't paler than kraft bags. Thus, the Daniels didn't get near the "better" colored churches and clubs. Except that Mom's grandmother cooked. When she moved from God's Eye to Louisville, that got her out of scullery and laundry work. Got her into fine, white folks' kitchens. Mom's father came to Cleveland following big steel money. When that wasn't enough, he ran numbers and a girl or two. His daughters, Mom, Riva and Jillian, those three full-featured and coffee-toned sisters with honey-brown wigs, they all wanted cream-colored men. Mom was lucky. In the 1940s, men married their baby's mothers. In our case, Dad loved her. Yes. As a family, we had to be careful who we let in.

After Lonnie died, I spent months on the road. Took my paints, pastels, charcoal. Worked night and day. Mainly in the desert Southwest and high plains. Then Cleveland amazed the world. The Cuyahoga River caught fire. Ignited two bridges. Flames blazed five stories high. Perhaps that news, more than anything, brought me back.

I kept painting. Stayed in bars. Girls' pants. My parents' lifestyle lost all dimension. Their world became so flat that I finally understood why Lonnie took me to old drummers. Their hands could make the skins praise, challenge, sing and cry. They pattered rhythms that covered like kisses. They had said that soon. Soon Lonnie would be able to follow his fiancée's leaps, dips and twirls with his own drum. Soon Lonnie and Abebi would dance with wide wings and stir the stars together. Soon even his little brother, even I would know the way.

I could see the way but didn't want it. Especially the colorful clothes. The whistling and singing. The hands clapping. The glowing faces. I didn't need to understand seasons. The symbols inside numbers. And what did they mean by *soon?*

All these years later, old hands keep inviting. They carry blackened pots of hopping John and gumbo straight from stove to table. The aromas make me ask: How come I'm well fed and starving? Why am I just suspecting what Lonnie knew? That without flies and mosquitoes coming through open windows and waterbugs under the sink, I don't know how to protect myself from the resentments and loneliness the world slings. Without root knowings and earth-crusted wisdoms handed down, I can't recognize my own ignorance. Without things that I can love, I have no life.

Ten years ago, Dad asked for help with his business. July 1969, the Indians played in Cleveland. Municipal Stadium needed more popcorn. I got to Good Sky around noon. Blistering heat all the way. No breeze in Faraday's parking lot.

Walking through the dust my truck raised, I see a dark girl. Cut-off jeans hug her slender hips. Her legs swing from the loading dock. Her hair is short and *au naturel.* A nappy embarrassment, Mom would say. No ladies our family knew wore their hair that way. Even Abebi, Lonnie's girlfriend, had braids. Kid sister Melinda got pressed and curled. Mom added peroxide lightening.

The young woman plays checkers with Marla, the manager's newly married and very pregnant daughter. Marla flips her long, russet hair. Her round face is fuller. Brown eyes and cherry lips smile. She's got a strong body. A back-slapping laugh. A probing mind. Surprising with her milkmaid appearance.

The young woman with Marla leans back. Accepts the sun. Unusual for one with dark skin. A yellow halter relaxes over her breasts. She raises a pretty arm. Shades her eyes. A smile lingers on full lips. She wears tiny, gold hoops in pierced ears. I sense meadow air. Sweet earth. Light flowers.

Marla says, "Hi, Jimmy. This is Willow. She's taking over for me. Bet you're thirsty." Hoisting herself up, Marla pats her belly. "I'll get us all some Cokes. Maybe a little more exercise will help get this bun out of the oven quicker."

I look at their checkers game. Ask Willow if she plays chess.

"No." A soft, level voice.

That summer and autumn, I never thought about how others, especially my family, might see only Willow's surface. I never thought we couldn't build a future until Mom's questions started.

"Where does she attend college?"

"Who are her people?"

"What does she look like?"

Then our baby died. He was barely four inches long. Weighed two ounces. His fingers and toes even had soft nails. I figured his passing was just as well. That way, Willow and I were bound only by feelings.

A month later, I kissed Mom in our kitchen. Walked through our dining and living rooms. Saw our house up a driveway, beside a flawless lawn, off a street, through a neighborhood where Willow had no reality. When I reached Evergreen Way, when Willow, beautiful and suddenly wrong, met me glowing, I was empty.

But in those magical months with Willow, I had loved. In my own fashion. I knew how. After all, I had loved being first in line and getting good parts in plays. I had loved morning light, softball and Christmas eve. I had loved the smell of French fries, new books and oil paint on canvas. I had loved little girls in Easter dresses and lilies of the valley. I had loved snowball battles, the touch of sable brushes, kissing warm brown lips and feeling a woman's heart beat close to mine. I had loved learning to drive, to sketch a hand and realizing that reality is just perception and perspective. I had loved a good jump shot and hook and how Willow was all of those things.

*Jimmy, guess I should let you know I'm starting to see someone now. That's a surprise too. Can't really picture liking someone like him because he's so different. But he's nice. His name is Clement.*

My art now expresses itself in balance sheets and other numbers that must match. Years after marrying Shelley, I wondered: When making the choices I did, do many men chase their taste on other Black women's lips? Lips like those that were fire hosed while praying for equal rights? Do they seek embrace in arms that Selma, Birmingham and Little Rock clubbed, cattle prodded and ripped with dogs? All that abuse so that I could think: What the hell, I'm a man, not a Black man. I married a woman. Not a white woman.

I needed to escape the icicles on Black women's sightlines. Sometimes straight-haired, college-educated, caramel and mocha-colored women got wine, flowers, dinner and slept with because I needed to be with women who were marching against their fathers' and brothers' lynchings. Castrations because they were suspected. But those men never winked or whistled and certainly never got their hands on the jewel inside white women's panties.

But I never chose dark ladies. Not the ones with mahogany creasing soft honey palms. None were small and delicate with lips that parted ever so slightly when smiling.

*Just know I will always be your friend and care about you, Jimmy, but do not send me anything else. After all this time, it's best to leave what we had where it belongs.*

*Your friend,*
*Willow*

I hear a knock. Open my door. See Abe Corsini. He's a math teacher. My neighbor. A bachelor. Likes regional history. Jazz. Collecting bow ties. He's five-eight. Curly brown hair that's mostly gone. Eyes so active, I wonder when Abe's brain rests.

Abe wears black sweatpants. Gray sweatshirt. Holds a basketball. Peers in the door. Says, "Haven't seen you in weeks, my man. Ever since Kim walked out. Or was the last one Amy or Odetta? What've you been doing in here?"

Abe picks up papers. Whistles. Nods slowly. Says, "Don't know why you waste your time crunching numbers. Who is she?"

I put away my pastels. Shrug.

Abe bounces the basketball in his palm. Tilts his head toward the door. Says, "Get your high tops. Let's go."

"Not now, Abe."

"It's a holiday, my man. Winter's long gone. Hibernation time's over."

Outside, I blink. Sunlight almost hurts. I ask, "What are we doing here, Abe?"

"Make it, take it." He sinks one from the foul line. Strolls to the ball. Tosses it in. Says, "And the Corsini Corsairs score again. Might have a rout going." Abe dribbles the ball close. Dodges away. Trots to the court's far side. Shouts, "So, how're things going?"

I catch Abe's air ball. Tell him, "Things are great. The job's stable. No hassles. Saving money."

Abe tries snatching the ball. I pass it behind my back. Run. Set up to shoot.

"Well, I'm sure those bank accounts keep you warm at night."

I miss. Turn and sneer. "Look who's talking."

Abe grabs the ball. Sets it at his feet. Opens his arms like he's hugging the sky. "Hey, I'm getting mine."

"Since when?"

"It's *Beshert,* James. *Beshert.*"

"What's that?"

"Yiddish. Didn't know I was Jewish, did you?" Abe chuckles, then points up. "*Beshert* means it's in the stars. Destiny. Fate. *Que sera sera* with an engine."

"What's that got to do with me?"

Abe struts to the top of the key. Hollers. "Check!" Spins me a bounce pass. Says, "*Beshert,* my friend, means we get what we're supposed to have."

I bounce the ball back. "Does that mean you and I are supposed to be sitting out here twiddling our—"

"Are you going deaf? Speakest for thyself." Abe shoves the ball at me.

I sink the shot. Eventually win the game. We go inside. Kill some of Abe's wine. Several beers. After again hearing about Italian influence on regional industry and his mother's knaidels and challah as well as eating cheese blintzes, I drag down the hall. Unlock my apartment. I light a cigarette. Stare into a night lit by court lights. Remember Abe saying. "It's *Beshert,* James. Try it."

"Get out of my face."

Abe laughs. Says, "Try it, you stubborn son of a bitch."

# 13

## Willow

## Sunday, June 10, 1979

## Moon: Full

The first time I ever saw Jimmy Anderson, me and Marla, we sat on the loading dock eating egg salad sandwiches and playing checkers. The dust that Jimmy's truck raised hung in the air. Through that haze, sunlight shone off him. The way Jimmy walked made me think of a bear. Mainly because Jimmy moved with a kind of strength and determination. As though, once pointed in a direction, he'd press on until a greater force aimed him different.

Jimmy's complexion was almost dark as mine. He wasn't tall. His white shirt and khaki slacks were neat, despite the long drive and heat. Jimmy was near my age, and I was seventeen then. But getting closer, the set of Jimmy's face made his soul seem more like thirty. Jimmy had eyes like Coca-Cola in a white cup. He had a nice laugh, real open and catchy, and pretty teeth.

Sometimes, Jimmy picked me up at Faraday's. The next morning, Frank Singer might catch me sweeping up overflowed popcorn and say,

"Perhaps you and Mr. Anderson should just stay up late on the weekends, uh?" Frank had watery brown eyes that peered through graying eyebrows. His hair was thin. His shoulders slumped and his mouth always seemed on the verge of a smile. Those mornings, he would grin and shrug. "But what can I tell young people? Look at my daughter, Marla. Didn't I counsel her? It's no use. Young got to be foolish. Maybe so when they get old, they got good memories." He winked, "Like me and Rose."

Jimmy rode me past the MileMaster Train and Bus Depot and Julio's Price Is Right Gas Station and out the highway past the cornfields. Some of it was popping corn, but I didn't think about things drying out or insides fusing from heat and swelling until they burst or much else, except Jimmy's broad shoulders and his arms and how good being with him felt. Especially while Ruby was visiting family that autumn.

By that next spring, I thought the relationship Jimmy and I had was tough as the shells on popping corn. Nothing could break what we had. Especially with the baby. Jimmy really seemed to want him. And if there was any heat and pressure, it could only create a bigger and better love.

The Andersons' home was freshly painted white. Lake Erie glittered in the distance. Two live oak trees grew on a grassy lawn bordered by white and pink impatiens. In the side yard, between two cherry trees, I saw a wood glider. Inside, their stereo played soft symphony music, nothing like Frau Edda's.

Jimmy's mother was a dark and plump woman with sandy-tinted hair. It was stiffly sprayed in big curls. Her full lips were colored dark red. She had high cheekbones and wide, watchful eyes. Mrs. Anderson wore a silky white blouse with lace at the collar and cuffs. It was buttoned to her chin. The taffeta lining swished under her gray skirt.

Jimmy's father had light tan skin. He was a short, stocky man with wavy black hair that was just a little gray. Mr. Anderson had a soft, cultured voice. He smiled. His eyes warmed when talking about his early years in the South. "I don't think my family's unusual, Willow. Colored people might have it hard, and getting a higher education isn't easy, but

I've come to believe it is very important to improving our situation. After all, fewer of us can survive on farms these days."

"Thank goodness," Jimmy's sister said.

I sat in the living room holding a delicate glass that rang when it hit my teeth. I kept trying not to spill or say anything stupid and wished I had soda pop in one of Momma's aluminum cups.

When we finally got to the table, Jimmy's mother traced a manicured finger around her gold-edged china. She said, "Some of these dishes come from my Aunt Bessie, Bessie Daniels Tyler. And this silver is from my grandmother, Josephine Harris Daniels. James' father's family and my people, the Chalfonts, the Daniels, the Tylers and Harrises, we place great importance on family and passing on the very best." Mrs. Anderson patted the creamy tablecloth. "You understand, of course."

I looked to Jimmy for some words or at least a glance to ease the weight of all those names. Jimmy just shoved his potatoes and wouldn't look my way. I wanted to run. I wanted to wipe that whole scene away as though it were chalk on a blackboard. I thought of my school days and saw fat brushes dip into tempera paints. They dripped pictures of Momma quilting and Daddy making big pancakes. I saw us eating Blue Meadow raspberries and chili with cheese and hotdogs with relish and baked beans on plastic dishes. I tasted grape Kool-Aid and smelled fish frying in margarine beside Corey Creek.

As Mrs. Anderson nodded over her minted lamb and pale wine, her pastel yellow dining room with matching satin and silk upholstered chairs became a dusty woodland road. Fuchsias and forsythias clustered on one side. Far off, I saw Momma and Daddy's old house with the windmill. The sun was setting. Through the tree branches, stars glowed. They got bigger and bigger until their lights were all that was left.

There was a bad storm when Jimmy drove me home. Hail cracked against the car. The way the wind rocked and lightning cut through the smoky darkness, it seemed the whole world was as upset as me. By the time Jimmy started back to Cleveland, the weather cleared. I figured except for some flooding and downed trees and poles, he got home okay. But Jimmy never let me know he was safe. I didn't hear from Jimmy until he called and took me to Vincente's.

The year before, when I got off that Greyhound bus to stretch my legs and get a snack, I was never sure how I smelled anything but pizza outside the MileMaster depot, much less Faraday's popcorn. And if I'd just gone into Vincente's, I would never have met Ruby and Rose. I wouldn't have been looking at Jimmy there in Vincente's with my heart flopping and little ice crystals starting to grow, and I wouldn't have been reliving the hurts that got me to Good Sky in the first place.

After Momma and Daddy died, my grandmother, "just" Lucille, had me come live with her. "Just" Lucille had a three-story, brick building across from the U.S. Steel mill in Homestead, Pennsylvania. On the first floor was her bakery. Lucille lived on the second floor and the third floor was empty rooms. "Used to rent them out," Lucille said. "I ain't in that business no more."

Working in the bakery was how I met Kinshasa Cinque Salaam. He towered over the other millworkers who came into Sweet Lucy's. Just like them, he wore the green asbestos pants and jacket and a hardhat with goggles.

Kinshasa was the color of walnut shells. He had a beard and mustache and watchful eyes. When I was ready to take Kinshasa's order, he bowed his head a bit and said, "Peace to you, sister, in all praise to our great Black Motherland." Then he ordered nut rolls, a couple of jelly-filled crullers and some Danish.

One morning, Kinshasa came in early. Lucille was in the back running the big mixer, and I was putting ladyfingers into a display case.

"Peace and blessings on you, sister," Kinshasa's voice vibrated inside me. He smiled, "You're new in the city, aren't you?"

I nodded.

"I've been admiring you, sister. I see in you the legacy of our great African queens."

All I'd ever heard about Africans was that they were backwards and cannibals with bones in their noses. They put plates in their lips and their children starved. Jungle movies and cartoons didn't show anything great about them. I felt myself flushing hot and hopeful.

Kinshasa said, "For over a hundred years, our full lips, wide noses and fuzzy hair have been presented as ugly or funny. But I look at you and wonder how our loveliness could be missed."

I fidgeted with a rag.

"Tell me, sister, why don't you let your hair express its natural beauty? Let it stand and hold sunlight around your face."

Then, I really blushed.

"I didn't mean to embarrass you, my sister. I'm just telling the truth. Think on it, my beautiful queen."

In the quiet until the next customer came, I kept touching my hair, thinking about Momma's straightening comb with its cracked, wooden handle. Most of the orange paint was gone. Every other Saturday night, its iron teeth clanged over the stove's blue flames.

That's when my fresh-washed hair, fluffy as cotton balls, was parted and greased, sometimes with lard and, if we had money, bergamot or Dixie Peach. Rags were scorched, testing the iron's heat. When Momma combed those hot iron prongs through my hair, the grease sizzled. The kitchen got so smoky, we opened windows, even in the coldest and stormiest weather. Burnt-crisp hair fell all over the floor, but the reward was shiny hair. It couldn't swing like the white girls', but at least it was straight.

The next time I washed my hair, I just patted and shaped it. Lucille fussed about my woolly, Ubangi-Zulu look, but she came around and even told me about a barber who'd trim it nice and not charge much.

When Kinshasa came back, he nodded and smiled. "You're a true inspiration." He said, "Why not join with some of your brothers and sisters. Come with me to some meetings. You'll understand why we're not 'colored' and 'Negroes,' and why we're getting rid of these slavery names. It's time we left the white man's ways alone."

I went. As we ate from bowls of fruit and I paid quarters for small meat pies and cookies, I saw slides of African people. They were beautiful in their robes and beads and paints, their headdresses and metal adornments. I heard the lectures and realized that people like me had a past that was great and honorable. In the drumming and the people singing, I found possibilities. Then, as they danced, a woman whose four-year-old called Kinshasa father introduced herself. A couple weeks later, I met a woman pregnant by Kinshasa. Then I met Kinshasa's wife and their two children. It was nation-building time.

Kinshasa was my second lover. Otto was my first. Otto who walked square and tall and moved his hands deliberate and purposeful. Otto whose gray eyes were like Frau Edda's, even with little rainbows sparkling. I thought about how I'd taken my homework to a leafy area along Corey Creek not far from a new cluster of wild raspberries. It was real private and a great spot if sudden rain came up. As I got closer, I heard Otto's soft whistling.

Birds looped in a wide, blue sky. Mice, chipmunks and partridges skittered through the meadow. Some tall grass dipped and rose in waves as the wind moved. That afternoon was the third summerlike day in a row that March.

When I called Otto, and he said to come on in to that special place, I felt good even before I saw him. For a while, we just listened to the creek and watched little fish. We'd swing our feet through the ice-cold water. Our thighs and arms leaned together. When Otto touched my hand, I felt like when Momma'd been baking all day, and those wonderful pie and bread aromas made my mouth water.

We didn't say anything for a while. Then Otto touched my face. He looked at me a long time. Surprising lights gushed through me. Maybe

I didn't even need to nod when Otto kissed me, then kissed me again longer and asked, "Can we do this, Willow? Is it alright?"

Being with Kinshasa wasn't like with Otto. Maybe Otto and I had been clumsy, but our caring made up for the fumbling. After meeting Kinshasa's wife, some other people drove me home. When I squeezed out of the car and watched it disappear, I realized that Homestead's burning hills had crusted too many cinders over me. I called Aunt True in Akron.


At Vincente's, when our food came, Jimmy looked at his hoagie like it was alive. Finally, he said, "I'm going back to college, Willow."

I said, "That's good."

"That means I won't be able to keep coming down here. I won't even be in Ohio."

I just kept staring at Jimmy.

"And there's a lot of preparations I have to make."

"I guess so."

"We won't see each other for a while."

I looked at the red, green and white squares on Vincente's floor. I wondered if in "a while" they'd put down new colors. I wondered if Molly O'Brien, the young woman serving us, if in "a while" she'd have children and grandchildren. Maps of Italy and pictures of Italian landmarks hung on the wood-panel walls. How much of that would change in "a while"?

"Your mother wanted you to go away, didn't she?"

"My mother, she's, well, both my parents, they're paying my tuition, but I'll have to work some to take care of other expenses. And there's so much catching up I've got to do."

"I could work."

"Thanks, Willow." Jimmy blinked. "It just feels like . . . don't you think we need a little space?"

In the months that followed, I'd keep noticing Mei-Yeh's laughing Buddhas. I'd remember her telling me that he actually had a name. It was Mi Lo Fo. "He is Friendly One," Mei-Yeh said. "Look at how big he is. That is because he knows so much. And being all wise, he can laugh no matter what happens in the world."

I'd look at Mi Lo Fo and try to convince myself that it didn't matter, Jimmy's going. In time, there were other lips that tasted and sounded nice and bodies that felt good. But after a while, I just wanted to be left alone. I wanted to roll. Roll without bumping or being bumped.

In trying to understand leavings, I thought about Mariah who died the summer I was fourteen. Mariah's dying was like someone who'd left in the night. Cause by nighttime, folks were usually tired. By night, folks either didn't bother or couldn't watch those departing, so the leavings seemed more invisible. Then, I thought about Frau Edda.

The last time I saw her, she was pale and thin. Her arms were too weak to hug us, but her gray eyes sparkled. Frau Edda gave us ten dollars and smiled as we presented our Honor Roll certificates and described the ceremony. Then Frau Edda said, "These are great steps you are taking. Look at how you're going from little to big."

But big seemed so far away. I didn't think I could ever do that.

"Very soon, you will graduate. See you not how you're about to fly so high into new selves? Your new life, maybe it is like the nighttime that you enter, not able to see, not sure what you will find. Remember Tristan and Isolde. Remember how she could not see that Tristan had died, only that he was transformed. It is like all stages of our lives, *ja?* Who knows what opportunities come, dear children, when old doors close so that new can open?"

After Frau Edda's funeral, Otto gave me a gift-wrapped box and said, "*Oma* wanted you to have this." I put the package on my dresser. For days, I watched morning light glow on the curly pink and green ribbons. That next Saturday, while Momma rested and Daddy cooked our sausages and pancakes, I finally peeled off the paper and lifted the lid. The book inside lit up the gloomy air. There they were, Parsifal and Brunnhilde, Lohengrin and Tannhauser. But they were all painted brown. Of all the things I never got from the house in Creame, Ohio, I missed Frau Edda's book most.

After Ruby handed Jimmy's Mother's Day flowers over the back fence to the Svenson sisters, in quiet moments, I felt myself burning and freezing. I wanted to know how come Jimmy was walking back through my waking dreams.

I had enough troubles. May and then June, they were like peppermints and vinegar. Clement had made every kind of bread, from apple buttermilk to whole wheat zucchini. Spending so much time with him, I was put off and starstruck. I was peeved and overjoyed. I got scared of Clement and then trusted. I didn't think I could stand the seesawing. What was I to do with the wanting and resisting all the time? In the shower, I'd imagine Clement's hands moving over me. While deliberately not thinking about Clement, I'd hope he'd phone. It was bad enough seeing Clement's dark eyes, his smile and the grace in his walk, but hearing his laugh, even his footsteps when no one was near, that was getting to be too much.

One night, Clement, he just stood in my door with his glowy skin and tarbaby eyes and hair like steel wool caught up in a thick rubber band, and he said, "Come on, Willow. Sunsets and full moons and the good-night whisper of new leaves don't wait."

Outside, the Svenson sisters fussed over the petunias in their window boxes. LaShawn and Bessie Carpenter shared sugar cookies with their dolls while Amos finished painting his doorsill.

Touching Clement lightly felt so good. And thinking on how I knew everyone on our street, I said, "You know, I don't think I've ever seen your landlady."

Clement walked a little faster and said, "Really? Seems I see her entirely too often."

When I first got to Good Sky, a FOR SALE sign hung on Clement's house. Later, a little board printed with VACANCIES got taped to a window. No one lived there until Clement. I said, "Isn't it odd that someone would leave a place empty so long?"

"That's why I'm here, my dear." Clement wiped his hands, reminding me of Momma when she finished kneading bread or cutting biscuits. He glanced at the house, then said, "Come on, sweet Willow. Let's enjoy summer's first eve."

"Summer won't be here for nearly two weeks."

"Mere detail."

Mill dust glittered on the embankment sidewalk. Lights from houses and cars way across the Calliope shimmered in the water. The clouds were orange and deep purple. A glorious full moon rose. Leaning over the railing, Clement said, "This moon is so beautiful, but the one I love best is dark. With its midnight rise, each night it becomes more frail as what it was drains away. Soon nothing is left but the chance for something new."

The coke ovens blazed ferociously. A tugboat hooted as it pushed barges. "You know," Clement said, "I always thought of fire as destructive. That's why it scared me. I could never get near it. Not even to toast marshmallows. Just thinking about fire made my skin feel charred."

"What did you do about birthday cakes?"

"Aha! Now, I can accept that fire doesn't so much destroy as change. Think what it does to those dry corn kernels you work with. And that coke out there, it used to be coal. When it got to the mill, it became fuel for ironmaking. The base for steel. But once upon a time, a dry seed grew into a great tree. When the tree died and fell into the earth, it became coal. With enough time and heat and pressure, there could have been diamonds." Clement's eyes sparkled. "And my father taught me that, on a night like this, a man first realized he could travel like thought."

"Your father must have been teasing you."

"Father said everyone could do it. He said that the people lived near where the Niger River now flows. Only the river wasn't there."

"I don't believe that. Where was it?"

"Patience, Willow. Father said that the man could take himself to the stars and back, like that." Clement snapped his fingers. "And, you know the big spider and the hummingbird and the other designs that are so large yet so symmetrically, even microscopically perfect that researchers can't figure out how ancient people carved them into the plains and plateaus of Nasca? Do you know that spider now exists only in a small part of the Amazon rain forest thousands of miles from where it was drawn? And you'd have to be miles high to get the proportions correct. Some think beings from outer space did all that. How ridiculous. But then the scientists have only recently realized that the continents here are mudpies that float and that Saturn has at least twenty moons. Anyway, although that man wasn't as interested in leaving signs as in mapping possibilities, he created a magnificent design. Just as with the pyramids and other ancient works, what people today fail to realize is . . ."

A silvery blue wisp crossed the moon. Warm as the night was, I shivered. Clement rubbed my arm and said, "We'd better go."

"But I want to hear more about that man."

"He died."

Clement's abruptness startled me. He closed his eyes for a moment, then said, "You know, some of the stars we see, they no longer exist. Their light was sent centuries, thousands of years ago. Though the light source is gone, their works continue. Just like long after this instant, others will see our light. Even after this planet and moon and Sun vanish, others will know that we were here."

Clement walked away and was, for moments, a silhouette. A figure without definition. When he came back, he only said, "Come on, Willow."

"But—"

Clement tugged me along, saying, "The pattern was magnificent. Miles wide and gorgeous. One of these days I'll draw it."

"Why can't I just go see it?"

"Hills have risen and others have crumbled. Rivers shifted. You'd have to be a good ten miles or more . . ." Clement tapped his jaw with his forefinger. He looked lost in calculations.

"How come you're the only one who knows about it?"

"The only one?" Clement looked perplexed. I waited for him to explain. Instead, as we turned off Hibiscus onto Evergreen, Clement said, "Why don't you come up to my place tomorrow? Let me play host."

"I won't be bringing bread."

"Just be my guest, sweet Willow. You know that really is a wonderful name. Did I ever tell you there was a place—"

"Yes, you told me."

"It was a magical world."

"Clement, I'll bet if I told you my name was Sequoia or Cedar or, or even Sumac, you'd come up with a story."

"And what would you bet, my dear?"


That next morning, when I stepped onto Ruby's stoop, at first I didn't notice the woman. Considering how she looked, that was amazing. She had on a stark white dress under a navy, bolero-cut jacket with bold, silver patterns that zigzagged. Around her neck was a chiffon scarf in shades of light and dark blue with silver glitter. She was as small as me, with creamy, mocha skin. She wore misty, navy-colored stockings over beautiful legs and was built—as Daddy's friend Mr. Porky used to say— like a brick shit house. Her dark, wavy hair had reddish highlights and her long fingernails were sparkly white.

I nodded and said, "Good morning."

Silently, with very dark yet vividly bright eyes, she looked me up and down. I got an odd sensation, like when I was eight years old and wading through big, heart-shaped leaves to find pumpkins. The wood fence posts, the rusting garden hoe, the parched cornstalks all had that crystal icing that the sun would melt and pull up into clouds. The purple and pink dawn was so huge that everything, especially me, felt as tiny as I did with that woman who wasn't young, but who didn't look old.

She tightened her small and bright red lips. Then without a smile or even a word, she turned and walked toward the Calliope. The ends of her scarf floated behind her like long, wagging fingers. Her white, ankle-cut, high-heeled boots sparked against the bricks. Otherwise, she never made a sound. In morning air that normally smelled of coffee and bacon, there was a sweet fragrance.

I looked back when I reached Cedar Avenue, and she was gone. As I turned the corner, I thought—maybe visiting the neighbors, maybe at the post office or at the Applegate Mall, maybe long ago, or maybe it was the darned full moon—but I'd seen her before.

# 14

## Clement

## Monday, June 11, 1979

## Moon: Full

From across Evergreen Way, my dwelling looked dismal. The neighborhood had all kinds of stories about the house's long abandonment. Folks talked of neglected building codes, a shifting foundation, curses and ghosts. They suspected that neither mice nor ants, not even cockroaches came in, which was true.

Why on Earth did I invite Willow? The reason must have been temporary insanity. The full moon had made me foolish. I was in trouble and starting to panic. Then, in one nanosecond of lucidity, some Self in me suggested: Get a grip! Acquire a broader, a more universal perspective. Reinforce your backbone. Develop guts and other manly apparatus.

I breathed deep. Lowered my pulse. Closed my eyes. When I just floated and convinced myself that those eructing, corporeal anxieties—including throbbing temples and a weak bladder—had very simplistic origins, the cold sweats subsided. When I thought rationally instead of in panicked fits, I understood that the cause of my distress was gravitational compression. I was reacting to the broil and friction of a weighty matter collapsing into itself. Actually, the phenomenon happened all the time and touched practically everywhere. Why was I so upset? When masses of little hydrogen atoms scrunched enough that they heated to, oh, twenty million degrees centigrade, *voilà*! Thermonuclear fusion. Each time four hydrogen atoms smashed into one, they became helium. A gamma ray photon erupted. If there were enough—and my little Sun fused just four hundred million tons per second—well, then a star ignited. During a gamma ray photon's several-thousand-year journey out to a Sun's surface, X-ray photons were sprouted, each of which could generate its own thousand photons of visible light. Earth intercepted about one in every half billion its star produced. But with Suns gushing light all over the place, those who could see, would. Of course, there were times when one wished one couldn't.

If one couldn't . . . see, then the presentability of one's abode wouldn't plummet so drastically when one was about to have company, real company, especially for the first time. One wouldn't wonder why the furniture was lackluster and the fixtures dusty. One would have noticed that the plaster walls needed patching, fresh paint and some artwork. One would not have been surprised by holes in the rugs and draperies. Looking at my sparsely situated furniture of odd and faded pedigree, I felt as though I'd just awakened after years in a thicket.

But frantic scrubbing and scraping weren't the only reasons my hair frizzled. I hadn't slept well. Willow filled my thoughts. And those images generated a tension. It was like little lightning strokes. They charged my nerves and scratched through my arteries. When I was with Willow and she frowned up at me, my arms, my fingers—well, certainly all extremities—tingled and rose to attention. I blushed so acutely I wondered where that much blood came from. My brain couldn't hold a thought smaller than Io. So, when I could remember that "one" and "two" were sequential and could add an answer like "Clement" to a question like "Who are you?," when I could accomplish such feats in Willow's presence, what did I think? I realized how I'd never . . . not in human form, I'd never had . . . times were different when I left. I'd been so young. I hadn't known anybody. There'd been no reason for, well . . . sex.

Like a bolt from the blue, albeit a tad late, I remembered my cure for responsibility, uncertainty and stress. Fly! Get out of there! Call Willow. Cough and wheeze. Postpone everything!

Downstairs, the screen door clapped. Because the doorbell didn't work and the knocker was gone, Willow called me, her voice tentative but loud. I froze, bug-eyed. When Willow called again, I didn't answer but eased down the stairs, thinking, just thought.

I didn't like trembling above character-building moments where I usually and joyfully did so poorly. But the alternative was rudeness. Once boorishness bullied in, vulgarity might arrive. No! Developing integrity couldn't be that bad. I got downstairs just as Willow turned to leave. With great effort, I blurted, "I'm so glad you came."

"Clement!" Willow jumped. Then she snapped, "Where'd you come from?"

"Pardon, my dear. I was in such a hurry, and I've gotten so used to this place, I didn't stop to turn on the lights."

Willow relaxed and looked around, noting that the first and second floors were more barren than bare. Cracked and torn tiles revealed the splintered floorboards. Black adhesive suggested long-gone carpeting. There were no doors. Most of the wallpaper had been either peeled or steamed off. Exposed plaster shone dully.

When we reached the third floor, I could finally smile. At least the newly sanded and varnished floors looked good under the braided rug. Although tattered green shades dangled behind curtains that looked like netting, the pitched garret walls were comforting. My sofa was old but elaborate mahogany topped with burgundy brocade cushions. A refinished door atop scrolled masonry made a coffee table. Tiny flames from thick, ivory candles flickered above gilded but cracked saucers. Lilac incense burned, mingling its fragrance with fresh-baked apricot bread. A clear mayonnaise jar held gold poppies and red geraniums. A little plastic chess set, two wineglasses and a colorful ceramic platter with cheese and apples finished the setting.

I dusted at the sofa. Next, I pulled a chair to the table, settled in and gulped some wine. Breathing easier, I checked to be sure that my smile felt relaxed, then said, "You look beautiful."

"Thanks." Willow's eyes swept the table. "Everything looks . . . nice."

I pointed to the chess set and said, "I've been studying quite a bit."

"Good for you." Willow wrapped her gum in tissue, bit into an apple and said, "Let's get started."

From the bog that had been my brain, a long-armed and hairy query slogged forward. It asked just exactly why I'd gotten so worked up about Willow visiting.

I answered, Because I cared. Because, ever since I'd first floated up Evergreen Way, having Willow with me was what I'd dreamed, schemed and hoped for.

I lost the first game. After the second, both of us sighed when I retired my king. Watching Willow assemble her pieces for the final game, I was struck for the one thousand seven hundred forty-third time by how centered Willow was. How did she manage to pack a life force as huge as Achernar inside her?

I said, "Tell me, dear Willow, if you could make a wish come true tonight, what would it be?"

"Money."

"No!"

"Lots of it."

My heart shrank to a cold bean. Her nonchalant smile mortified me. I squinted and asked, "And what would you do with . . . with money?"

"Depends on how much I got."

"A pragmatist. Yuck!"

"Yuck you, Clement."

I glared at Willow, and then at the board. "My dear, that means war."

Midnight was minutes away. Watching Willow's king surrender was like seeing a sequoia fall. Bracing her elbows on the table's edge and her chin in her palms, Willow quietly surveyed the squares.

"You know," I said, entering Willow's silence like a swimmer who understood still water, "for me, every time a piece gets taken, it feels like I've lost a part of myself. It doesn't matter that some pieces must be sacrificed so that there's room to maneuver. Except I'm not concerned about the bishop—that sneaky sidestepper—or the queen. But a pawn, a rook"—I paused—"and certainly the knight. I care about them."

Willow smiled . . . just a little.

"I don't want you to be sad, Willow. Maybe we should find a new game."

She was about to answer when I said, "You know, this chess, it's like life. There are challenges, some grand and some subtle. And I was thinking," I smiled, "two nations were going to battle out on what was once called the Jebel Abyad Plain. It was a great plateau under the Moon's mountain. The kingdom's soldiers wore dark silk and matching turbans with silver bands. They kept jeweled daggers in silver girdles. They made music with their footsteps and with drums. The queendom dressed in flowing white fabrics woven with gold thread. They marched with whistles and clapped their hands. It was thrilling."

"Is this near where the willow trees grow?"

"Sort of." I was so pleased that Willow remembered. I was also intrigued by the beginnings of two of me. One sat upright and talked with Willow while the other me reclined, as though sinking into soft pillows, and called the story to the shell of myself that Willow saw. The reclining me felt warm and very hued, as though my heart pumped Jell-O-bright blood cells. I said, "As the two armies approached, the queen-dom with their whistling songs and clapping and the kingdom with their marching rhythms and drums, when they were close enough, their melodies mingled, and a marvelous thing happened." I felt sure by then that my voice drifted like incense and my eyes sparkled.

"What?"

Willow's question broke my reverie. I was upright again and my thoughts spun like a pulsar.

Softly, she said, "I'm sorry, Clement. I didn't mean . . ."

Shaking my head and reorienting myself, I said, "That's okay. I shouldn't wander like that. Here, let me show you something." I took Willow's hands and led her to a doorway covered by white muslin. We entered a short hallway, passing red velvet embellished with glass beads followed by drapes of orange brocade, a yellow chintz and green satin. I said, "I've never shown this place to anyone."

"What happened to the marchers, Clement?"

I grinned. I pursed my lips. Then I said, "They laughed. They touched. They realized themselves in each other and celebrated."

When Willow touched my hand, I wanted to hold her as I had read about in books and seen at movies. My body was willing, but my mind kept reminding me that I didn't really know what to do. I was a grown and mature-looking man who'd certainly read enough about sex, exhausting the Good Sky library and several others. They offered technical information. There were shops and theaters in larger cities that provided vivid demonstrations. There were all manner of materials providing romantic, emotional, even spiritual insights.

Still, there remained the delicate issue of experience. I suspected whole worlds of difference between the information and the actual doing, and I wanted everything for Willow to be right.

## Mother

*In May, one hundred twelve tornadoes struck over twenty-three days. In Kossuthville, Florida, an eighty-three-year-old woman was crushed. When the tornado writhed down from the ink-black sky, the woman thought herself safer in a concrete-block shed. Meanwhile, the mobile home she'd abandoned was the only one out of two hundred not damaged.*

# 15

## Willow

### Monday, June 11, 1979

### Moon: Full

I'd asked my daddy once why he hadn't married a lighter-skinned woman. That way I'd a been lighter, too. Daddy's eyes went blank. He sat back. Then his big, tanned hands held mine tight, and he said, "Honey baby, ain't nothing wrong with your momma's color nor yours. The problem, the shame if there is any, is with mine."

My Daddy was seventeen and Momma was fifteen when they got together. They lived in Bridge, Kentucky, with Mariah. The few times Momma talked about my brother, Julian, seemed like she had to go back through the years and build my brother up and love him again before she could tell me how he was fair, how he really looked just like Daddy. She'd sigh and wipe her hands together and say how, even as a tot, something about Julian suggested he'd a been tall too and probably thin if he'd had the chance.

Then Daddy got the wander bug. Daddy was partial to Cadillacs, no matter how raggedy they were. Back then, he, Momma and Julian traveled around in a Fleetwood roadster. "Built in 1931," Daddy boasted. "Nearly as old as me, but the best car I ever owned." I'm sure it was, least ways, until it broke down just past Creame. That's how we wound up there.

Julian is buried by the peach trees. He got pneumonia and died two years before I was born. He's real to me, though. Sometimes I imagine Julian as his baby self. Sometimes as a boy and then a man, always three years older than me and, like Momma said, favoring Daddy.

The only time I ever thought of Daddy as not being totally colored was at twilight when I'd run through the yard expecting to see no one, especially not white people, and realize the folks on my porch was Daddy and Aunt True.

"It don't matter, brother. Why should I fret about anyone that didn't want me?" Aunt True shrugged. "They did enough just getting me here. And that old man, you know he was so crusty, he probably couldn't a smiled if the devil tickled him. Can you imagine letting anything come between you and your flesh-and-blood child? So our mother made a mistake. She probably couldn't help it, knowing how things were back then. There she was, working for those white folks when she was so young. Living in their house. A few years later, there you come, brother. They give her some money, let her go and I come out your spitting image in '29. Served them right, whoever they were, to lose everything when the stock market crashed."

"He should have practiced what he preached," Daddy grumbled.

"But what did being a Garveyite and all that Black Star stuff have to do with turning their backs on Cleopatra and her babies at a time like that? I don't think it was part of the teachings. I think Granddaddy just took things too far. Do you remember Cleopatra taking us to her mother's funeral? Remember how Granddaddy wouldn't even look at us? I felt like a little ghost. Orneriness, pure and simple," Aunt True started laughing. "That's all it was, Union, and I think you inherited some of that."

I wanted to hear about my family, so I didn't say anything and stayed on the other side of the hedges.

Daddy mumbled, "It wasn't right. Not none of it."

"Well," Aunt True sighed, "things worked out. Remember those old Black women who used to watch us? They loved our pale skin. Gave us better than they gave their own. We had things pretty good, at least until Cleopatra married Mr. Enright and started another family."

"He hated us."

"You got it worse than me, brother. But, you can't exactly blame him for not wanting another man's children."

"You mean some white man's bastards."

"Union, hush!" Aunt True stood up and scanned the yard. "Where's Willow? Where's Eddie and Jeffie?"

Wasn't until I was on my own and visited Aunt True that I saw an old brown and white picture of Cleopatra. She was a tan-colored woman with curly hair and small features. Maybe that's why, riding that Greyhound bus toward Good Sky years before, one thing I thought was that up my family tree on both sides, and with life in general, folks couldn't care. And what did that do but make oceans between people when there shouldn't have even been a creek?

Saturday mornings, Daddy and I packed cheese and baloney sandwiches, Kool-Aid and cookies, and he took me, Terry and Otto fishing.

One time, we drove clear to Lake Wendover. The air was crisp. Shadows were still long. Unloading our gear, we heard geese calling. I saw one bird struggle and fall away. The sky never seemed as big as when the space between that bird and the flock kept growing. Another goose flew down to the weak one. Then the whole flock came around and hugged the tired one in before they flew on.

Walking to the lake, Otto asked, "How come they did that?"

"Cause they're smarter than people," Daddy said. "The ones up front take a beating cleaving open air channels so it's easier for the ones behind. When they tire out, others move up and do the work. They honk to keep each other going, and if a goose gets too bad off, he never goes alone. No sir. Two stay with him. If he dies, then the pair has each other until they find another flock. And somehow they stick with their partner for life. I don't know how geese come to be called silly."

Just like Daddy always cooked link sausages with apples and made skillet-sized pancakes that I soaked in dark Karo syrup on Saturday mornings, Saturday nights he fried hamburgers and potatoes with onions. Every day of the week, even Sundays, we ate our chili with cheese or hotdogs with relish and baked beans off the same white plastic plates. We had tin forks and those bright-colored aluminum cups. We used paper napkins and sometimes paper towels.

Sunday mornings, Daddy ate his oatmeal and drank his red enameled cup of coffee early. Then he yanked on his oily leather cap and started up whatever piece of Cadillac he had.

Momma and I would eat a prayerful poached egg and unbuttered toast. When Daddy drove us to church, the shiny, black case with his pool stick was always in the backseat with me where Momma wasn't supposed to notice.

One Sunday, I moaned and coughed and whimpered until Momma went without me. Later, I begged and promised never ever to tell if Daddy would please, just that one time, take me to Mr. Porky's.

"Willow, you oughtn't deceived your Momma."

"I was sick, Daddy. I, I'm better now."

"It's the Lord's Day, Willow. Watch what you say. And that's a gambling place. Ain't fit for a child. Sunday or no."

"But it'll only be you and Mr. Porky, Daddy. Please. I want to see."

"You're real curious, ain't ya?"

I nodded fast.

"You probably been thinking on this a while. Probably got some fancy notions about the place."

I nodded again and put my hands together, begging, "Please, Daddy. Please."

Daddy frowned. His mouth screwed up like he'd just sucked a whole lemon. After a minute, he said, "Well, maybe . . ." Then he scratched his head. "Doggone. If your momma finds out . . ."

Porky's Place was a wooden shack on concrete blocks with hand-written signs on the walls and porch posts saying, REFRESHING DRINKS OF ALL TYPES INSIDE. NO SPITTING. NO GUNS.

Mr. Porky was as wide as he was tall, and brown like coffee beans. When he laughed, his sides jiggled. Mr. Porky had hands like pillows, and he always had nickels for me. When Mr. Porky wasn't at his place, he joked with the men who smoked and chewed tobacco at Creame Grocery & Hardware or who sat drinking pop and beer at the gas station where Daddy fixed cars and trucks and tractors. And Mr. Porky was the only person who could call Daddy "Whitey." Even with Mr. Porky, a hardness set in Daddy's jaw.

Following Daddy through the door, my legs felt like pudding. Inside, sunlight glowed through the whitewashed windows and fell onto some flimsy chairs and tables, the bar, an old ice box, a sink and a shelf of glasses. I didn't like how the place smelled and was holding my breath. My eyes were big as doughnuts.

We couldn't see Mr. Porky when he boomed, "Welcome brother Union, and howdy-do, Miss Willow. What a pleasant surprise."

"I'm feeling good this morning, Brother Pork." Daddy strode into a bigger room with peeling wallpaper and bare lightbulbs dangling on wires over two pool tables. Mr. Porky snatched down a yellowed calendar with white women showing their titties and behinds and frowned at dust piles and pyramids of empty bottles on the floor.

"Jerome, why didn't you sweep that stuff up before you started eating?" Mr. Porky stared at a broad-shouldered, muscular boy who looked too young to drink legally but too old for school.

Trying to get his mouth around a huge fish sandwich, Jerome said, "Sorry, Porky. I was hungry."

Mr. Porky's nose twitched as he fumed, "Ain't it a little early for something like that? Where'd you get it?"

Daddy clapped Mr. Porky's shoulder and said, "Let up, Porky. Dust brings me luck. So, are you ready to lose again?"

"Lady Luck's been good to you lately, that's true. But I got something for you this morning." Mr. Porky swaggered to the rack, his big hips rolling. After he pulled down one stick and then another, a scratchy voice called, "Hey, Porky, you fat son of a bitch, you seen Elmo? That nigger been in here?"

Before Mr. Porky could answer, the bowlegged old man hobbled over to Jerome. His leathery face jiggled as he sniffed and said, "What you got that smell so good there, boy? It smell like pussy."

"Hey man, watch it! I got my kid here!"

"You meant it smells like food for a pussy cat, didn't you . . . fool!" Mr. Porky patted my hand and said, "You know how much cats like fish, Willow. And, naw. Elmo ain't here. Probably won't be in till Tuesday."

"Okeydoke. Tell Elmo I'm looking for him."

Daddy and Mr. Porky racked the billiard balls. Then they began a leaning dance around the table, saying things like, "Oh, no, no baby, don't go down there. Just look. Take a peek!" Daddy and Mr. Porky, they talked a lot about a fat lady clearing her throat and singing. Their fingers crooked in weird angles, sliding the poles across arched thumbs and through finger tunnels.

Later, I figured maybe Jimmy, Tyrell, Kinshasa and some of the others wouldn't have hurt me so bad if I'd thought about how no matter when or where the billiard balls rolled over that nice, flat green and no matter how scuffed they got, their bright veneers defined where whatever they were began and where whatever they weren't stopped.

# 16

# Clement

## Monday, June 11, 1979

## Moon: Full

After the bright blue silk and a translucent indigo, a hundred lights glimmered through a violet veil. Willow gasped as we stepped into an alcove shimmering in a topaz haze. My candles, dozens of them in different shapes and colors, flickered atop a chest of cherrywood and tulip poplar inlaid with star-shaped mother of pearl. The candles sat in wood and clay holders that I'd painted with poppies, marigolds, penguins, peacocks, egrets and fish. Votives sat in foil squares atop papyrus. The large mirror behind the chest had etchings of moons and suns.

Willow glowed. "Clement, this room is beautiful."

"These candles are my angels," I said, pointing to a pale mauve taper. "There's Ezgadi, who helps with the successful completion of journeys. There's Isda, who nourishes humans, and Tubiel, who returns small birds to their owners." I pointed to a spiraled ink-blue candle with silver tracings and said, "That one is for my mother."

Willow looked up and said, "Clement, how sweet of you to think of your mother this way."

I looked away and whispered, "It's important that I remember Mother and all that she does."

Seeing questions form in Willow's eyes, I held her wrist and pulled her through the drapes. Outside, as Willow planted her feet, I asked, "Do you dance, my dear? Is there anyplace where we could?"

"We'd have to go to the city, Clement. We could probably find places in Akron or Canton or Youngstown, but it'd be better if we went to Cleveland." Willow crossed her arms, "Why did you do that?"

I raised my shoulders and eyebrows.

"What are you hiding, Clement? Why is everything about you such a secret? If you can't tell me about yourself, how can we . . . we . . . And anyway, why don't you get along with your mother?"

"Get along with Mother?"

The concept evoked a river, azure with an opal bed, not as wide as the Calliope but deeper. That river flowed to a hyacinth and pearl ocean. As those waters evaporated, their mists became tremendous clouds. Thinking of that much water looming over my head, I said, "If I could be objective, I'd admire Mother. She's a brass-tacks, hard-as-nails, Napoleonic little woman who's always been pushy. And right in through here, probably for the first time in both of our lives, I won't be shoved."

At first, just my head and shoulders and then my arms swayed. My waist, hips, knees and feet got going, suggesting the tango. I said, "Mother and I are working through this adjustment. It's not been easy for either of us."

I stopped moving. I considered that statement's implications and added, "Things will probably . . . No, knowing Mother, they'll definitely get worse before they get better, Willow. And if that happens . . ." I lifted Willow's hands. "You suggested that I didn't trust you. That's not true. Trust is inseparable from how I feel about you. I'm just being careful. I don't want you hurt by . . . by anything. Sometimes, in the heat of the moment, some family members forget what they . . . they don't think. I trust you, Willow. I need for you to trust me."

Willow was stalled, but quickly regrouped and asked, "What does your mother want?"

I looked slowly around the room.

"What does she want, Clement?"

How was I supposed to tell Willow about Father? How could I explain the levels of wisdom, insight and patience required, that I didn't have and never wanted? How should I discuss the compassion that was necessary when assessing souls for their next experience? Especially when the task wouldn't be much fun.

I guided Willow to the sofa. "Remember the first times we played chess? Remember how fascinated I was with the queen? She moved with so much freedom, so much power. That's also why I wanted to lose a piece so superior to the others, who could strike with such devastation from almost anywhere and leave with impunity."

"I wish you wouldn't use big words. What's *impunity*?" Willow smiled. "At first, I thought you were setting me up, Clement. But what are you saying? That your mother's dangerous?"

"Mother is what she is. Willow, please don't ask me more. Not right now."

Willow touched my hand. She shook her head. Tears actually budded in Willow's eyes as she tried to keep from laughing. "Clement, you're absolutely amazing. I never met anyone who exaggerates things like you, and then has the nerve to get worked up about them. Do you really want me thinking your mother is a wild woman? She's probably very sweet. She probably sits home watching soap operas and worrying about her only child who doesn't call often enough. She probably bakes cookies and crochets booties for the church bazaar and the grandchildren she hopes for."

"Actually," I swallowed hard, "Mother's a little more active than that."

"Anyway," Willow smiled, "I kept wondering how you thought you'd win if you gave up the queen so easy."

I answered, "The only way I can respect the queen piece is when she comes from a pawn."

"What about the king?"

"Ahhh. Like so many I've known, he's a grand and powerful man who filled his life with fine accomplishments. He was revered, obeyed, protected. But he can hardly move. Just one square at a time. I love him, though. And I love the knights for their elegance and because they can leap over others without destroying. It was so hard for me to understand the way they moved. Then I so very much wanted the knights to be in the forefront, to lead. The rooks, they're good guys. Straightforward. Rank and file. And the pawns are those brave little nothings that can become anything by persevering."

Iridescent patterns flickered in the melting candle wax. Watching the lights dance across Willow's face, I said, "One day, you will understand, Willow. Because I love you too much, now, it's inevitable. When that happens, all I ask is that you trust what you know of me."

Willow's face softened. She leaned toward me. Softly, I caressed Willow's neck, her shoulder, her breast. I inhaled her warmth as our lips touched. We kissed a long time. When my clock chimed midnight, Willow, her body moving into me and her mind drawing back, whispered, "I have to go."

As we worked our way down the stairs, I tried not to notice the hint of honeysuckle and juniper, but Willow asked, "What's that smell, Clement?"

I mumbled, "I really couldn't say."

"You know, this morning I think I smelled the same thing outside." Her eyes lit up. "Yeah! There was this incredible woman."

"Oh?" My voice quavered.

"She had on a wild jacket, and—Clement, are you okay?"

"Okay?" I felt like I would faint but laughed, perhaps with too much bravado. "Why, I'm as okay as . . ." I didn't mean to, but my voice trembled. I paused, then asked, "Willow, this woman, was she small? Light coloring? Long fingernails?"

"Yeah."

"Well, I . . . I've . . . are you sure you've never seen her before? She seems to drop into the neighborhood frequently."

"Do you know her?"

I shrugged and tried to appear nonchalant. "About as well as anyone." While Willow thought that over, I asked, "Can we play again tomorrow?"

Completely ignoring my question, Willow asked, "What does your mother want, Clement?"

I could tell that Willow hadn't connected the woman on the street to Mother. Still, my thoughts scoured Callistro and orbited Rhea before I said as lightly as possible, "Mother? She wants me to resume my father's work."

"That's not monstrous. In fact, that's perfectly motherly, Clement, especially considering what you're doing now."

The streetlamp lavished Willow's skin with silver. As I looked into Willow's upturned face, I nearly melted. My feelings tumbled like Syfess weeds from the Aldebaran system. Pieces of thoughts ballooned so quickly, I thought I'd burst. Slowly enough to spell each word, I said, "I am going to be what it is that I am. Not just what is expected. No matter what."

Willow blinked, then patted my hand and whispered, "Clement, you do make such mountains out of molehills. You're very sweet that way. Strange, but sweet."

I watched Willow cross the silent Evergreen, and it occurred to me that the Sun's light was almost a thousand times weaker when it reached the soft, blue, eighth planet than when it touched the third, my also-blue Earth. And I realized that the farther Willow moved away, the more constricted my heart became, as though it were sinking into a Neptunian sea . . . into a frozen ocean that warmed when Willow waved briefly before closing Mrs. G's door.

Gravity, where content counted more than size, that's what I thought about as I sat far from Evergreen Way. In a place where the sky was still blue, where the clouds were thin but abundant, I watched the Sun set again and thought about its hold. Neptune had the mass of seventeen Earths. Saturn had the mass of ninety-five Earths. More than three hundred Earths could be made from Jupiter. Tossing in Mars, Mercury, Pluto, the asteroids and meteorites, given all the content in our solar system, everything added up to only one percent of the Sun. That's why everything stayed. Whatever had the most pulled the best. Was that why I couldn't leave Willow?

The full impact, the marvel and wonder of Willow's first visit to my rooms filled my thoughts. I recalled Willow's presence as though the feelings were ginger blossoms evanescing on midnight air. Remembering our walk through my rainbow corridor, how the candles lit her eyes, how the mirror reflected her face, the sensations that Willow aroused . . . I wanted more. The need for a joining far more tactile than our social interactions obsessed me.

I would see Willow, and my temperature increased. My heart beat faster. My breathing accelerated. My pupils dilated. Sometimes, when I spoke to Willow, when we stood close, my skin flushed, my nipples hardened. When I inhaled her fragrance, felt the brush of her blouse or hand, my testicles rose and my penis filled and firmed. Something had to be done. Despite that culture's espousal of women's liberation, I knew that as the man, I had to get things going and see that things went right. With all that in mind, how could I possibly approach Willow as a virgin?

After significant cerebration, I was nonplussed that the solution hadn't occurred sooner. Of course! The best way to know how to please Willow was to *be* Willow. I had all the parts. Some just required enlarging, as with the breasts (actually specialized sweat glands), the vagina masculina and, to do things right, the seminal colliculus. I could shrink down to Willow's more petite stature, withdraw the penis, delicately limit the scrotum and add a marvelous and juicy new opening. Then pull the testicles up to become ovaries, develop the uterus and fallopian tubes, a tight waist, pleasant legs and a cute behind.

Gawking at my Willow self in the mirror, touching the wonderful softnesses and curves, I got so excited I could hardly stand. Breasts. Such delightful jigglers. Of course, I would augment mine to be just a little, oh well, a lot bigger. Exploring my Self and discovering so many physical treats, I wondered why Willow had been holding back. Why did she hide herself under unflattering apparel? Why didn't she decorate herself and shine?

I moved my hands around the breasts, enjoying the marvelous flesh-iness. When I worked slowly, firmly toward the nipples, when I rolled them, squeezed them between my fingers, I swooned. It was delicious, almost too sweet hearing Willow's sighs pass through my lips. My eyes kept rolling and glazing. One hand circled slowly downward, entering the soft pubic hairs and then parting the breath-stealing lips. On the way, I touched and touched again that tight and nerve-rich cluster of petals, that tiny but potent and sweet little case that floored me.

When I recovered consciousness and had returned to my Self, ec-static and smiling like a lunatic, I realized that far more research—alone but certainly with partners—would be essential.

## Mother

*June would total one hundred fifty tornadoes over twenty-four days. Among the worst were the ten that swept through north-central Iowa. One would hit Manson, Iowa, widening to one thousand feet and destroying one hundred ten homes, a school and twenty-five businesses. Another struck west of Palmer, razoring everything in its half-mile-wide trail for thirty miles.*

# 17

## Jimmy

### Friday, July 13, 1979

### Moon: Disseminating

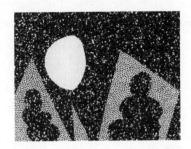

Standing by these rivers feels like a Black Hole. Like space is curved and time is swallowed. Forever. This Monongahela River has one hundred twenty-eight miles of water. It pushes, pulls, dries up, floods, levels. The Allegheny curls northwest into New York. Then it carves south and west. After three hundred twenty-five miles, the two meet like arms asking why. They birth the Ohio. It flows west. Dark. As though a woman easy to watch.

I think, Eighty-seven miles from here, the Ohio receives the Calliope. The Ohio grows and goes on swaying through green-carpeted mountains. Reflecting seven hills. Cascading over limestone falls. Before filling the Mississippi, *La Belle Riviere* visits a thousand miles of little towns with names equally as odd as God's Eye, Hindsight, Bridge, Creame and Good Sky. Villages with two stop signs and no red light. Places where Saturday night out means the VFW hall.

I used to wonder. It seemed so backwards. People living that small.

The rivers look weary. The hills like unmade beds. My eyes sweep past bridges and skyscrapers to J&L's fires. Four miles farther, clouds reflect Homestead's heat. Beyond, there's Braddock, Duquesne, Clairton, Elizabeth. Twenty miles of steel mills. I wonder, Was Willow as shaken as I am when she looked for valleys that didn't drop off so steep? Did Willow's heart feel coated in river sludge when she got wise to the nation-building brother? Beneath it all, was she as angry?

I actually believed the success deal was: Plan. Prepare. Perspire. Persist. But if all that counts, how come this country launched a nine-story, eighty-ton construct called Skylab and didn't know where it would fall? How come this town's industrial back is breaking?

My reports ended jobs today. Is this why I went to college? If they'd told me my title included "hatchet man," would I have turned down the job or merely asked for more money? As doors clang and footsteps fade, I become lost in desert sunrises. I feel sable brushes and fine-woven canvas. There is no time at all, despite how shadows grow from empty chairs. How they merge. How they flow through an orchard where I once painted pastel lilac on Willow's toes. Where I drew the sun's warmth in her face. Where I never suspected that's all the success I needed.

I watch dust motes dance. As office lights dim, I wonder if Willow still wears surprise beautifully. Because Willow would shut her eyes. Cover them with her hands. Laugh softly. Pull her body close.

Remembering, I rise. Hit the desk. The boom becomes too big. I get out. Drive to a cinder-block bar where smoke hovers so thick my eyes water. Where the tinny jukebox deafens. Where someone's played the Platters' "The Great Pretender" so often, I can sing it by heart.

I hate how the cracked ice in my Tanqueray clinks. I detest the man on the next, patched-up, Naugahyde bar stool, especially his ugly green T-shirt with the Day-Glo words *Hell No, We Won't Glow. Three Mile Island Must Go.*

People talk, smoke, joke and laugh as though life is fine. Just when

I need to shout, "What's wrong with you?" the barmaid pats my hand. Smiles a gap-toothed grin. Says, "Hi, cutey. Never seen you here before."

I stare at her chipped nail polish. Grease on tired blue apron. She flops down paper plates with barbecued ribs, collards, black-eyed peas, hamhocks. Jokes with the green T-shirt man. Wouldn't know a daiquiri from a dishrag.

I refuse to look in the mirror. In that tarnished glass, I might see chiseled lips. A lazy smile. Coarse, wavy hair. Eyes like a cat half sleeping. Skin colored like taffy. Butter pecan wrapped in reefer haze. Six-foot-two. Easy stride. This bar is Lonnie's kind of place.

Real young, I knew I'd never be as tall as Lonnie. Not as talented, charming or good looking. Lonnie slept like an angel. Face up. Arms and legs open. Only he got away with napping on the sofa. Even the baby, Melinda, couldn't compete. Not in life. Never in death. And we didn't mind, Melinda and I. Not much.

Lonnie's big hands tore down engines and built them back. Lonnie played football. He raced his copper Challenger and caroused the Flats. I remember the summer vacations. 1967. 1968. Lonnie taught me how to change tires and engine oil. Check radiators and fan belts. We loaded trucks. Met customers like Frank Singer and Mrs. Faraday. When the draft board certified Lonnie fit for war, he headed for Canada. I started Ohio State. Christmas 1968, we both came home. I drove. Lonnie was in a box. I learned Willow's parents had died that April. I figured maybe people wore hard grief in ways that only other sufferers saw.

I finish my drink. Slap five dollars on the dull wood counter. Stomp through the smoke and noise. At door, see the sign. On peeling black background, gilded red letters warn, HOLD ON. THIS IS A DARK RIDE. I stumble over the threshold. Stand in deep shadow. Realize . . .

*There's another train coming. Will I feel it shaking the ground?*
*Will I hear it? Will I see winds pluck and shred the steam?*

Ten years ago, Richard "I am not a crook" Nixon and convicted criminal Spiro Agnew were the presidential team. We didn't know that President Eisenhower ordered public confusion about atomic fallout. The National Audubon Society hadn't warned that DDT soaks into the soil, runs into streams and kills more than insects. The theory of continental drift wasn't fact, and yet William Shockley, codeveloper of the transistor, stated that Black people were genetically stupider than he was. Now, Tanzania produces four-million-year-old, humanlike footprints. The Supreme Court reverses. Allows "voluntary" affirmative action. Two hundred miles east, four hours by car, Three Mile Island's nuclear reactor nearly melts, and I feel like centuries of salted earth.

Ten years ago, Willow told me how her bus stopped four times before Good Sky. While mail was loaded, she could have gotten a quick root beer and pizza. But Willow smelled popcorn.

Maybe Mrs. Graham and Mrs. Singer didn't realize that Willow left a Greyhound waiting. Willow told me how Mrs. Graham served fried chicken and candied sweet potatoes that night. I imagine how she must have weighed Willow's words against the spaces where she, her husband and their children once slept. Certainly, having a boarder would help. After all, Mrs. Graham spent each autumn visiting relatives. She stopped home a few times. Beyond that, Willow was on her own, which made October through Christmas nice for us.

Why was it so long ago that we walked along a rise toward a pine grove? Gazed over a stream curlicuing through an apple orchard? That we lay on a blanket as Willow told how once she nearly burned down her parents' house? She'd pulled corn from her mother's garden. Sliced kernels. Dried them. In a big iron pot, Willow heated lard. The corn charred. Smoke filled the house. Later, her daddy said that not all corn could pop. The kind that did was special.

I told Willow of an eighth-grade science project. Lonnie helped. Told me the corn's tough skin. The moisture. Air inside. That made the difference. When the starches got hot, regular corn couldn't contain the pressure. Popping corn had strong shells. Their pericarps withstood the stresses and strains just long enough.

"Perry whats?" Willow laughs. "What kind of carp is that?" She kisses me. The wind and sun, the scent of apples, the soft pine mattress and Willow feels good. I pray that we melt. That we expand and strain and burst.

Memories of Willow keep sneaking up on me. They attack like muggers. Grab my arms. Shake me. Grin over what I abandoned. Snatch from my pockets. Leer as I raise my fist. As I shout, "I want everything back!"

Startled pigeons flap away. Inside the bar, someone replays "The Great Pretender." I find my car. Gas rationing? I don't care. I drive until lights from the bridge above shine on broken bricks and window frames. Past the huge and empty cable reels are acres of rusting metal, old wire and weeds. Beyond that, the rivers gleam.

I trip on old wood. Rocks. I lean over the water. I listen for its song. I need boatloads of it. A fat woman in loud purple taps my shoulder. Says, "Boy, you oughtn't stand out all night like this." She turns to a man my age. Says, "Tell him."

He grins. He wears a Panama hat pulled low. A fringed vest. A large cross shines on his bare chest. He drawls, "Look what you done to them clothes. Folks with sense wear boots and dungarees for mess like this."

"He needs to go home," the big woman grumps. "That's what you oughta said."

Small bells ring. A tiny woman swings in playful circles. Under her yellow pinafore and long dark dress, little feet skim the bricks and broken bottles. Silver is woven through her black braids. She whispers, "Yes. You go on home. You get some rest, baby. You need it." A man walks up. He's in ragged overalls. Tattered straw hat. As he lovingly takes the little woman's arm, she shooes me like I'm a child. Says, "You've been down by these rivers long enough. You go on back now."

They disappear. My stomach knots. Far off, my car blinkers flash. I stagger over rotten rope. An anchor. Rusting chain. I decide I've been asleep on my feet.

*There's another train coming. Like Lonnie, will I feel the sun's heat shooting from snow so iced it does not melt? As pearl and navy clouds charge across the sky, will I also see angels swinging low? Through smoke richly inhaled, with its wisps curling before and behind my eyes, will a stray leaf so captivate that I do not hear the horn? Will shadows come and go so exquisitely that I also sit suspended above earth and cares but not the vibrating rails?*

I reach the car. When the engine starts, I'm amazed the battery lasted. That police haven't ticketed.

East Carson Street glistens. Passing the J&L mills, I feel the heat and brutality that force ores and coal into steel. After the scrap metal yards, the wind's fragrance becomes damp dirt. Fungus under stone. Skunk. Raccoon. Winding asphalt. Rotting wildflowers.

Homestead starts at Mesta Machine. The town is brown and gray and black. The U.S. Steel mill smokes, booms, chugs and crashes. Hills rise like shoulders. Hug in the oxides. The sulfurs. The ammoniated air.

I turn off Eighth Avenue. Creep down blacktop over brick. Splash through puddles. Pass cafes offering kolbassi, kraut, barbecued chicken. Bars that sell shots of whiskey chased with Iron City or Rolling Rock beer. There are Laundromats. Hotel rooms rent for five dollars a night. Windows glow purple. Some amber. Some red.

At Sixth and Amity, I find the yellow-brick building. Sign says SWEET LUCY's. Small red and white awning over door. Upstairs, the porch has a glider and old kitchen chairs. The view: A soot-coated train station. Cyclone and barbed-wire fences. Lamp-lit yards. Men in heavy boots. Worn-down sidewalks. Five-story sheet-metal walls. Flatbeds and dump trucks, barges and trains. Ashen rain. Fiery chimneys.

After her parents died, Willow stayed with Lucille. Lucille with the eyes. Eyes that see so much.

Lucille is small like Willow. With cropped and gold-toned hair. Honey-blond skin. Spit curls at the ear. Large, hoop earrings. Bright scarves at waist. Open blouse.

Lucille's eyes can be purple. Gray. Green. They look straight through. I feel like nothing when she winks. When she drags hard on her cigarette and says, "Now don't you go breaking my grandchile's heart." This pronouncement from the woman who left her infant for a pimp.

I steer carefully through potholes and the gray dawn. Cross the misted Homestead Bridge. Am home in half an hour. The phone rings. Mom says that Dad's had a stroke. While I pack, I wonder, What if blood burst in my brain? What sum would my life add up to? What deductions for not having really, deep-down laughed? For not having touched sunflowers, Gesso and love in such a long time?

The turnpike cashier says that gas stations are actually open. Unlike Pennsylvania, Ohio doesn't have odd/even days. I turn up the air-conditioning. Reset the cruise control.

From Pittsburgh's one Black radio station. I get vintage Civil Rights speeches. Amiri Baraka. Stokely Carmichael. Malcolm X. I remind myself: Blacks have never been this country's only slaves. More than Black people must remind ourselves that we are beautiful. Black folks aren't alone in trying to strain truth from nonsense.

At a Howard Johnson's, I splash my face with cold water. Try to avoid the mirror where Lonnie looks back. Soon enough, the one with stubble, ashen skin and soured mouth seeps through. Only the eyes. Lonnie's eyes remain.

I drink black coffee and drive. The car rolls so smoothly, a sweet ease drifts down. I switch on the radio. That Pittsburgh station is static. I'm out of touch. Just like when I thought only my talent should be noticed. Thus, I spoke softly. Minimized gestures. Wore gray. If associates heard non-European idioms slip from my lips, they would at least not think of me as common, urban rot, ring-in-the-nose Black.

I had sugarplum visions of becoming a corporate Ralph Bunche. I wanted *Forbes, Business Week, Wall Street Journal* success. Whatever the hell that was.

My head ticks like a needle fallen off an LP's rim. I rub my eyes. Put in a Ramsey Lewis tape. "Les Fleur" plays. I note the exit that leads to Good Sky. To a cobblestone street where tree roots rumple redbrick sidewalks. Where folks play cards on summer evenings and children jump rope. Where nosy neighbors cook cabbage. Corned beef. Barbecue. *Chǎo sǎn yàng*. Red beans. Macaroni and cheese.

At the Calliope River, children and old folk feed ducks and geese. They fish. Old men play crosswords, checkers and backgammon. They joke and tease with accents from across this country and the world.

I light a cigarette. Suck the smoke in deep. Wonder why it stings. By noon I am home. Melinda says that Dad is stable. I can see him soon.

I try to sleep. If I dream, it is of the old warehouse. Parking lot dusty in summer and fall. Bogs in winter and spring. Smudged and yellowed windows. Lopsided blinds. Dark green loading dock. Through the door . . .

*There's a yellow train. Its light blinds. Its whistle crests the hemlock- and laurel-covered hills. Its wheels crush. Its steam rises like ghosts. It chants: Death-chah-chah-chah. Death-chah-chah-chah. Death.*

# 18

## Willow

### Thursday, July 26, 1979

### Moon: New

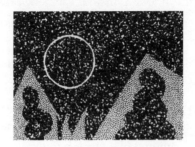

From out of nowhere, rough winds blasted Good Sky. Lightning and thunder slammed so hard, Faraday's building shook. Hail cracked windows. Rain flooded the parking lot. Trees came down and power went out all over the region. Just when I was good and scared, the clouds cleared. The sun came back.

Marla had helped me bag a large, special order that morning. Thank goodness. When we couldn't run the conveyor belt, the sieve or the little escalator, we waded through the parking lot and went to the Applegate Mall. With no air-conditioning on such a muggy afternoon, I was frazzled when I got home. I sure didn't need Clement at my door with his eyes all red and his hair all wild.

I was already sour about how contented Clement seemed with eating at Ruby's, walking around Good Sky with me, playing chess and going home. His kisses were wonderful, especially the one after he'd shown me his little room. Maybe if I hadn't stopped things . . . But that was over a month before. I had hoped for more. Matter of fact, my nerves were right on edge. For at least two weeks, I noticed I was itchier, more snappish and crankier by the day. It was all Clement's fault.

I shoved some wine at him. After he finished, and his skin got slightly less blue, I listened to Clement ask, "Did you hear us?"

"I just got home, Clement. Hear what?"

Quicker than I'd ever seen Clement move, he pulled me out the door and downstairs. His normally quiet and graceful stride could have punched holes in the floors. Outside, Clement breathed like a steam engine. Sparks flashed in his eyes, and his jaw tensed as he looked from his car to his house.

He yanked open Cabrilla's door and whisked me into deep seat cushions embossed with the Thunderbird insignia. As I ran my fingers across the padded dash and sun visor, I noted the round clock, speedometer and other gauges that circled the steering column. Each one had indicator arrows that pointed like clock hands.

In the little round mirror outside my window, I watched Clement fuss with the soft top, fuming, "I should have done this first." Clement's removing and packing the roof brightened more than Cabrilla's chrome and white interior. By the time Clement plunked into the driver's seat, he was calmer.

When Clement turned the key, Cabrilla hesitated. He worked the gas pedal and muttered, "Come on, Cabrilla. We've got to go." The little car vroomed to life. Shifting the gear stick, Clement steered Cabrilla down Evergreen and onto Cedar. He didn't even wave to the Svenson sisters, the Carpenters or Rose Singer, who stood outside her shop talking with Amos. We passed the gas station and the MileMaster and rattled over the train tracks to where the highway opened.

We splashed through puddles and over tree branches and cornstalks. The fields had that rain-fresh smell. As Clement drove, his mouth stayed firm. His jaw jutted. The crinkles around Clement's eyes deepened. For about twenty minutes, the road and the wind ripped past us. Then Clement shouted, "Hold on, Willow!" He swerved onto gravel.

Mud, water and rocks flew around us. Things got really messy when the road became dirt and the car bounced and scraped bottom and slogged up the rutted and overgrown trail.

Clement stopped in a small clearing bordered by woods. I saw no signs of the storm there. But sometimes weather was funny. Several times, it rained across from Faraday's, but we never got wet.

The remains of a cabin—an old wood and concrete deck—lay on rocky soil. The tall grass and pink and gold wildflowers rustled. Birds twittered in the trees. I heard clanking from the coke ovens and watched a blue engine slowly pulling coal cars. Its thick steam gushed toward orange and scarlet clouds. We were still sitting in the car when Clement asked, "What do you think?"

Startled, I said, "Do you mean about how angry you are or the drive out here or . . . ?"

"Whatever."

Clement spoke so fast, my mind had to hold on and stretch the word out until I understood and lied, "I'm glad you brought me, Clement. It's a nice view."

Clement rubbed his face. He moved his shoulders in circles and breathed slow. Then Clement shook his hair loose and got out of Cabrilla. When Clement opened my door, his hand felt warm and soft. His skin glowed. His eyes were calm.

Clement strode over the pebbled earth to the cabin's deck. The wind lifted his hair and played with his clothes as he stood watching the sun. Then he sat tailor-style.

Sunlight bathed Clement as he tilted back his head. When I got near, he reached up and pulled me close. Softly, he said, "In many ways, perhaps too many, Willow, I had a wonderful childhood. I was very indulged. And yet that always came with the sense that, one day, a lot would be expected. One day, I would have my father's very high standards to live up to. I never asked for those responsibilities. When demand was made, I put a lot of distance between me and those expectations." Clement sighed. "Since I left home, I've lived a life even more full of gifts than my pampered childhood. And, for the most part, I loved it."

"It's your mother again, isn't it? Something's happened with her that's upset you."

"Mother's just so used to having her way. She won't accept that others have their own lives to live."

"Have you been fighting?"

I thought Clement heard me, but he answered, "What's wrong with having a little fun?"

"Clement, what are you talking about?"

"What's wrong with exploring new things? So what if we get bumped around a bit. Life is about taking chances. The down times are what make the up times better. The occasional bruises help build character and fortitude. Pressure's okay. It's what makes the stars shine. And, anyway, who was I hurting?"

I repeated my question louder and real slow, "Clement, what are you talking about?"

Clement got up and paced the deck. He kicked a stone and watched it click across the rocks and into the wildflowers. When Clement sat down again, he sprawled on the weathered boards like a child making snow angels. His hair spread like a huge halo. He sighed and said, "I thought I knew who I was. If I didn't know, at least I was happy. Now too many expectations are weighing on me. None of them are mine. And even if I was willing to go along with the cosmic plan, I don't know how."

Inside me, I felt what had been confusion boiling into anger. I snapped, "Clement, I just got home from working all day. Something you don't have a clue about. That storm messed up a lot of things. I'm tired. Hot. Need a bath. Excuse me, but, doggone it, my period's just about due. On top of all that, you came over looking like you stuck a finger in a live light socket. Then you haul me way out here and go blabbering all this stuff that doesn't make sense. You don't even answer me."

Clement touched me so tender, I could have melted. For that, I hated him, except for how he gazed over my face, across the skyline and back into my eyes as he said, "You asked who I am. Well, look Willow. Look carefully. What do you see?" Clement's eyes were childlike and sad as he waited and then said, "I'm not very much. Not much at all. Just opportunity waiting to become real."

Even in the red air, I could tell that Clement blushed. Then he kissed me so fully. So delicately. When Clement's hands came up and held my shoulders firmly . . . when our bodies touched, I knew all I needed. I wanted him then and there. That time, Clement pulled back. He shook his head and said, "Come on, Willow."

Stars were twinkling through the dusk. By the time we got back to Evergreen Way, Clement again gripped the steering wheel so tight his knuckles gleamed. A few kids still played in the late light. Others sat on stoops licking Popsicles, reading comic books and playing cards. When Clement helped me out of Cabrilla, his voice was stiff as he said, "Would you come upstairs with me? For just a minute?"

I looked at Clement's house and thought how the place seemed so lonely. That night, the bricks and rough paint around the eaves seemed even grayer and made me want to stay away.

"You'll be okay," Clement said. "Nothing's wrong beyond the air that's still tense. And as usual when Mother and I disagree, things levitated."

My mind grabbed for reasons not to go. But I just couldn't make myself say, "I need to eat" or "I'm tired" or "Clement, your place scares me."

Inside, stuff on Clement's first floor crackled as we walked. Plaster dust made me cough. The cool air felt brittle. Groping up the dark stairwell, our feet kept crushing things that sometimes shattered with a fine tingling. Finally, as though someone else in the house might hear, I whispered, "Clement, what are we stepping on? Why don't you turn on the lights?"

"I'm sorry. I should have cleaned this up. The lightbulbs are broken." Clement's voice shook.

My eyes got real big. Slow and soft so as not to sound like I wouldn't be back, I said, "Well, Clement, I'll just go get some more."

Clement tugged my hand. "Please stay with me, Willow. I've got candles."

When we got to the top of the stairs, the streetlights traced silver onto Clement's overturned furniture. The sofa, chairs and little tables looked like dead animals heaped around Clement's room. After rummaging about and finally lighting a candle, Clement moved to his living room's far corner. I watched his eyes flit from the chair with the missing leg to the slanted coffee table to the broken dishes. Weird shadows drained Clement's face. He reached for a cracked lamp, then grabbed a broken vase. He was too jerky to hold on, much less fix anything.

The flowers covered with broken glass, the shattered plates that he'd painted and the general mess made my anger take over. I said, "Clement, what happened?"

Startled, Clement looked toward me. Then he shook dust from a slipcover and watched his chess pieces scatter. His eyes were blank.

I grabbed both of Clement's arms and shook him, shouting, "Damn it, Clement! Come back here!"

A light crept back around an empty corner in his eyes. For a while, Clement looked like he didn't know where he was. My chest felt so tight, and my heart beat so hard, I thought I'd have to breathe or bust. Then Clement dropped his head and sighed.

I'd never been to the Great Salt Lake or the Dead Sea, but I'd heard that people could float in those waters without sinking. That's how I felt with Clement. Like we were in a warm and buoyant place. I lowered my eyes and mumbled, "Guess I got a little carried away."

Clement touched my hair and tilted my face. He said, "I was so upset when Mother and I finished, I hadn't really seen how bad this place was. I'm thankful you helped me, Willow. So thankful."

A flush spread down my neck and through my shoulders, zinging to the edges of every place that I was. I looked down, but Clement lifted my face and said, "There are things that you deserve to know. But I don't have a way of telling you. One day soon, I'll explain. I want you to understand. Your not knowing, it's selfish and it hurts me more and more to hold back."

Firmly I said, "Tell me, Clement."

He looked around his destroyed living room. He shook his head sadly and said, "I want to, Willow, but it wouldn't come out the way I'd like for you to hear it."

For a while, we just stood there. Then, Clement's eyes sparkled. I hated seeing it.

"Gracious!" he said, "You must be hungry. I'll go and get something."

"You've got enough to do here, Clement. I can make us some TPJs, Toasted Peanut butter and Jelly sandwiches. Get some more candles lit up here. You're going to explain while I help you clean up."

"Although the menu sounds truly gourmet, I'll pass."

"You're not going to eat?"

"No big deal."

"For crying out loud, Clement. You straighten up some, and I'll be right back."

As I turned to leave, Clement touched my hand and said, "Please don't be worried, Willow. When Mother's upset, there's nothing like her. This afternoon, she was in outstanding form." Clement's eyes mixed joy and pride as he said, "And you thought Mother sat home crocheting."

I hadn't even gotten out the peanut butter and jelly when Marla called. She said, "Willow? My God. I'm so glad I got you. Where've you been?"

"I went for a ride. What's up?"

Real cautious, Marla said, "Fuses kept blowing. Dad found some bad wiring. Electricians'll be working out there tomorrow. Probably all day. Mrs. Faraday said you don't have to come in, but Dad's having conniptions about the lost work. Be ready to roll up your sleeves Monday. I'll be there to help."

I thought Marla would say good-bye. When she didn't, I said, "Is there anything else?"

"Willow? Um . . . Willow, what about that guy who lives across from you?"

"What about him?"

"Have you learned anything more? I mean, do you know who his people are? Where he's from?"

"He's just a nice guy who's having problems, Marla."

"He's a mystery guy, Willow."

"Everyone's a mystery. Sometimes it's best that way."

"And sometimes it isn't."

"What do you mean?"

"I mean, oh hell, Willow. You're happy. We all can tell. I just don't want—"

"I'm not a kid. Marla, what are you getting at?"

"Willow, I thought you should know we got a call. Buckley Anderson had a stroke. One of their drivers was in an accident. With all this OPEC stuff and the trucker problems, Jimmy's coming back. He'll be here Monday."

"When did you find out?"

"It hasn't been long."

Seemed I held the phone an hour before Marla said, "It's been a while, Willow. Did you know that Jimmy's divorced? Are you okay?"

I breathed slow and said, "Sure."

"Take care, Willow."

"I will."

"Call if you want to talk."

"Okay."

Two hours sped by like a movie going too fast. Somehow I'd cleaned my bedroom, bath and kitchen and had two clear thoughts. When I looked at my chess set, I remembered the day Jimmy went to the Red & White Thrift Store to get it. I knew Jimmy wasn't the secondhand type. He'd probably never been in such a store. But Jimmy went because I asked.

The second thought was about what a hard time Clement was

having. No job. Family problems. That house he lived in. How could someone so deep-down decent have so many troubles? That's when I remembered the sandwiches.

The night had gotten warm instead of cooler. Wondering if I was too late, I looked up at Clement's window and saw a bluish and silvery light gleaming. Thinking it might be a fire, I hurried across and called up Clement's stairs. Too late, I heard a woman's voice.

They got quiet, then Clement called down, "Willow? Goodness, what are you doing here?"

Feeling stupid, I said, "I promised I'd bring food."

"I'll be right down."

Clement's flickering light swelled along the stair walls. When he arrived, his face was flushed and happy. With delight, he lifted the sandwich wrappings and said, "How truly thoughtful. Thank you, my dear. It got so late, I thought you'd taken your well-deserved rest. Gracious, you'll have to get up in a few hours."

"I got a call from my job. We talked a while, and I got distracted." I bounced the toe of my sneaker against the floor, and said, "Turns out they've got electric problems. There's no work tomorrow." I backed toward his door.

"Ah, so the good fortune cookie gets a long weekend? We can start right now. Come upstairs. Mother is here. You've got to meet her."

"I . . ." My heart and lungs went flat. I said real quick, "I can't."

"Why not?"

"I-I'm . . ."

"Oh, come on." Clement reached for my hand. When we touched, an electric snap made both of us jump.

"What was that?"

Shaking his hand, Clement frowned and said, "Just some static. Come on, Willow."

Staring at my tingling hand, I mumbled, "I-I'm really not dressed."

"Oh, psshaw! Mother's finicky, but she won't be rude."

Something in my expression must have helped Clement understand what I felt. He said, "I know what you've seen and heard about Mother might worry you, but things are fine now. She never stays angry long. Everything's okay."

Clement touched my hand again. I was ready to jump but felt the very opposite of that electric snap. I felt drawn to Clement. Softly, he said, "You've asked me who I am. All I can answer right now is, Take me as you see me and consider the possibility that I am from a place that is like those magic tricks I used to do. As you learn what to look for, you can find the illusions and see what's real."

"Clement," I said, "just say what you've got to say."

"Remember when we were by the Calliope one morning, and I told you how the river loves for us to send sounds to her, and I told you other things?"

I nodded, trying to remember.

"I was very sincere, Willow. Remember that morning."

I said, "Okay," and waited for Clement to explain.

Instead, he kissed my forehead, then my mouth and asked, "Are you coming up with me?"

"I can't, Clement. Not tonight."

Clement's smile had neither joy nor sadness. He said, "Then most important, in walking away from here, think of beautiful things. When you go to bed, think of what has made you happy, sweet Willow. Think about, yes, we will have a picnic tomorrow."

"I don't think I—"

Clement glowed. "You've been very patient. You saved me tonight, and I'm grateful." He kissed me again, then said, "But I don't believe the word 'wait' is in Mother's vocabulary. I'm going to have to go, darling. I'll see you tomorrow. We'll start early. And thank you for being with me. Be happy, Willow. I love you."

# 19

## Clement

## Friday, July 27, 1979

## Moon: New

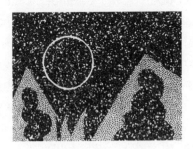

Ever since my female awareness, life had gone so well I sometimes had to pinch myself, or at least squeeze and nuzzle. A woman's body was such a treasure. I even experienced menstruation. Briefly. The filling to feed life and then release, that was astonishing. How fascinating the way the female form had specifically sexual locations while the male's apparatus was multipurpose. The male hardened and thrust. The female softened, received, accommodated and at times grew whole new possibilities. What a difference.

In places like Marseilles, Amsterdam, Singapore and Tokyo, I enjoyed breath-stopping bliss. I tried an encyclopedia of techniques and reached three marvelous conclusions. First, varying the interactions definitely added ginger, cayenne, curry and mint. Second, when practiced with joy and caring, sex was tremendously liberating. Third, whether male or female and whether with opposite or same gender, every millimeter of flesh was sensational. Just the two facial lips had so many nerve endings, it's a wonder they didn't self-ignite. The back was a pleasure plane. The soles of the feet, between the toes, around the ankles, the scalp, temples, forehead, the earlobes and nape, so many rapturous reservoirs to be tapped that I thought I'd finally found my life's work.

Toward the end, I really did remind myself why my research had begun. I restricted experimentation to Willow's form and hoped she would never visit Lagos, Lusaka, Rio de Janeiro, San Juan, Caracas. . . .

I'm not sure how Mother surprised me. I usually sensed her honeysuckle and juniper hours away. Alexander, a muscular, wavy-haired Australian, and I had attained that moment when he probably thought we were generating the sparks flying in the room. The room's air got so itchy that people would get goosebumps as long as the building lasted.

Mother went back and forth from ethereal to physical so often back then, she could have managed the transition instantly. But, no. She took her time. While Mother's form was still as vague as smoke, we both saw her say, *"Quiero hablar contigo. Ahora mismo!"*

No doubt Mother did want to speak with me. But why did she have to scare Alexander? He barely grabbed his shirt and pants. He left his socks, shoes and underwear. The intimidating tactics that a despotic little woman like my mother sometimes employed were appalling.

*"Hijo mío!"*

I hadn't been eye level with Mother in quite some time. And never female. I said, "Mother, could I have just a moment. I'm at a greater disadvantage than usual."

While Mother turned her back, her patting little boot shook the block.

When I was more myself, Mother stared up at me, eyes flashing, and snapped, *"¿Qué pensaría tu padre?"*

What would my father think? Buying time, I frowned, hopefully conveying how carefully I considered her question. During those seconds, I actually did see Father's dark, lined face. His obsidian eyes. His cottony brow and hair. Father looked so tall. He looked so solemn. He looked like respect. Responsibility. I sighed. All in all, Father looked too far away for me to know anything except his magnificence and love, so I answered, "I'm not sure, Mother."

"My son!" Bolts from Mother's fingernails burned the floor. The air heated up and the building quivered. Out the window I went, heading for Good Sky with Mother raising squalls the whole way. Her anger was peaking, fortunately, when we crossed the Rockies. By the time we reached home, Mother only drew sparks from weak wiring, exploded lightbulbs and overturned my rooms.

*"Nunca mas, mi hijo,"* Mother said, departing. "Never again. *Esta ha sido increíble! Imposible! Escándolo!"*

Mother left me so shaken, I kept sputtering and otherwise pathetically fizzing in and out of corporeal form. It took hours before I could maintain physical integrity.

I'd be forever grateful for Willow's presence that evening. I was sorry she didn't meet Mother. Mother would have been cordial even if abrupt. Perhaps Mother's being in a peace-making mood was why Willow's picnic day was perfect.

Thin cumuli floated across the bright blue sky. Willow wore shorts. As I so well knew, she had lovely and strong legs, and how the thighs tingled when feather brushed. Willow's feet were entrancingly accented by pale leather sandals that tied around her ankles. How those little toes curled when kissed. How those ankles loved firm massage.

I lay towels on Cabrilla's leather seats, then put Willow's chess set and lunch in the trunk. When I pulled on sunglasses, Willow blew a minty pink gum bubble and asked, "So, where are we going?"

"Your pleasure, my dear."

"Well," Willow tapped a light staccato on the windwing, "not far after the turnoff for that cabin we went to there's a nice spot."

I turned the key, and Cabrilla's supercharged, three-hundred-twelve-cubic-inch displacement V-8 roared. When I shifted gears and backed up, Cabrilla's one-hundred-eighty-one-and-four-tenth total length inches of low-slung chassis with X-type frame turned beautifully.

We passed Mrs. G and Mr. Akkadian, and they called, "Have fun, kids." May Belle, who was watering poppies in her shop's windowbox, winked and smiled. After Willow and I rolled past Vincente's Pizza Shop, the MileMaster Train and Bus Depot and the cars backed up at Julio's Price Is Right Gas Station, I floored the accelerator and Cabrilla's free-turning, overhead intake valves sucked air while her Holley carburetor, two barrels in front and two in back, gave added power. The short-stroke, low-friction, deep-block, three-hundred-horsepower engine moved Cabrilla's one-hundred-two-inch wheel base with ball-joint front suspension, ride stabilizer, wind-up bumper on the cross member over the axle nose and five-leaf rear springs smoothly. Out on the highway, I couldn't help myself. I yelled, "Yes!" And as the road flew under Cabrilla's Firestones, I felt like I was on that honey-colored pearl called Saturn with thousand-mile-per-hour tailwinds.

At a weather-beaten sign whose chipped-away lettering spelled MEROPE'S ORCHARDS, we churned up a rutted, cinder trail surrounded by dandelions, crabgrass and Queen Anne's lace. Soon, we crested a small rise. A shining stream curlicued through the orchards below.

Feeling decidedly rejuvenated, I hopped from Cabrilla and opened Willow's door. She smiled up at me and said, "Seems like you and your mom got along pretty good last night."

I hummed a light tune. "She apologized, although we're still very much at odds. But why dwell on someone you don't know?"

Willow looked sincere when she said, "Next time your mom visits, Clement, I promise I'll . . ."

I shrugged and smiled, then said, "This is a lovely place."

Willow gazed across the shallow valley and said, "There's a couple reasons I chose it. One is that I used to pick apples here. Momma and Daddy would drive up from Creame, but we never came into Good Sky. We lived about three hours south and west. We made good get-by money. Every month, all through summer and fall, we went out harvesting things. And from the apples the Meropes always let us keep or buy cheap, Momma made terrific cobblers and applesauce. This place hasn't changed a bit, except they've painted the buildings and there's sections where they've cut down old trees and started some new."

As we pushed through foxtail grass to a pine grove, Willow pointed to a squat brown building beside the barn. She said, "There was an apple press in that shed. The Meropes made the best cider I ever tasted."

We spread the quilt over pine needles. Squirrels and small brown rabbits hopped through the grass. Crows cawed overhead. I enjoyed how sunlight danced through the heavy green boughs and played on Willow's face. Most of my life, I hadn't thought much about giving just for giving's sake. Occasionally, it happened . . . inadvertently. But that day was my gift to Willow.

We played a game of chess, which Willow won. We ate some lunch and set up the chessboard again, casually studying the pieces. Not quite ready to start, Willow said, "Clement, it's wonderful that you can just take off and do whatever you want."

I breathed deep and full, patted my stomach and said, "Yes, it is."

"But where does . . . ?" Willow frowned and started again. "I want you to know I only ask because I'm concerned, and I know you don't have to pay rent because you're fixing up that house." Willow stopped again. "Clement, how do you pay for other things?"

I waited for Willow to make another and different sort of query. When she just stared at me, I looked over the orchards and answered, "When my grandmother . . . when she died . . ." I let the scent of pine and young apples quell the emotions that missing my grandmother always stirred. I started again, "Grandmother Beah was the kindest, funniest—oh, the stories she could tell—the best friend a little guy ever had. Mother, on the other hand, knew that she would tolerate having one child and one child only. Mother adored Father. She would do that for him. And that child had better be a son.

"Father didn't interfere with Mother much and with Mother being who she is, my only out was Grandmother Beah. Mother and Grandmother Beah must have been the most polarized pair ever. And yet they were amazingly alike. Grandmother Beah was velvet-covered iron, and

Mother is iron-covered velvet. From Grandmother Beah, I get a stipend. I suppose it was Grandmother Beah's way of helping me prepare for the future. It hasn't worked yet. I go broke pretty quick."

Willow leaned forward and asked, "Do you have any money now?"

"Not much."

"So, what are you going to do?"

I was amazed at how nonchalantly my voice managed to say, "Oh, live, I suppose."

Willow's probing was pulling us seriously away from my intentions. Gradually, the blue sky, warm breezes, bright sun and soothing shadows, the birds and food and the chess game, had become inconsequential. With rude aggressiveness, my universe centered on Willow's plump lips and her breasts, which pressed against a thin, sleeveless blouse. I was coping as best I could with some very familiar physiological changes when Willow asked, "How?"

Swallowing, I answered, "Well, Mother gets a tad cranky, but she won't see me starve. At least she hasn't so far."

"Clement."

I wondered if practice would improve my ability to experience the physical compulsions that threatened to explode me while maintaining polite and unrelated conversation. "It's just possible," I said, "that maybe what I'm doing now is trying to show Mother and prove to myself that the world really can go on without grand strategies. You see, Father knew who he was. He understood his mission and, whether he liked it or not, he accepted his place in the order of things. Mother, no doubt about it, she pursues her role with vigor. Me, all I want to do is—"

"Clement, don't you—"

"Willow, I thought we came out here to relax. This afternoon isn't about me."

"No. It's about us, isn't it?"

I considered her question, then said, "Look, Willow, see those orchards."

Annoyed, Willow asked, "What's that got to do with anything?"

"They're neat. Orderly. Farmer Merope has taken a natural process and removed the random opportunity. Seedlings that take root out of the designated rows are plowed under. Those that sprout in the, oh, proper places have their trunks cropped and their branches pinned to wires so that they grow only in carefully defined and convenient ways. And by convenient, I don't mean for the tree. Who knows how tall and wide and amazing they would have become if left on their own? They might have grown to be like my wonderful sycamore. Ah, well, see what happens when I get philosophical? Come on, Willow," I touched her hand, "make your move, or should I?"

Willow's eyes flickered, but she kept going, "I don't agree with you, Clement. These trees are kept healthy. Animals and insects can't chew them up as easy. Irrigation systems protect them from drought. Smoke pots save them from the cold. At least they get everything they need to be—"

"To be productive."

"I wasn't going to say that. But that's what they were made for, to bear fruit. The farmers just help them do it better."

"They were given an opportunity to live, Willow, and whatever happens is the life they live. Why force things? Willow, do you really see yourself as one generation produced by and producing another that will become that drab utensil called 'adult'?"

"Somebody's got to do it."

"It seems to me that the world functions well enough all by itself. The planet spun just fine, well maybe a tad quicker, long before hominids ran things. Why won't people just let their lives be?"

"Excuse me, Clement. Maybe worrying a lot isn't a good idea, but groceries, a paid-off mortgage and keeping the lights on, that can be helpful."

"There's so much more to living."

"Most people can't cope with the kind of surprises you seem to enjoy. Most people want life a little more predictable."

"Well, they should loosen up."

"You mean like you, Clement? Hah!"

"Now that we've got this aspect of our philosophical outlooks clar-
ified . . ."

We both watched an ant hike across the chessboard. After a while
I breathed deep, shook my head and said, "Have we had enough of this
depressing subject?"

"But—"

"Willow, this is your special day. Don't worry about me."

"I don't."

"I'm more durable than you think."

"That's your concern. Not mine."

The mood had definitely deteriorated. I asked Willow if it would be
safe to walk down and see the cider press. She shrugged. When I returned, I pretended not to notice Willow's slightly reddened eyes and
runny nose.

I asked, "What are the other reasons you chose this place, Willow?
Why did we come here?"

Willow looked out over the orchard and was quiet a while before saying, "I wanted to make sure I only remember happy things
about this place." As she smoothed her hand over the quilt, Willow's
words were soft and fluid and starkly final. While Willow repacked
our food and I put away the chess set, I said, "Why don't we go out
tonight? We could get all dressed up and go to Cleveland. It's on the
lake, isn't it?"

"Yeah."

"We could go dancing."

Willow didn't answer.

# Mother

*Two hundred and three funnel clouds were recorded that July.*
*Wyoming had the worst in its history. There were thirty-nine*
*tornadoes in North Carolina, twenty in Iowa, fifteen in Colorado*
*and eight in Arkansas. Texas got fifty-nine.*

# 20

## Willow

### Friday, July 27, 1979

### Moon: New

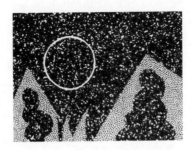

After I put on a little eyeshadow, lipstick and mascara, pretty underwear and perfume, I started feeling better. I wore a fuchsia dress with little rhinestones and matching shoes. I'd almost forgotten how heels, even low ones, made me walk so that my hips swayed. The swishing skirt reminded me of how pretty looking good could sound.

Clement had on a white shirt with thin silver threading and buttons. His pearl-gray pants also had silver threads. Clement's open collar showed off the star, crescent moon and knight pendants. With gold prices leaping like crazy, I figured they were getting real valuable. Summer had raised a mocha color from Clement's skin. The small diamond shone in his ear. His long hair was pulled back in deep waves, and I smelled a wonderful cologne. When I asked its name, he said, "My grandmother loved raising flowers and herbs and gathering roots and seeds. She dried them and mixed in oils and spices and made all kinds of concoctions. This time of year, we always had spearmint and peppermint, sage and thyme and rosemary. So, in addition to getting on my mother's nerves and making good sense, Grandmother Beah made scents. Well, enough family history. Are you ready?"

Clement pinned on a corsage of buttercups, and we stepped onto the sidewalk. Girls jumping rope, even boys playing kickball stopped and whistled. Ruby grinned. Amos rubbed his chin and said, "Veeery nice."

I hadn't felt that good since . . . well, maybe I never floated that free and light. Not even as a kid ripping through Blue Meadow. I placed my hand on Clement's. The Calliope unwound like a ribbon pulling us past cornfields and woodlands that floated a sweet fragrance. We sang everything from "Row, Row, Row Your Boat" to "Dancing in the Streets" to "Hold on, I'm Coming." I couldn't carry a tune, but Clement's voice made me sound great.

Stars twinkled through the sunset when we reached Cleveland. We danced a lot. Clement's grace, his energy and joy, his strength lifted me. When the clubs and cafes started closing, I said, "Let's try the Gold Tiger. It's like the old-time gangster clubs, you know, with a little window in the door."

"You mean they check you out before they let you in?" Clement grinned real wide. "Do you think we have the look?"

"Yeah."

"Well," Clement said, "let's go check *them* out!"

The Flats was a smoky, low-lying plain with gray-glassed warehouses, grubby buildings and railroad tracks. Across a waterway, steam shovels and cranes hauled ores on and off barges and Great Lakes freighters. The blackened metal decks of moving bridges groaned. Their whistles and bells rang and lights flared. Ashy flakes floated in the humid air. Stopped at a light, Clement leaned over and asked, "Are we in the right area?"

"There it is."

I pointed to the yellow neon sign on a building that churned up as much smoke as the steel mills. Clement parked, and we strolled under lights and through the shadows. We could hear the jukebox a block away. When we reached the swinging double doors, I breathed deep as Clement eyed the sizzling ribs and chicken on crusty metal grates. He looked over the cooks. One was a big, bald man who wore a reversed baseball cap and a ripped T-shirt and smoked a cigar. A thin guy in a sagging chef's hat and food-splattered apron worked the row of deep fryers. As though Clement were talking about a light summer rain or how nicely Ruby's flowers were growing, he asked, "Does Cleveland have a health department? Do they ever come here?"

I laughed and said, "Clement, this place is an institution. Come on, let's get some food. We can take it downstairs. That's where the band is."

Carrying our steamy white bags, we nudged through crowds who ate at stand-up counters. Below the dim and very narrow steps was the door lit with a red lightbulb. On the way was a fat brass railing. I said, "Look, Clement. It's still here. Isn't it wonderful?"

Clement peered at the railing like a toddler discovering a grasshopper and asked, "Why?"

"I always wanted to slide on it."

"Really?" Clement looked delighted.

"Yeah," I said, rubbing the metal. "It reminds me of the time Momma took me to this big store in Cincinnati. Oh, how I wanted to slide down that railing."

"Did you?"

"No!"

"Why not?"

"It just wouldn't have looked right."

"To whom?"

"To everyone. Momma was very concerned." I whispered as two couples squeezed past, "You know how it was back then. Colored people didn't usually go in those stores and when we did, Momma didn't want to draw more attention."

"You mean that all these years you've wanted to slide down a railing and you've never done it?"

"I was a child, Clement. That's behind me now."

Clement blinked and asked, "Why is it all behind you now? And is there a pun in this?"

I put my hands on my hips, "Can't you see me standing here all grown up?"

"Well, actually, no."

"Look again, Clement."

"So, you don't want to slide down this brass marvel?"

"When I was young."

"I'm not talking about twenty years or even twenty minutes ago, Willow. You know, this whole growing-up phenomenon is a truly obnoxious expectation of longevity. I am convinced that maturity is just a figment of some spoilsport's imagination. My dear, you're young as long as you can manage it. I, myself, as you may have noticed, manage it a lot. So, go ahead, *mon cher.*" Clement played his fingers on the railing as though it were a piano. "Do it, babe."

"I'd feel ridiculous."

"We deserve that sensation daily. Smart folks manage it more often." Clement took my food.

I glanced around. Music from below mingled with the restaurant chatter and loudspeakers above us. I sat on the railing, then hopped off.

Clement moved his face so close to mine that his two eyes became one. "Willow," he said, "would you please slide down this thing. Our food is leaking, and anyway," Clement smiled, "please."

I eased onto the railing. Clement sighed, "Oh, what a lucky rail." I pushed at him. A little squeal broke from me until my feet touched down.

As more footsteps creaked down the stairs, Clement asked, "Now what do we do?"

We both turned and gawked at the door with the little window. It was shut tight. Finally, I said, "Well, we . . . we . . ."

"You knock." A short, dark man with a floppy cap tilted low over one eye reached between us. He rapped the door hard. When the small panel slid over, he snapped, "Open up! Ain't got all night." The woman with him, Oriental and several inches taller, smiled and shrugged.

When the door opened, at first all I saw was smoke, red cigarette tips and candles burning in amber glasses. A mirrored ball pattered sparklers across the rough-plastered walls. We found a small table. I sat swaying in my chair, studying the other people and waiting for Clement to dance. When I looked at Clement, he nodded mechanically, as though he couldn't quite catch the rhythm. By the time the band stopped, even in the darkness, Clement looked like a ghost. I thought his face would flop into his deep-fried vegetables. Rasping, Clement said, "Willow, I'm sorry. I can't . . . I, I've got to . . ."

Clement staggered toward the door where the bouncer said, "The bathroom's that way, man."

"I just"—Clement's chest heaved—"I've got to get some air."

Halfway up the shadowy steps, Clement braced against the wall. "I'll be okay Willow, honest. As soon as I get outside." But Clement only moved a few inches up and then started sliding down. Finally, embarrassment burning red spots into his cement-gray face, Clement whispered, "I think you're going to have to help me."

Steering through The Gold Tiger's crowd took forever. Outside, Clement choked and couldn't breathe. I was about to go hollering for a doctor when Clement whispered, "Wait."

He relaxed against a wall. With his head tilted back, he closed his eyes and was quiet. Finally, Clement looked at me with a rickety smile.

"I tried, Willow. I really did." Clement was hoarse. "This is my Achilles' hell, I mean heel. Feeling shut in is a real problem." After a long breath, Clement smiled more easily and said, "I'm fine now."

Clement pulled me close and hugged me so tight, I nearly smothered. I felt his pendants and even smelled his cologne under the smoke. I cherished his thumping heart as Clement kissed my hair and said, "You were really enjoying yourself, and I ruined it. But when I couldn't find windows, and the doors were locked, I felt trapped."

I rubbed his chest gently. "Clement, you should have said something."

"This problem . . . I panic, you see. I'll definitely discover a cure. This can't go on."

"Clement, how on Earth do you manage in your candle room? It seems to have everything that you're afraid of. Fire. Small space."

"That room is different. It calls for opening up. Didn't you feel that?" As Clement's dark eyes caressed me, I nodded. Then he asked, "What would you like to do?"

I worked my hands past Clement's sides and around his back. Clement moved his hand on my back until I felt like I was sliding . . . up . . . up, up, up into a warm and beautiful place.

Startled by how I'd slipped into just plain enjoying Clement's embrace and remembering the times I'd felt that way before, I pulled away. We stood there. The world felt like it held just the two of us, and we were on a narrow wall. It was not high but rising. On one side, I saw brilliant night. On the other side was fog. Sooner or later, Clement and I would either fall or leap. But, which way?

Clement tugged my fingers, and we walked to the car. He drove to a beach with large, egg-shaped rocks. We stood there until the birds rustled. Until there was a vibrating that I'd always thought was the night birthing a new day. Trees, dogs, grass, rocks, buildings, everything held its breath, awaiting the first light.

Clement and I soaked up Lake Erie's sounds, freshwater smells and reflections. Boat hoots and buoys rang across the water. As Clement held my hand, I asked the day just beginning to open a place, a good and warm, a safe and trusting space for us in each other's heart.

# 21

## The Tree

## Saturday, July 28, 1979

## Moon: New

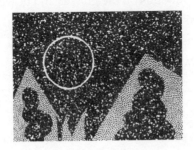

Winds delivered me. Lightning heated and hollowed my place. Rain wrapped earth around me. I reached. My roots touched others, and I learned. I dug, tested strange soils, adapted and anchored until I was strong enough to rise from darkness and above the mists.

I knew Clement and Willow from the moment they left the lake. As they came closer, Willow peeked at the horizon, wishing she could wake enough. Willow wanted to see the sky's fresh lilacs and carnations.

He was pale, tall and thin. Coarse brown hair tossed around his old and yet young face. His features were full and rounded. His eyes were like night.

Amazed, Clement saw me glittering in the rose-hued light. Fascinated, he watched my limbs drop long, silvery fronds that stirred the vapors and glistening grasses. He asked Willow, "Do you mind? Could we wait and watch the sun rise?"

Willow barely heard the car stop. She hardly noticed Clement open the trunk, pull out a quilt and say, "You know, on mornings like this, when clouds kiss the earth and make the world sparkle, they say that the pixies are out. Brownies are bashful beings, you know. They usually hide from us."

Willow was small and dark. Her features were fuller than his. Clement's talk of fairies roused her. Willow saw the river shimmer, softening from amethyst into pale violet, wisteria and mauve until, in the east, water, earth and air glowed coral. She heard the wind singing through dew that was like diamonds on the grasses and flower petals. As Willow walked, little fingers tickled her ankles. She jumped.

"It's just the grass." Clement smiled. "I envy the grass."

He lifted Willow and parted my drapery.

## Clement

At first, I was just aware of gleaming silver and emerald, the river songs and wind sighs, the earth fragrances and undulating mists. The tree rose as though from prayer, sparkling and magnificent. And Willow was so warm and wondrous in my arms. As I carried her through the catkins, I admired how the tree's roots reached out like star points. I spread the quilt between them.

Lying together, Willow rested her face above my heart. I smoothed Willow's hair, then caressed her shoulder. Her softness and her flower-sweet, earth-salt scent electrified me. Willow's luminous eyes held the sky. In them, I understood that I either had to give myself honestly and completely or not at all.

I became a tiny cell. I became even less, an atom. When that small, the giving of my Self became nothing and entirely too much.

Inside, I was hot. But a cold sweat burst from me. I backed away. I wanted to run. Run like three children. I saw them. They were racing the rain.

I wanted to fly fast enough to leave the galaxy, and far off, I saw a flame. I thought about how sight was never simultaneous with the perceived and wondered how long each bursting bit of light needed to travel from its source to my understanding. I wondered how Willow and I could love and, instead of responding some fraction of a second later, our receiving would be one with our giving.

The flame became a candle. It was night, and I circled, fascinated by the light. I was frightened of the heat yet compelled, thrusting my whole into her fire and exploding spectacularly. Disintegrating, darkness swallowing me, I felt more than Willow as a hot, divine part of myself. I realized that I had surrendered. From Willow, I withheld nothing and received.

I received.

## Willow

After years of running from who I really and completely was, cooling and then chilling until my ability to love had crusted with enough ice to sink Good Sky, I tasted spring. A drowsy peace lapped over me. A melody bloomed from my center. The song tingled in my abdomen and surged through my heart. It bubbled into little stars that broke through my skin.

I remembered what could follow. I tried to hide the lights. I couldn't let their brightnesses bring summer and then autumn. Winter would surely follow. I couldn't take the chance that the good giving, the sweet taking, that the happiness Clement brought could clack and roll away.

The shadows of long-gone men fell. I looked into Clement's face and saw that he recognized Jimmy, Kinshasa and others. And he ran like three children with the rain moving fast. We both ran with the wind pressing our backs, tussling our hair and lifting us so high I was breathless watching the trees and Corey Creek and the barns and houses get smaller until the Earth, the Moon, Mercury, Venus and Mars became like billiard balls and night was my rocket ship.

Clement kissed my forehead, my temples, my ears. He kissed my calf, ankle, thigh, my center and my breasts. He kissed like sunbeams. When Clement pushed into me, I rose up. I met him. I absorbed Clement's giving. I gave back and died. I dissolved into raptures so beautiful that I couldn't breathe. My body became like roots that pulled out of the ground. My fingers and toes were leaves that fluttered away. My arms and legs became diamond dust, and I fell up . . . joyously. I knew for sure that, centuries later, people would come there. They would find my bones. My bones would sparkle. They would be jewels.

## The Tree

Platinum lined the bright pink clouds as Clement cradled her. Mists slipped under and through my branches like little feathers when he whispered Willow's name. As he tenderly traced her mouth, Clement looked skyward and whispered, "I love her." Then he sighed and pressed the center, just above Willow's lips. Clement kissed her as sleep took hold.

The arms and hands are warm and strong. Willow wonders how their embrace could feel so forever. She recognizes the whisper. It sounds like, "Shhhh, child. Shhhh." Willow watches. She understands but will recall only tiny faces peeping under my leaves. The faces, the grass, the stars beyond, they all smiled, making Willow feel like a little creature, a gecko colored topaz, ruby, aquamarine and opal. She rode a big lily pad and there were many luminous and fragrant white flowers. They clustered atop a forest pond. Willow saw the delicate tissues of grass easily and watched her reflection in raindrops that cascaded for miles.

When the rain stopped, Willow was herself again. She walked along a pillow-soft beach. The mists and water trickled. Seagulls coasted above the inlet. A rhythm, at first faint, drifted from beyond the chrysanthemums, poppies, Stars of Bethlehem, lady's slippers and peonies. Through papaya and mango, coconut and banana trees, Willow heard drums and feet marching and hands clapping songs. High and sweet voices called and deep, strong voices answered. Their music grew louder until Willow felt she should have been able to touch the singers.

Willow thought she knew them, like cousins, great-aunts and -uncles. Men appeared first, bronze and brown and black. Some wore helmets like tall cones that curled forward. Fringe hung off the head-pieces like horse manes, with diamonds where the eyes would be. Silver straps crisscrossed their bare chests. Dark, silver-trimmed wraps hung to just below the men's knees. They were barefoot. The first marchers tapped thin sticks against small drums nestled beside their ribs.

Others appeared pounding larger drums strapped to their sides. More men came. Their rich voices answered calls from distant women. Soldiers appeared. Their heads were wrapped in dark, silver-trimmed cloth. The ends bounced against their shoulder blades. Long daggers were fastened at their waists. Small, silver shields were fixed to their wrists. Their thick hair strands danced as their arms swooped low, then skyward. The men formed a large circle, and the women entered.

The women's heads were wrapped with gold and white cloth that pushed their thick hair into rounded and sparkling puffs. Their hands swung rhythmically above their heads. Some snapped their fingers. Others clapped. Their milky, gold-flecked garments floated. Beneath their sheer blouses, cloth and cowrie-shell halters cupped their breasts. Their swaying hips carried thick shell belts and beads and stones and bells of brass and copper. Fifty women filled the circle. They sang to the men. Their feet, jingling with gold and silver beads, stamped harmony. The men and women mingled sensuously but never touched.

More men appeared. They wore feathers and hats of thin woven woods decorated with shells and beads. They swept brushes made from long grasses behind them, then toward the dancing women. More women arrived wearing tops like cowrie-shell brassieres. Straps crossed their lustrous backs. Their skirts were leopard and gazelle and zebra skins. Those women also brought drums, some small, held at their sides. They tapped with their fingers and with long, thin sticks. The women bringing the largest drums stopped, snuggling them between their legs as they pounded, and let the little bells bouncing from their drum skins ring.

Willow struggled awkwardly to join their dance and song. The harder she tried, the fainter they became. When Willow reached after them, their forms faded. Willow's heart beat faster. Her palms sweated. She panted. Desperate, as they almost vanished, Willow froze. In that still moment, she understood, "Just enjoy, child. Know delight and love."

At first, Willow's steps were tiny and uncertain. Willow swayed and swirled and swung her arms freely. That's when the others joined, and Willow danced in soft earth, her copper, gold and silver jewelry ringing. Cowrie shells covered Willow's breasts. Sheer, white cloth circled her, floating and kissing her skin. Willow tapped a small drum with her fingers. Her drum was carved with suns. Pretty beads and stones and shells jingled.

With the women, Willow chanted, "We seek our child." The men answered, "He has been lost." The women sang, "He guards our souls." The men responded, "We are ready to guide him home."

Arching and rolling her body, Willow became as they were, butterflies fluttering in silken and brilliant blue and pink, orange and purple, yellow and green. Willow rejoiced in how her hips swung slowly down and up. She bounced through the Anlo Ewe people's Gahu and exhausted herself with the Mongo hunters' Bofenia, ending with the Lutuk, the Mbala people's moonlight dance of caring and sharing.

Within that night, Willow felt whole and eternal. Torches were lit and the flames swept across the ground and into the air. Through the thinning and sweetly pungent smoke, a hooded figure crossed the crystal-black horizon. He wore iridescent robes and walked with a shepherd's crook. Bright and bountiful stars followed like ribbons. His head was low, as though heavy with thought. The people cheered, then drew back glowing.

Clement and Willow were not gone long when lichen enveloped my trunk and moss covered my roots. They were not quite home when I expanded out and up until, far below, the meadow grass glittered as my being, by then golden motes, rained.

# 22

## Willow

### Saturday, July 28, through

### Monday, August 13, 1979

### Moon: New–Disseminating

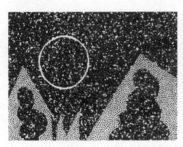

I opened my eyes to see the man with the stars better and woke up in bed. Rubbing my eyes and then shutting them tight, I tried to pull back the dream. Where was everyone, especially Clement? I wanted the loving and the dancing back. I wanted to burst open again and find Clement and me more whole. Right then, there and always, I wanted Clement opening more surprises within and around me.

By Sunday morning, Ruby must have gotten tired of tapping the ceiling with her broom handle. My phone blared, and she huffed, "Chile, ain't it time you got up? You got to be hungry. And you know I can't abide slothful. Get down here. I'm not letting this food sit and spoil."

I plunked downstairs. Groggy and holding my head, I endured Ruby's stares and Amos' gentler glances. After Ruby clattered my plate onto the table, she said, "Chile, chile, chile, that must have been some night."

Staring into my water glass, I said, "I'm sorry, Ruby. I hope we didn't worry you or—"

"Did you hear her, Amos? She hoped we didn't worry."

"It was a really wonderful evening. Clement was . . . he was just . . ."

"I guess he was." Ruby leaned back and crossed her arms. "Ain't seen hide nor hair of neither one of you since he brought you home. High noon Saturday of all times. Right when everybody is out there washing cars and windows and shopping." Ruby eyed me harshly, then her voice softened. "But he was so very sweet. Wasn't he, Amos?"

Amos grunted and dipped a biscuit in gravy.

I whispered, "How can I face everyone?"

"Chile, long as you been living here, I thought you'd a noticed. Ain't no saints on Evergreen Way. Maybe up there on Cedar, around on Birch or Hibiscus or over there on Laurel, but ain't none here. And haven't you learned yet? Each tub's got to sit on its own bottom. Lord knows, misery'll dump on us by the truckload. Ain't got to ask for that. But we do have to fight for joy. I've had my good times. So mind me, girl, during life's winter times, them happy rememberings can—Well, I'll be darned!" Ruby clapped her fork on the table. "Willow, you ain't heard a word."

"I was listening, Ruby. You were talking about, about winter."

"Don't try fooling me. Where was your mind?"

"I was thinking about . . ." I blushed really hard. "I was thinking about Clement, Ruby."

"No kidding."

"But I was also thinking . . ."

"What?"

"Marla called. She said Jimmy Anderson's coming to Faraday's tomorrow."

Amos stopped chewing.

Ruby frowned and said, "What's he going there for?"

"His father's sick, and they're having trouble with the business."

"Ain't he got a job somewheres?"

"Maybe I won't even see him."

"What's it matter if you do? He ain't been sending more flowers, has he? He ain't been calling?"

I shook my head. I felt dizzy. Whirling around me was the question, When did you ever stop loving someone? Jimmy had painted and sketched me a few times. I still had a couple small ones. They were in my bottom dresser drawer. They were under things way in the back. I hadn't looked at them in years. I wasn't sure when I would.

Ruby pointed toward her front door and said, "What about that boy across the street?"

I couldn't think of an answer. All I could do was sense Clement in and around me, and I melted.

Lips soured, Ruby said, "Willow, when a man and a woman parts company, you're supposed to turn the whole thing over to time. Every day, when there's nothing feeding the feelings, a little bit and then a little more's supposed to go away. One fine morning you wake up and realize ain't nothing left for that person. You mean you ain't got there yet?" Ruby leaned over the table and looked at me hard. "You got any plans for tonight, gal?"

I thought about Clement and dissolved even more.

"Good," Ruby said. "Glad to see you're free. You're coming with me."

I was listless all afternoon and didn't get to my regular chores, like washing clothes, dusting, painting my nails and shaving my underarms. Rose Singer came by after dinner. I had hardly touched Ruby's salmon croquettes and cheese-topped broccoli. Rose had some tea, then drove us to the end of Evergreen Way, where she looked at her shop, then turned right and took us past Faraday's and up the little hill to Corinthian Baptist Church. On the way, Mrs. Singer said, "The tall young man who lives across from you, he seems like a nice person."

Glumly, I answered, "Yes."

"Well, you deserve someone nice, Willow. From what he says in my shop, he likes you very much."

"He does," Ruby added, cementing the feeling that I was a small bug under two huge microscopes.

The Flying Needles had a quilt frame in Corinthian's white paneled basement. Children's toys and books and little chairs were at one end. A kitchen with counter was at the other. That night, Jessie Bloom brought peach upside-down cake and made the coffee. Ruby said little to Jessie, mainly because the former elementary teacher had kept the same dress size for forty years.

Mary Hanover was a plump blonde with eyes that made me think of a chicken. She brought cherry cobbler. Mary Hanover lived three doors from Ruby going toward Primrose, but Ruby stopped riding with her six years before when, as Ruby put it, Mary stuck a mop handle out her second-floor window one Christmas and hung a banner appliquéd with a decorated tree. Before long, everyone except Ruby had banners until the fad faded a couple years ago.

I hadn't quilted in a while and spent some time watching Bethany Walsh, Sue Chin, Ruby and Jasmine Moonglow gently rock their needles forward, joining the windmill-patterned top, the warming batt and plain muslin bottom fabric. I listened to Bethany answer questions about her upcoming wedding.

"Yes, I think you and Darryl are going to make a lovely couple," Anna Perkins, the children's room librarian said, looking over her bifocals.

"Marriage, it is not an easy thing," Mia Svenson said.

"How would you know?" Ruby asked.

"I watched my parents. It was hard. That's probably why Astrid and I, we stayed—"

"Sometimes that's the best way," Mabel O'Brien cut in. "Keep them out of your heart *and* your pants."

"Speak for yourself," Jasmine said. "I like having a man around. I say: Use it or lose it. What about that guy on Evergreen?"

"What about him?" Ruby huffed.

"Is he available?" Jasmine looked straight at me. I felt my own face heat up.

"He's a polite and courteous young man," Ruby answered. "Means he had a good upbringing."

"I didn't ask about his upbringing." Jasmine smiled as she brushed back her straight blond hair.

"I reckon the rest is his personal business." Ruby butted in again.

"Oh, you mean like coming in with Willow here yesterday morning was private?"

"I think," said Astrid Svenson, "new feelings finding their way is a beautiful thing, and we must wish well all those who enter into such."

A melody of odd but lovely harmonies dipped and rose and swam around me. I thought of how Momma sat with Terry's mom on Sunday evenings listening to church music and preachers on the radio as they cut and sewed little bits of fabric together until there was a whole new cloth. I thought of how those Flying Needles members sat together each week while the world whirled in oil problems, trucker strikes, inflation, record-breaking gold prices, trouble in Iran and the cold war that always threatened to go nuclear. With all that gloom and doom, those women joined bits of cloth as though in a hundred years their quilts would still warm someone.

After a while, I barely heard the women gossiping. Matter of fact, I didn't hear, eat, drink or sleep anything but Clement for quite a while. Even after seeing Jimmy. Even with Jimmy's sending flowers all the time. Cause Clement kissed, moved and touched in ways that I never imagined. We were like children playing, exploring, daring and delighted, never knowing when or how something magical would ignite, then settle around us like cuddly blankets. I near forgot what aloneness was and didn't ever want to be without Clement again.

Then I got home from work and found a letter from "just" Lucille. Feeling real happy, I carried the note up to Clement's rooms. Sunbeams looked like smiles fidgeting through the holes in Clement's half-drawn shades. Clement's wiry hair hung loose. His skin was like vanilla fudge. We hugged and kissed and enjoyed touching. Just touching. After we tumbled into bed and played and laughed and exhausted ourselves, I told Clement, I said, "I don't ever want this to end."

Clement kissed right above my heart and answered, "It won't."

I said, "I've got good news."

Clement's face brightened as he asked, "Must I make three guesses?"

I couldn't wait. I gushed, "Lucille is coming."

"Who?" Clement was about to laugh. Then he sat up and asked, "Isn't Lucille your grandmother?"

"Yeah." I was all aglow.

"Didn't you say she has these eyes? This special vision?"

"Sure. But Lucille never sees much that bothers her around here, Clement. No ghosts. No spirits."

Clement looked away and asked, "How long has it been since you visited your grandmother?"

"About eight years. I haven't been back to Homestead since, well since 1971."

"Perhaps you should visit your Lucille this time."

"Would you come with me?"

"I, um, we'll see."

"Oh Clement, Lucille's coming this way anyhow. She always does. And you wouldn't like Homestead. It's smoky. Noisy. Besides—" Clement was so quiet and shadowy, I said, "You'll like Lucille a lot. She tells the funniest stories and . . . Clement?"

In the space between us, I felt something like a castle bridge heave up. An iron gate clanged down. An icy moat made an emptiness too wide to cross. I said, "Clement, are you okay?"

A week later, I saw spectacular lights flare in the night sky. They were just like the glittering sprays I'd seen that morning around Christmas except the color was more like a beautiful reddish purple. After that, although there were days with Clement that were lovely as sunflowers, there were other times when he was like a hound out in the dark sniffing for trouble.

## 23

## Jimmy

## Tuesday, July 24, through

## Saturday, August 18, 1979

## Moon: New—Last Quarter

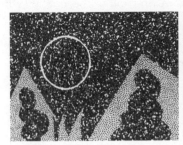

Abe says that "holocaust" is about sacrifice. It's when the fruit, the lamb, the effort surrendered is completely accepted. It's what the fire totally consumes. That's not good enough. I need to know why Lonnie was on that bridge. When did Lonnie see the train? How hard did he fight for life?

Lonnie's grave marker is gray and rose granite. The holly trees we planted are tall. I offer small sunflowers, forget-me-nots and star tulips. I offer incense. Beads and shells. Pears. With these gifts, this earth and air must return more than images of blood clotting on snow.

In the silence that surrounds me, I remember a little boy asking Lonnie how fireflies lit up. Where the Tooth Fairy lived. If I might need a second trowel to dig my way to China. One last question comes, How am I supposed to accept your death, big brother? I gaze at Lonnie's sandals and staff. I touch Lonnie's drum and shakere. My lungs won't swell. My head aches. I want to ask why he went south alone. How he managed to come back laughing. Rougher and more relaxed. Satisfied, much like Dad. Disregarding our crisp-cut landscape. Narrow pinstripes. Ignoring the need for thin features. Hair for fine-toothed combs. Pale skin.

When I go back to my car and check the rearview mirror, the man with the curling, silver and black beard strides from the north. He wears a torn straw hat. Patched overalls. Uses a smoothed tree branch for a walking stick. Pigs and chickens follow. He sings deep and hearty.

The small woman's singing rings like tiny bells. She comes from the south, two-stepping through shining puddles. Rain glitters in her silver and black braids. On Spanish moss. A tin-roofed house. She swings a soup ladle like a conductor's baton. Measuring spoons are pinned to her yellow pinafore. They jingle. Her long and dark blue dress bounces. Underneath are bright pink slips.

The man lifts the dancing woman against his chest. Swings her around, then sets her down. He laughs. Shouts, "Ha! Ha! It is a marvelous place!"

She nods thoughtfully. Asks, "Even if it isn't?"

He bellows. "Who cares how others name it? Those fool enough to leave should not look over their shoulders."

The big woman. Huge bosomed. Broad hipped. She comes from the east in fierce purple. Her red umbrella has a brass handle on polished wood. She points toward the couple. Demands, "What do you know?"

"Actually, Momma . . ." The setting sun silhouettes the man wearing the Panama hat. Fringed buckskin vest. Hanging midway down his muscled chest is a white cord with a cross. He's dark brown. Handsome. Sly. Jeans worn low. A sheathed knife in his woven leather belt. He says, "They care as much as we do. They know what they love. They hold true like us."

"If that's the case," the big woman thumps her chest. I feel the thud, "They understand it's the heart that counts."

I think, Is this all you've got to do?

They all stare. The big woman laughs. Says, "Don't mind us, child. We got our ways. But ain't none of us fools."

They're gone, leaving only a sound. Real faint. Like the rhythm of my tires on the road.

Tha-Thump.

Tha-Thump. Tha-Thump.

The return trip is five miles. Nothing stops me. Still, the drive takes most of my life.

When I get home, late light caresses trees. Bird songs. Boys passing in baseball gear. I imagine an old German woman holding little black hands. Telling stories until they become real. Again, I hear . . .

Tha-Thump.

Tha-Thump. Tha-Thump.


When I call Faraday's, a woman answers. I nearly choke asking, "Who is this?"

"Marla. Who are you?"

"James Anderson. How's your baby?"

"We're fine, Jimmy. And he's not so small. Alvin has a little brother now. A lot happens in nine years. Oh. Here's Mrs. Faraday. You called for her, right?"

That Monday, I drive beyond Cleveland's metal and glass. Beyond the mills' fires. I stare into long and longer miles and realize I've spent most of my life strategizing. Studying profit and loss. Plotting economy of word and deed. Figuring how to win efficiently. I thought that was success. I feel like Abe Corsini must have coming home from a school board meeting saying, "James, my man, if there's one thing I've learned, it's impossible to make anything foolproof. Fools are too ingenious."

I turn off the air-conditioning. Lower the windows. Silos and corn bins top the horizon. Farmhouses. The vast fields bake. Sweat drops like putty. Looking for what I've done right, I need binoculars.

A goose rises from cattails. The bird coasts beside the passenger door longer than I think possible. Another accompanies until the road veers me away.

I pass the Merope Orchard sign. The Calliope Coke Works. The MileMaster Train and Bus Depot. Vincente's. I see May Belle's Antiques & Collectibles, the Big Star Picture Show. Prisms from the leaded and stained–glass shop windows sparkle. Maple trees still rise above red-wood benches. Through her open door, I see Mrs. Singer laughing.

I drive past the post office. The produce store with baskets of let-tuce, tomatoes, peaches and plums under awnings. The Red & White Thrift Store.

After Akkadian's Junkyard and Longacre Grain Distributors, I park. I stare at Faraday's yard and building. At each weed, nail, knob and handle. I note the new glass-block windows. Cleaned and pointed bricks. The bigger, circus-letter sign. I smell corn popping. I walk and feel the gravel. Touch the loading-dock railing. Each wooden step groans of broken dreams. Brokered promises.

The door opens. Frank Singer has the same bushy eyebrows. His gray eyes study me cooly before offering a firm handshake. With all-purpose wedding and funeral smile, he leads me to Mrs. Faraday's office. Marla is inside. She's pudgier. Her eyes are just as sharp. She offers coffee. Both leave.

Mrs. Faraday still has the bamboo plants and ferns. If possible, there are even more laughing Buddha statues and rollicking dragons. Crystals shine at the window. The room smells of lilac, but her new desk is sleek, black wood with a glass top and a red felt blotter. Two wire baskets hold mail. Pencils and pens jut from a cloisonné cup. Mrs. Faraday now has barrister cabinets for her books and the carpet is Persian.

I think about Dad's start behind Tiny's Cafe. A wooden garage. Tin signs advertise Coca-Cola. Gold Dust Soap with those black pickanin-nies. O'Baby Chocolate Drink with a Black man grinning. Tongue licks wide, thick lips as he says, "Ain't Dat Sumptin." Inside, a big bank cal-endar has red and gray pencil circling birth dates and anniversaries.

Phone numbers on margins. Oily rags. I see Dad's dark-red truck as I wipe grit from the headlights. Feel the bouncing, creaky suspension and the wonder that after nine years, I've returned.

Mrs. Faraday enters. *"Nǐ hǎo."* She nods and smiles. "It's good to see you, James. You look prosperous."

"Thank you."

"How is your father?"

"He's tough. Things won't be the same, but he'll make it."

Mrs. Faraday nods. "That toughness is important, isn't it?"

"It's an ingredient."

"Yes."

"One of many."

"I see."

"It's good to have when needed, Mrs. Faraday. What I'm learning is," I pause, "I'm learning some things aren't needed all the time."

Mrs. Faraday gestures to a chair. Offers small licorice-flavored candies. Says, "So, James, it's been nine years. What else have you learned?"

Through Mrs. Faraday's window, a rectangle of light shines. It has moved from a flowering magnolia twig in a glass vase to a pair of elaborately painted, white porcelain statues. When I thank Mrs. Faraday for her time and stand to leave, she rises, bathed in light, and smiles at the statues.

"Do you know what these are?" Mrs. Faraday asks.

I shake my head.

"They are He-He Gods. They look so happy because they are of summer and prosperity. They carry lotus flowers so carefully in their jars because they treasure purity and spiritual grace. They are cherished as symbols of balance and harmony in marriage. I often think all couples should have them." Mrs. Faraday tilts her head. She smiles. Her eyes sparkle as she adds, "But what the gods desire for us is one thing. What we allow is another."

Mrs. Faraday offers her hand. Guides me back between shelves of candy, paper and Styrofoam cups. The room where Willow works is quiet. Frank Singer stands beside the loading-dock door. He says, "Tell Winona to let us know how we can help, James."

I mumble, "Thank you." Step outside. Shield my eyes. See Marla and Willow with oranges. I go down the five steps two years at a time. Perhaps the Earth stops, but I keep spinning. Willow says, "Sorry about your dad, Jimmy."

When my heart pumps again. When I have strength enough, I say, "Thank you."

Willow swings her legs back and forth. Peels her orange.

I say, "You look like life's been good."

"Yeah." Willow's calm eyes punch the breath from me.

"I thought you might be married and gone. That new man you're seeing, what's taking him so long? Not even an engagement ring?"

Willow looks down. Separates an orange segment. Sucks juice from her thumb then her forefinger. Shrugs.

"I'll be back, Willow."

Willow's lips press tight. I walk away, then turn. I tell the sky. Mrs. Faraday. Frank Singer and Marla. I tell Willow, "I'm going to get you back."

Every week since, whether I see Willow or not, I leave roses at Faraday's. Yellow for joy and friendship. White for innocence. Light pink for grace. Orange for fascination. Lavender for enchantment. Coral for desire. Dark pink for thankfulness. And red for love and respect.

## 24

## Clement

## Sunday, August 19, 1979

## Moon: Balsamic

Who could see the magnificent arc in the sky that was our wheel? Our great circle of circles. Our one among billions of sparkling discs. Were it not for the spin flinging the weight of their moons, planets and stars outward, gravity would collapse galaxies into and through their own masses. Oh, the delicate and precise balancing required to keep things the same. Yet none of the universe's amazements surpassed the landscape of Willow.

Thinking of Willow was like dawn flooding the sky. Clouds were no longer Mother's gloomy messengers. They were marvelous sailing vessels. Hints of Earthly potential carried aloft. I could enjoy the way mists lay on bodies of water so that bits of heaven filled the rivers and particles of sea ascended.

I had attained just such a buoyant and clearly vulnerable mood one night when Willow smiled beatifically and said, "May Belle's got a wonderful chess set."

All I could manage was, "Oh?" Then, against my better judgment, I asked, "How wonderful is it?"

"Well, the squares are cream and black marble with a jade border and a mahogany frame." Willow pursed her lips, fighting a grin and said, "You've got to have seen it, Clement. The pieces are gold and silver. On one side are men and the other are women. They're in beautiful costumes."

Examining my fingernails as calmly as possible, I said, "Tell me, my dear, they're not real gold and silver, are they? It's not real jade?"

"Maybe."

"Well, given my suspicions about its price, what's it worth to you?"

Willow snuggled close and said, "Five minutes of my deluxe."

"Five minutes? Why just five?"

"Well, most men can't . . ."

My eyes sparkled. "Can't what?"

Willow could barely answer for laughing.

"Wait a minute. Do you mean that what I've gotten up until now has only been legumes and tubers? I haven't had dessert?"

Although I knew Willow's body, I didn't know her capabilities. Intrigued, I continued, "Well, five minutes of more than I've already experienced, the value is beyond calculation. But to buy this assemblage, I may actually have to become . . ." Unable to face that implication, I said, "How about us making this a little more interesting? What if you take two out of three," I nodded toward our chess set. "But if I win two . . ." I smiled broadly.

"Honest work's never been fatal, Clement."

"Please Willow, not that subject again. Let's just play."

Around eight-thirty, several moves into the tiebreaker, I asked, "Would you like to see some magic?"

"You're not distracting me, Clement."

"Maybe this really isn't magic. Did you know that my left hand is magnetic?"

"Well, I thought there was something, um . . . extraordinary there."

"Really?"

"No foolishness, Clement. Forget the tricks, and no weirdness, unless it's, well, there is this one wonderful thing you do. I really like it."

I knew Mother would adore Willow. They were two of a kind. Just a bit of difference in wattage. True to her gender, Willow had effectively undone me. The game didn't take long. I was too busy figuring out what the odd thing I did was.

After that blissful evening, I thought my biggest problems would be finding a job and staying away from Willow's grandmother, but the next morning my screens rattled. My sycamore scratched the window. Far off, thunder boomed. Electricity flared from a flash-blue and silver cloud churning like a battleship across the horizon. The wind was heavy with honeysuckle and juniper, and I couldn't help thinking how my beloved clouds, the realm of the wisps, sometimes flexed their muscles when bridging sky and earth.

White high-heeled boots sparking as she paced, Mother demanded, *"¿Cuanto tiempo piensas que tu padre trobajara sien ti?"*

As delicately as possible, I acknowledged that, yes, Father's work couldn't be left hanging indefinitely. Then I asked if someone else couldn't handle the tasks.

Mother's beautiful, heart-shaped face tightened. Her smoking eyes glared up into mine and her vermilion lips firmed. Despite her flared nostrils, I lifted Mother's small hands. I swallowed hard and continued softly, saying, "Mother, wouldn't you agree that my first commitment must be to make myself whole? I don't feel as strong as Father. I don't think I'll ever be as wise. Can't you see? I'm not ready."

The air got itchy. The nap in the rugs and upholstery rose. The begonias stiffened. The wallpaper crackled. My iced tea, even napkins and the salt and pepper shakers climbed toward the ceiling. Electric wires sparked, and I thought I smelled smoke.

Over the years, I'd had the joy of trying Mother's temper in highly imaginative ways. It was fun evaporating her low tolerance. Especially when I could run to Grandmother Beah. Meticulousness was one thing Mother prided herself on, and a properly raised child fell right in there with crisply defined squall lines and effective wall clouds. If it hadn't been for Father's mountainous influence and Grandmother Beah's intercessions, and the little reality that I was Mother's only offspring, I might not have survived.

I released Mother's hands. Her bituminous eyes flickered. The room's snapping tension dissipated. The begonias sighed. My iced tea, the napkins and salt and pepper shakers settled. The upholstery and rugs rested. The buzzing in the wires stopped.

Mother studied her glinting fingernails. Then, she took my hands. She stood on tiptoe and smoothed my hair. The moment was as exquisite and fragile as fine crystal when Mother said, "My son, I have been very patient. You are of the man that I have loved, and you have responsibilities to him. You will fulfill them. Whether you want to or not. Whether you are ready or not . . . you will."

Mother paused. She walked away from me. As though talking to herself, Mother continued, "You were a difficult child to raise, and your father's mother didn't help things. Perhaps if you had had brothers and sisters . . . Whatever. It's obvious, I failed to make you understand that there is a way that things must be. Sooner or later, what must happen, will. You are now a man, my son. Time grows short. I, too, have obligations, and you are not the only one who has needs. I have been far too indulgent. But because I believe that you are moving toward something meaningful, I will indulge you one . . . last . . . time."

Mother's voice got arctic as she said, "You have a month. You have until the Moon and Sun again travel together to accomplish what you tell me you need. When these days have passed, you will come home. You know the way. I don't expect or want to have to return for you. But if that becomes necessary, my son, you will not be the only one who regrets it."

When Mother was gone, I walked to my window. Watching the last of her envoy sail big and blazing beyond the horizon, I thought about how moving at two hundred fifty kilometers per second, nine thousand three hundred miles per minute, my Sun still needed two hundred forty million years to orbit the Milky Way. Eight million human generations could come and go between solar birthdays. I wished I had that much time.

I thought about the approaching solar eclipse. From Earth at that time, both the Sun and the Moon appeared the same size. Although the Sun was four hundred times wider than the Moon, the Moon was four hundred times closer. Without that exquisite relationship, eclipses as Earth knew them would not have been possible.

My sycamore's rain-bright leaves flickered golden green, creating a shifting ceiling above nearby buildings. I pulled up a chair, leaned back, feet on the sill, arms behind my head, and gazed out my window. I shook my head, glad to have survived Mother's visit, and then thought that maybe I hadn't. Perhaps I'd spent far too much time resisting family expectations and not enough time developing my own. After all, except for my love for Willow and my fondness for people like Mrs. G, Granny Mei-Yeh, Amos Akkadian and May Belle, I was still hollow and adrift, entirely too ready to vanish and manifest light-years distant.

I decided to let that sycamore's spirit mentor me. I'd develop the attitude that downpours did more than drench. They cleaned and refreshed. I'd master the sycamore's technique of letting the roaring winds flap its branches until the million leaves harmonized with the thunder. That would be my strategy. Plan A: Make adversity work for me. If that didn't work, then Plan B: Which I had yet to develop.

Then I watched magenta streamers ignite the midnight sky. There was no mistaking The Afreete's tracers. Far overhead, the showers raced in a great glow beyond my horizon. Seeing them, I realized the swelling of time, the contraction of space and the development of backbone had taken on whole new meaning.

We had touched. I knew much but not all about The Afreete.

Perhaps It could also shrink time and collapse distance. Maybe the months of joy I'd known with Willow had actually been millennia. Whatever the explanation for The Afreete's quick arrival, there was no escaping the fact that I'd led horrible danger to all that I cherished.

Using one candle, I lit the others in my alcove. I drifted my worries across the flame tips. When I thought of Willow, melodies of faith, enduring love and perseverance reminded me that, despite their strengths, humans were very fragile.

In the days that followed, I wondered what The Afreete must be learning and where It might be. I headed toward the Coke Works and walked along the railroad tracks. The Calliope's song reminded me of Pulai, with its mercury seas cresting gently under Chartreuse skies. How sweet yet bitter to recall its moons following and leading, filling, draining and regrowing over and over again the light of their star. Had The Afreete left any life there?

Bumping my foot against tree roots, easing down the slippery bank, I looked into the blue-gray water and saw two heads on my shoulders. One was ugly enough. Its lipless mouth roared in multiple voices, saying that I should have left Willow alone. That I had no right to disturb her life. That I knew trouble would come. The second head with mottled purple and green skin and empty eyesockets, that one berated my weak integrity and limp character. I kicked dirt into the water. The two heads fractured into hundreds that babbled and berated until the river reflected nothing but clouds. Beyond all of that were dark depths where nothing was certain or safe.

I faced the fact that, despite my cowardly tendencies, I could not abandon my home to The Afreete. It would destroy Earth if I fled. Yet I could not participate in another's destruction. Death was the reason I shunned Father's work.

Maybe Father could have handled The Afreete. For sure, Grandmother Beah could. But both of them were gone. Certain that Mother or Auntie Carmelita and all the others couldn't stop It, how could I?

During my travels, I'd heard murmurs. Other beings like myself had encountered The Afreete and run. But what did The Afreete's or Mother's threats matter? My greatest fear was that Willow's grandmother would arrive soon and see what I was.

# Oull

*So this bluish planet with just one moon is my Pursued One's home. This dust speck and several others are held by an insignificant sun far out on one of this galaxy's arms. My translucent mass laced with fine sensory nerves flexes and moistens. My undulating form covered with retractable talons itches. I will cherish every detail.*

*The colors here are intoxicating. The fragrances so varied. The sounds so stirring. There are textures that soothe and arouse. Succulent tastes. And beneath all of this loveliness, death and destruction. This planet offers so many opportunities, if only because the surfaces are so deceptive.*

*I become a cylindrical being. Currents pass that cool and warm. Vibrant life-forms swim. Rippling sunlight disorients victims. Like my self, this coelenterate has no bones. Victims are intrigued by tentacles with nematocysts that wriggle around my mouth. After approaching close enough to become entangled, prey are stung, paralyzed and pulled down my throat. They cannot resist. Their conscious fright thrills.*

*I glide across earth cooled and shadowed by large forest leaves. This might be, yes . . . the form pleases. The nonhearing actually enriches. Sunlight glistens on the dew and shimmers on my mosaic scales. I see a tiny, fur-covered creature. It is alive yet still, frozen in its awareness of my approach. My long, slick tongue flicks past fangs. My muscles contract and ease, curving my body toward its terror.*

*From planet to planet, slaughter became so routine, I barely* planned attacks. Before finding Earth, I had believed that my Pursued One was the only worthy prey. Here I have discovered many ways and incredible forms.

Yet this world contains life that does not destroy to live. The passive and the aggressive actually replenish each other. After annihilating the Pursued One I now call Mine, I could contentedly remain a stationary, chlorophyll-based heliotropic life-form. I would enjoy creatures crawling into me and experiencing their disintegration.

Discovering how developed Mine's home world is surprises. Mine has always avoided worlds where inhabitants complicate and compromise their environments. I prefer such places. As long as prey rely on physical devices, their apparatus may delay and sometimes irritate, but the populations always succumb.

# Mother

During the last quarter century, the United States had more than twenty thousand tornadoes. More than three thousand people perished, averaging eight deaths every ten thousand square miles.

On Friday, August 10, 1979, a small tornado ripped through Worcester County, Massachusetts. During most of the vortex's ten-mile journey, it skipped above treetops. At Gardner Airport, planes were torn from their moorings and cartwheeled across the landing strip and through fields. But at the Treasure Valley Boy Scout reservation, a ten-year-old and a seventeen-year-old died when winds snapped and uprooted fifty-foot trees. Bright green from leaves the funnel had consumed and accompanied by vicious lightning and flooding, the assault began and ended in minutes. Lookout towers, waterfront and *the chapel were destroyed. A tree was shot into the campfire's circle as though it were a bull's eye.*

*On August 28, a tornado would rip a mile-and-a-half-wide path through Iowa. Landing in Mills County, the column would take a surprising southeasterly course, bearing straight for Tabor, but lifting over the town and landing a mile south of Randolph. There, a tractor trailer would be crumpled and thrown one hundred fifty yards, the dead driver fifty yards farther. While one couple would find safety beneath their obliterated home, another woman would perish as her's collapsed.*

*That year, the United States endured more tornadoes in its eighth month than any other August in history. The Virgin Islands had their first and Iowa, Nevada, Oklahoma, Wisconsin and Wyoming broke their August records.*

# 25

## Willow

## Saturday, September 15, 1979

## Moon: Last Quarter

I was snuggled in Clement's arms. We lay together quiet when he asked, "Willow, have you ever been this in love before?"

I thought how I'd been overflowing the hopper in the popping room. I just kept walking back and forth filling those kettles and thinking about how Clement's coarse hair fanned out over his pillow. How his skin still had such a nice summer glow. How sweet he tasted. Next thing I knew, I'd avalanched the place.

I glanced at Clement's red polyester shirt with the yellow stitching: "Vincente's Pizza, We Deliver the Best!" His wonderful dark eyes were so open and trusting, I knew I shouldn't tease, especially with how worried he'd been. Before answering, I nestled closer and asked myself, Well, what was love, really? L O V E. Lots of Various Enjoyments. Living on Vigorous Energy. Letting Only Victory Enter. Little Opportunities for Valuing Everything. Coming up with those sayings, I felt like my brain had upped its brightness.

I remembered Otto, who had loved me once at Corey Creek, and Tyrell Webster, who moved to Denver to make his dreams come true. I thought of Kinshasa and Jimmy. I recalled the part in the marriage ceremony where the man and the woman pledged themselves through sickness and health and whatever else. I pictured Frau Edda leaving her homeland when the Nazis took over so that her Jacob and Otto's father would be safe.

Love was Daddy cooking on Saturdays and taking time just for me while Momma rested. Love was him sitting with Momma when she was sick and holding her Bible where she would see it. Love was Momma being so religious and home centered and Daddy loving to drink and travel around and gamble until he lost the emerald ring that matched Momma's earrings. Not that Momma was partial to jewelry. Besides, Daddy won them gambling. But the only other nice thing Momma had was her wedding band. Daddy thought we could get caught up on the bills if he had something to stake him in a game. When he came home red-eyed and slump-shouldered, Momma teased him about his torn-down looks. But she didn't say a word about sin and ungodly behavior. And I often heard her fussing at the wrongs she read in the papers or heard on the news. Momma just heated Daddy some coffee.

She would scrimp to buy me lace and ribbons for the dresses and blouses she sewed. For a surprise, Momma made my favorite gingerbread with raisins and coconut when we didn't really have the money. Even though she was tired, Momma would sing "Gimme That Ol' Time Religion," "Jacob's Ladder" or "Zekiel Saw de Wheel" for me before blowing out my kerosene lamp.

The last time I saw Daddy, he had on that old leather jacket and the cracked leather cap. As he headed outside, we heard geese. Daddy looked into the gray sky and said, "Ain't but two, honey lamb. Flying real strong. They won't be alone long."

Momma, she had on a green dress and a washed-out brown sweater. She held her raincoat and her umbrella that flapped and sagged. There'd been a downpour earlier. By then, the sun had opened blue and gold holes through the clouds. When Daddy pulled the car up front, Momma had just finished singing "I'm gonna rise and shine and give God the glory." She said, "Just look at this day, Union."

Daddy said, "It's fine all right, but nothing compared to you, babe."

Getting back to Clement's question, I had to figure that love, to me it meant eating bean soup with watered-down catsup and drinking Kool-Aid just the same as if it was nice wine served with minted lamb and little red-skinned potatoes. It meant Daddy's listening to Momma's hell-fire lectures and a smile coming over his face like he really did see heaven and once in a while shocking Creame, Ohio, by sweating through a church service.

I thought about the first time I ever saw Clement. How peculiar he looked, like he didn't really know what he was doing shoveling that snow. Then there was Clement at the library, his face shining while he watched little ones fidget and tumble and some even sit quite still while listening to *The Ugly Duckling, Old Possum's Book of Practical Cats, The Little Engine That Could* and *Corduroy*. I smiled thinking of Clement clanging his keys on the Calliope's railings and his beautiful candle room and the ways he made love to me that went miles beyond what he did for my body.

I remembered when Mr. Akkadian, who cheered for the Cleveland Browns, and Ruby, who rooted for the Pittsburgh Steelers, taught Clement the rules to football. Later that night, when it was just the two of us, he smiled and said playfully, "Do you know, my dear, that if the grape-seed-sized Pluto were placed at one end of a football field, on average, the grapefruit-sized Neptune would rest at the seventy-six-yard line? Uranus, roughly the size of a pomegranate, would go just inside midfield. Lovely, yellow-amber, honeydew-big Saturn would nestle at quarter field. Jupiter, large as a big pumpkin, would rest at the thirteen-yard line. Mars, like a plump pistachio, would sit inside the four. Earth would be a stout grape inside the three. Venus, a smaller red grape, at the two, and Mercury, a petite currant, at the one. And then the Sun, burning and big as one thousand huge watermelons, would glow at the goal line."

I shook myself free of those memories and figured that, to answer Clement's question, I couldn't look at him. I had to just let myself soak up his warmth, the quiet way his hand rested on mine and how he just waited as though my pause were seconds. I wanted him as well as me to enjoy how peaceful that moment felt.

Sometimes Clement had a strange, far-off look and rubbed his face so hard he turned red. Clement was even sprouting gray hair. Worse, he talked about leaving for a few days.

I'd teased him. I'd said, "Clement, stop worrying about Lucille."

"I'm not," he'd say, while chewing his lip.

"There isn't much, probably nothing at all to that special vision Momma and Daddy talked about."

"I'm not worried," Clement would say, sounding edgy. Then, he'd find a way to smile and change the subject.

So, had I ever been that in love before? I rolled in Clement's arms and faced him. I let myself enjoy how good our nakedness felt. Then I said, "Before what?"

Clement looked startled. Then he grinned and kissed me so tender, my life dreamed past. When Clement studied his effect, he looked entirely too self-satisfied. So I said, "I don't think that was a fair question for you to be the first one to ask. In fact, you ought to tell who you loved before you loved me."

"Well, that's not exactly what I asked."

"It's close enough. Who was it, Clement?"

"My dear, you wouldn't believe it."

"Yes, I would. Don't tell me what I wouldn't believe."

"Well, if you insist." Clement smiled. "There was this Faia near the southern peninsula on Kuvit who had the most divine—"

I snapped, "I get the picture."

Sometimes, I'd shrink when people used words I didn't know. In fact, the list of things that made me feel bad at one time or another could have rolled out my kitchen, down Evergreen and across the Calliope. It would have had items like: Dark skin. Nappy hair. Never actually graduated high school, although they did mail me my diploma. Wears secondhand clothes. Short. Poor. Can't cook.

I wasn't sure when ends of that list started tearing off. Maybe when I woke up breathing and the sun bothered shining the morning after Jimmy left. I thought the least the sky could have done was rain. More of the list flew away after I got each raise at Faraday's. Other pieces tore off when I looked into children's faces at the library, especially as they grew up, and I knew I had helped them. When they asked questions, I could find answers. Maybe the list just didn't matter after I slid down that brass railing at The Gold Tiger.

I asked, "Is she Cabrilla?"

"My thunderbird?"

"No. The person you named the car after."

Clement's eyes opened bright and laughing as he hugged me close and said, "Oh, Cabrilla was the closest sound I could find to describe a Soet I once, well, knew."

I was getting hot. My sense of humor really was leaving. I tried to push away, but Clement held me snugger.

"This one in particular, we had a, oh . . . an interesting time together scampering across the countryside and otherwise just existing. That's really all we did, which made it so good to be there then."

I said, "Where is that place anyway?"

"Too far, sweet Willow." Clement kissed me gently and long.

I just had to ask, "Clement, why do you love me?"

"Aha! Now I can keep you waiting." Clement looked delighted. Then his face straightened. As plain as if he were telling me the temperature, he said, "I just do. Maybe last January when I'd see you in the library or you'd pass me on the street and absolutely ignore me, maybe as recently as June or July, I could have told you why I loved you. But the reasons have become so many that I can't pick one, or even two or three. They've collapsed under their own weight and just are."

Clement relaxed. A faraway look misted his eyes as he asked, "Do you know how galaxies start?"

I lay my head against him and said, "Do you mean in the sky or Mrs. Singer's car?"

Clement laughed and said, "Thank you, sweet Willow."

I played with Clement's fingers as he said, "Before there are galaxies, there are amazing clouds. Galactic wombs where stars are born. But, no matter how big or powerful, everything goes away. Everything, except love. And when there is enough, and it doesn't take much, just a seed, then a universe that's gone so far into itself that not even a molecule remains, with a little love the whole thing blooms again."

Clement looked at me and asked, "Do you believe that love can last forever?"

Forever? That was like storms roaring in the night and Daddy and Momma not able to tell if a twister was coming. Forever was like fire bells, and my first night alone in Good Sky. Nothing scared me more than forever. Folks couldn't live forever, but they sure died that way.

And forever seemed like my great-grandmother telling me that all folks cared about was themselves. Once, twice, maybe a hundred times, Mariah preached that smart people saved their breath and didn't waste their energy on feelings. I felt Mariah's energy so strong, the withered woman actually rose right there in the bed between Clement and me. I needed every bit of goodness Clement and I shared to clear all that away so I could answer, "What I got for you, Clement, it will last. I don't care how long them stars out there burn, just know that my love will be here longer."

It was Saturday night. I could stay with Clement. I could comfort him when his secret worries sometimes made him mumble and jerk hard in his sleep. It was Saturday, and I could hope that my birthday, my new year as Clement called it, would get us off to a fresh start . . . to the peace that Clement seemed locked out of just then. 'Cause sometimes Clement's eyes got big, and he'd go to the window suddenly, look behind a door and watch along the ceiling. I thought if Clement didn't get a grip on himself, we'd have to lock him up.

It was Saturday night, and we could both sleep in. We could wake up stronger and love some more in the morning.

# 26

## Clement

## Wednesday, September 19, 1979

## Moon: Balsamic

As the Sun ignited dawn, I sat in deep shadow. I moved pieces. I re-moved pieces, mostly mine, until it was clear that my side's strategies, skill and experience were pathetic. There stood my black rook on queen's one. King on queen's bishop one. Knight on queen's bishop three. Pawn on king's bishop six.

They were opposed by white's king on queen's one. Queen on queen's bishop one. Bishop on king's rook five. Bishop on queen's rook five.

The universe was filled with such hopeless-looking situations. The moon called Miranda was only nine hundred miles around and barely as big as Ohio. Miranda had chasms that dropped eleven miles down, twice as deep as Chomolungma was high. Little Miranda had been bat-tered, bludgeoned, even blasted apart and yet managed—several times—to pull her pieces back together and reestablish an orbit. Even Miranda's master, the enigmatic and aquamarine Uranus, had been assaulted fiercely enough to knock him sideways, arraying his halo around him like a clock rim. I thought, Maybe I should just turn the chessboard.

I went walking and studied the thorns on rose canes, fading tiger lilies and birds picking the last seeds from wilting sunflowers. I remembered a story Willow had recently read at the library. The tale told of a vain prince who'd meanly refused a hag begging for food because she was ugly. The insulted but wise woman turned his body into a beast's while leaving his mind human. To learn his lesson and break the enchantment, the prince had to convince a woman to love him despite his appearance. Perhaps it was also that witch who arranged a wealthy merchant's circumstances so that his lovely daughter might meet the prince. Thinking that over, I wondered how Willow would have handled the Beauty's situation.

I noted how iron-gray clouds reached over the sun. I heard a door closing, pigeons' wings, a truck's brakes. For the first time, my world's huge spirit could not blind me to how small Earth was, circling with other particles in the vastness of space.

In our last conversation, Mother said, "My son, these humans, how can you stand their bodies? Their minds? *Esto es muy desagradable!*"

I answered, "Mother, it's not that bad. In fact, I think you'd be a lot happier if you got out and back to our roots more often."

I'd always resisted outbreaks of character and integrity. I didn't like standing up for things, especially with Mother. Who knew better than I that Mother, well, except for Father and, of course, Grandmother Beah, she didn't know how, she couldn't comprehend not having her way. But by then, a peculiar heat burned in me. At times, it left me incapable of backing down. Even as Mother's scant sense of humor evaporated and her boots spiked electric.

By mid-September, that new energy had me gazing into candles and grasping things that should have been mysteries. I would touch the cherrywood and tulip poplar chest and know exactly where the tree had grown, how sunlight felt when it warmed the bark, how like birth was the bursting forth of its leaves, how easily sleep came each autumn, how old the wood was when cut and how capable the carpenter's hands had been. I could alter things without touching them. At first, just small maneuvers like sliding a fallen leaf along a window ledge.

What was happening to me? I could listen to people and hear their great-grandfathers as well as generations yet unborn. I hadn't sought these abilities. They slithered into me like viruses. They grew slyly and fast and were of me before I knew to resist. They made me feel lower, like a foundation, and deeper, like a sea beneath ships.

Since the first of that week, I wasn't sure if it was by will or happenstance that those tendencies hadn't manifested in ways that human beings could see. Before long, I feared that cats, dogs and squirrels would do more than eye me guardedly. I would not be able to disguise tendencies that were fast becoming second nature. I might spontaneously and without thinking, answer questions before they were asked or turn on lights without touching them. Each day, I woke wondering what newness had happened. Had my hair become Saturnine wigglies? Did my eyes float like the fish folk near Betelgeuse? Would I roll out of bed in another universe? One morning, I looked in my mirror and Father gazed back.

I saw snow falling in the Yukon. I felt below-normal sea surface temperatures along the equatorial Pacific and the North American coast. With those conditions, I knew Mother's emissaries could bring the polar jet far enough south along the coast to blast cool, moist air off the Pacific and over the Southwest. Those winds colliding with hot desert air would detonate spectacular storms over Arizona and New Mexico.

After that, Mother's journeymen could race the polar jet stream around low-pressure centers seven or so miles above Greenland, central Russia, Japan and the southwestern United States and finish the circle by lifting the screaming winds over eastern Canada. That way, cold air would spill into New England, the Appalachians and the upper Ohio Valley and move south over Good Sky, heading toward eighty- and ninety-degree temperatures rising from the Carolinas, Virginia and Maryland. Before long, all of Mother's forces would be in place.

The New Moon was two days away. As I crossed Evergreen Way, I thought about how, for the past week, sometimes I just sat quietly while Willow read the newspaper or stitched small squares and triangles of fabric together or watched her little black-and-white television. Sometimes, I got so morose that Willow held my hands or my face. She'd sit on my lap. She'd hug me and ask what was wrong. Where were words for Mother's plans? Who could describe The Afreete? And how was I to explain that after "just" Lucille arrived, Willow would see me exactly as I saw that monster?

When I knocked at Mrs. G's door, she called, "Come on back to the kitchen, dollbaby. The Kentucky Wonders and corn on the cob's still hot."

Willow came downstairs. She slipped into my arms and answered, "He's coming up with me, Ruby."

In Willow's kitchen, the sheer, white curtains crisscrossing the window, the wooden table with one short leg, the yellow and green checkered tablecloth and Mrs. G's deep red roses in a green water glass, everything looked so normal I trembled. My heart ticked. I felt so flammable that I focused on the flowers until I cooled enough to say, "Willow, I know I've been a little difficult lately. It's just that . . . I just . . . I . . ." I sat down and flopped my hands on the table.

Willow smiled and kissed me, saying, "I ought to know by now, Clement, that if you want to tell me something, you will and then some. If you don't, there's nothing I've been able to come up with that'll make you talk . . . leastways so I'll understand what you're saying. Don't worry. I'm here for you."


Later that night, I stood in my sanctuary. I thought about how I hadn't wanted to come home. But the farther I went from Earth, the harder I was drawn back. Once I determined that the returning was from need, not desire, I thought I'd left The Afreete bulldozing through haystacks so distant and complex, It would never find Earth.

I stared into the candle flames. How their flickering colors and warmth appealed. How their destructiveness repelled. How their catalytic and transforming capacity fascinated. I allowed their little fires to draw me in and overcome The Afreete's chill. For the past few days, I'd felt It's nearness. When It exhaled, I took in the next breath. Where would It strike? How could I defend all that I loved?

I thought about one of the first children's stories I'd been able to read. It was about a rabbit that had challenged a construct of tar. In striking the entity, the rabbit found himself stuck. The more the rabbit assaulted the tar creation, the deeper he sank. I couldn't muster the courage to envision what, in the unlikely event I did battle and stop The Afreete, I would become as a result.

Inside my sanctuary, evanescent particles glued together awarenesses that I'd never considered. As dawn crept across the land, another understanding wrapped me like spider silk, making me wish that I knew nothing at all. Such visions had never come before. I had not felt the next moments so imminent. I hadn't seen the passage from known but unsure to unknown but certain. When I did, I rushed to the window and saw Mrs. G.

Knowing what approached, I gripped the sill. I looked until the pain became too great. I rubbed my face so hard it hurt.

I should not have known. I did not want it. I knelt and whispered, "Father, please hear me. I need you. Make it stop. I can't handle what's happening."

The first tear formed. My clenched fists pressed into the floor. Again, I begged, "Please."

# Oull

*I am repulsed by the pod-nature of these Orcas, but I like the way they generate fear. Soon enough, they detect my difference. Transforming quickly, I frighten before they attack. I travel alone. I savor the speed, the size, the strength. I like hunting the planet's largest animal. Despite her incredible size, the female blue is faster. It has taken weeks to trap her against a glacier.*

*I am a beautiful and lustrous brown. A rounded female arachnid barely a half inch wide. I spin fine silk lines and suspend myself. In the twilight, I lower an adhesive ball and float a scent suggesting the virgin female moth. Soon enough, a male flutters near. I sit very still. He comes close, moves away, then close again. I swing the glue, and he is caught. I embrace and take my time seeking his tenderest spot.*

*Aware and too confused to flee, a lamb watches an eagle's shadow grow. A wildebeest drowns in a crocodile's jaw. A piglet hears a jaguar scream. An injured moose smells the approaching wolverine.*

*Yet I have always known this place. The longer I stay, the more familiar this world becomes. Everything new seems like forgotten awareness. This information and wondering distracts. It takes time. Time that means nothing. Like the nothingness out of which I realized myself. Time that means everything.*

*Mine knows that I am near. He awaits me atop his dwelling, though he is not sure when I will come. I know this. Why?*

*In trying to understand how I read his thoughts, the final hold for Mine is discovered. I see a child. In a garden, something frightens him. He screams but cannot move. Through bright green vines, just beyond the red fruit, the creature appears. Again, I wonder how I know this of Mine. How?*

*I see Mine embrace a female. I watch her and experience a lightening and lifting, a swelling of my form. I desire her, too. These feelings disgust. I withdraw past the elms and oaks and maples whose greenness is turning red and yellow.*

*At the stone embankment, I soak in the setting Sun. As the stars emerge, I look for myself in the river and see Mine. He is gaining strengths. Soon he will realize what I now know. That cannot happen.*

*I return to Mine's door. I glare up at his windows. The lights there are as feeble as he. Mine is helpless, and I will strike with much pleasure.*

*I hear no sounds except Mine's thoughts. I enter and ascend. I will have my satisfaction, my freedom and my revenge.*

## Mother

*Mother doubled the normal September tornadoes for Florida, Maryland, Georgia and Wyoming. Early in the month, with a boost from Auntie Carmelita, Mother's tornadoes bludgeoned Delaware, New Jersey, Pennsylvania, South Carolina and Virginia. Her slow season approached.*

# 27

## Lucille

## Thursday, September 20, 1979

## Moon: Balsamic

Glad you came along. Yes, you . . . sitting there holding this book. You don't have to believe I see you. Plenty a people don't accept my vision. They should. It could save some misery. Might even bring some joy. Or at least some peace.

My name's Lucille. Lucille Thompkins. My mother, Mariah, when she raised my daughter back in Bridge, Kentucky, she told Verdell to call me "just" Lucille. "Just." Can you imagine? Like I wasn't worth being thought on. Like I was insignificant. (I like them big words.) Insignificant like hell. But some folks do want to stomp you down. Mariah tried. She did a pretty good job on my Verdell, and I'll get to my granddaughter shortly.

I'm riding the bus because no matter what the advertisements and government reports say, you won't catch my ass streaking through the skies. No sir-ree. I'll take the train or ride the bus in a minute. Anyways, this Greyhound's been out of the Pittsburgh station a half hour. It's nice getting away from that Homestead smoke. As for downtown Pittsburgh, it feels good leaving a city with little streets and tall buildings. Makes for too many shadows. I like this here daylight coming through the windows. Wide-open country does a soul good.

You don't need to know, but I'll tell you anyways that whenever I'm on one of these trips, that's when I especially miss my man, Daddy Boston. Can't help myself. We went lots of places. Made good money. And if Daddy Boston was still living, I'd want to know why he went and got himself killed. I'd shake a fist at wherever he was. I'd tell him he shoulda cut that simple woman aloose. Shoulda let that crazy nigger have that piece of wish she could hustle. Who ever heard of a man like Daddy Boston getting killed over pitiful pussy like that? Look what I been left with all these years. Wouldbe and wannabe lovers. Can't none of them touch me like Daddy Boston did. Soft when I needed it. Hard when I needed it that way. Thirty years gone by, and if I think on Daddy Boston too long, like now, I still get creamy.

With me being a smart high-yellow gal, people used to wonder why I took up with a black-skinned sporting man like Daddy Boston. After all, being light skinned goes a long way, even if you're otherwise oogly. But me being pretty, I could have got me an undertaker or a doctor. They warned me the babies might come out looking like anthracite. All I figured was that we could just let them little chunks of coal come on. 'Cause once Daddy Boston smiled at a woman and took her out and bought her presents, once Daddy Boston said things the way he said them, then he got up in there and rubbed and licked and filled a woman up with himself, the real puzzle was why any woman wouldn't want him. That's why that stupid nigger stabbed him. Now what did that accomplish? The trifling bitch still didn't want that nigger and then there was Lord knows how many women settling for hotdogs when they used to have prime rib. You see, I understood Daddy Boston. You had to or he'd be gone. I just made sure I got mine first. And if I didn't get Daddy Boston's stuff first, leastways, I got it best.

That's how life be sometimes. And everybody's taste in things ain't the same. Some people want the best books. Some want the best houses. Some craves good potato salad and ham. Don't matter. It's when people don't know what they want, that's when there's trouble. It's even worse when folks know what they want, and they won't go get it. Stifle themselves. All you can do going through life that way is come out behind, the hard way. But long as folks face up to their goodly and natural desires and don't hurt nobody else, well I do believe that makes the world better. Me, I ain't never had no problem knowing what I wanted.

My granddaughter, she done inherited Daddy Boston's color. She be black as night in the country. But she ain't got not a hangnail's worth of his ways. And Daddy Boston's ways, they were mighty fine. 'Cause Daddy Boston wanted to live good, and nothing about his being Black stopped him. Daddy Boston wasn't going to beg nobody to clean their buildings or open their doors or drive somebody else's big car. He'd do right by himself and let the chips fall wherever they landed. So we had the cars. Fur coats. Good jewelry. And we traveled.

Don't be shocked with me, honey. We're all whores out here selling ourselves for something. The concern shouldn't be what I'm doing with my box. The question ought to be, after all the screwing's done, Who's coming out on top?

But let me get on with what I'm doing here. You see, my daughter Verdell, she was the exact opposite of me. But then Mariah could dehydrate watermelon. She did a pretty fair job on my granddaughter, too. Maybe Mariah thought if she dried things out enough, they wouldn't spoil, and she could keep them better. So Mariah had my daughter and my grandchile call me "just" Lucille. Just what? Just better at living and having a good time and getting good loving is how Mariah shoulda put it.

You see, light-skinned bitches, and I'm one of them so I know, all we got to do is lay up and whimper and a Black man, he be satisfied. But a Black-skin gal, she got to jump to it if she's going to hold onto somebody. Shame to say, but it's the truth. I don't care what them fools was saying a few years back. "I'm Black, and I'm proud." That always was bullshit in the bedroom. Them niggers wanted to see who they were eating, with or without lights.

So, you there. Yes, you. The one holding this here book and getting hot under the collar. I'm telling it the way it is, in the language that it is. And you know, it's funny but really sad 'cause there's some Black folks out there that's absolutely obtuse and lost. Like that Anderson boy. He sure was one turned-around Negro. Hurts sometimes to see them that way. When their intellectual parts blocks their nature. But it's sorrier when that short-circuiting tramps over someone else. Just no way you could save them. Neither one of them children. Life'd just have to whop their asses til they got tired of holding on to notions that weren't worth nothing.

And it's taken Willow long enough. Nine damn years. Can you imagine? Now I missed Daddy Boston as much as anybody, but life still went on. And I know what she was doing 'cause there was times when I was in the same situation. Matter of fact, got a drawer full of doodads. Some battery operated and some, as you might say, manual. Them little things'll take care of about any situation. But you shouldn't need them all the time.

You see, I wanted to teach my granddaughter to keep a few pieces of men around and make them pay for it. Ain't a man born ever appreciate a woman that give it up for nothing. You got to make him earn it. I mean, if he's broke, have him paint the walls, mow the lawn, cook. And if he can't do that, and you want him anyway, honey, make him crawl. Any woman ain't got that much sense ought to have "welcome" stamped all over her ass 'cause men'll sure enough wipe their feet there and on anything else she makes available. But ain't that life? Fortunately, I'm getting good vibes from my grandbaby. Seems like somebody finally got her up and running. Problem is he's living in that house.

Damn. We in Ohio already? Well, as we're getting close, you got to know two things. One, I didn't never feel right about that place across from Willow. I didn't feel bad about it neither. It's just them doors and windows never had no normal-type aura. Now, I know you're wondering what I'm talking about. And I'll explain just once. So listen close cause if I have to tell you again, it'll cost you.

You see, by aura I mean a glow, like a halo. Like when something's in front of the sun and the light melts out around it. That's what I see sometimes, and apparently most folks can't. Sometimes them shinings is so horrifying, I don't know how other folks can't just plain feel the nastiness and how dangerous the situation is.

And then some of them auras is beautiful, and I can't get enough of them. Now, all I see is the lights. Some folks claim they see spirits. Others hear things. Well, ain't nothing I couldn't see never spoke to me. I just figure there's more going on than meets the eye. Some folks, if they can't see it, they don't believe it, which makes them kind of crippled. But maybe if I couldn't see what I do, I wouldn't believe a lot of this hocus-pocus stuff myself. But what really spooks me is folks who say spirits took them over. That, I leave alone.

And if the truth be told, I'm not so sure this knowing's a blessing. Sometimes, it's more like a curse seeing the things I do and knowing what it teaches about people and places. But I do know these abilities been in damn short supply since babies started getting them chemicals in their tender, new eyes.

Well, getting back to my Willow, common sense got to tell you that any house abandoned for years, now that place stays empty for a reason. So, first thing I plan to do when I put my feet on Evergreen Way is check out that used-to-be-empty building. Whoever'd live in that place is gonna have to be, well, don't get me started.

Now, the second thing I been thinking about is how my grandchile's gonna be thirty in two years. And if she don't get moving, she'll wind up high and dry. Took her a long time to get over that Anderson rascal, and I could see he was going to hurt her as plain as day. He wouldn't be low down and mean like that slag heap Kinshasa. And he wasn't a limp sausage like Tyrell Webster who claimed he needed to go find himself. What was wrong with his hands and a mirror? Nope. And that Anderson boy, he wasn't ready for himself either. So all you can do in situations when people ain't got sense enough to fight for what they want is shake your head. 'Cause if they won't stand up for what they need, what good are they?

My-my-my. Time sure flies when you're on a tangent. We're already in Good Sky. I'll give Willow her birthday present (a card and some cash). Fuss over her a few days. Then I'm on to Chicago, Las Vegas, Reno, New Orleans, Atlanta, D.C. and home. But what's this Anderson boy doing at the station? And the news he gives me about Mrs. Graham! Have mercy.

Now, I've seen some stuff that would straighten the kinks out of wool. But Lord, when I get to Mrs. Graham's house, when I see what I see, and it's standing there holding my grandchile just like it's one of us? Well, I always figured I'm as tough as they come. Now I know I have my limits.

# 28

## Ruby

### Thursday, September 20, 1979

### Moon: Balsamic

I am.

I am a whole lot of things.

I am Ruby LaMyra Jenner who became Mrs. Ellington Graham. I am the child who played with the sand and the pebbles, who made mud pies and splashed naked as the fish with other children in the Otter River. Brown Sugar Babies, that's what we was down under thick-leafed trees that opened sometimes and let sunshine dance with us on moss-covered rocks. I shelled peas and churned butter by the time I could walk. I starched clothes and ironed them so stiff they could stand on their own and skated up hard dirt roads to school.

I got done my first time under the wild grapes near the mailbox a quarter mile from my house. Maybe I was eleven. Maybe twelve. Whatever, I can still see the countryside with the pear orchards and tall pine. I can smell the grass and taste the wine we drank. But that's the stuff of summer. And although I've also found beauty in apple blossoms and ice patterns on window glass, I prefer a big old harvest moon with frost on still air.

I come to have the man Ellington Augustus Graham because his big hands felt good. Because I loved the way his shoulders dipped when he walked and how his pants fit. Ellington tasted like tarragon. He was warm and strong. Yes indeed, these pleasures of the flesh, even for folks like me, there's a lot to be said for them. It's worth giving a lifetime to.

Ten years back, when Willow came, I knew the minute that little girl stepped into Rose Singer's store that whole worlds of possibility were wrapped in her. There she was, a little shy, a little bold. After Mei-Yeh Faraday offered Willow the job, that child came looking through my rooms, eating my chicken and sweet potatoes, trying to make sense of how roots got set down for her so quick. What can I say? We wanted her. Given that Willow child's upbringing, we always had.

You see, when I was a girl, I learned early what it meant to put tomato and pepper seeds and onion bulbs in my mother's garden and keep them watered and tended. When folks care about a growing thing, they turn over the soil and put in things that make it nourishing. I knew what it meant when those seeds got neglected. And I knew what happened when wind or rain, heat or cold and especially if vermin overwhelmed them. Yes, I've watched that seed business work and fail, in all kinds of seasons all through my life. Personally, I feel I've done an excellent job. That's why I want to celebrate. I want to fill my lungs, puff myself up and testify!

I am!

Ain't that wonderful?

I am!

'Cause in this life, I rise in the dark on Sunday mornings and bake pies. I fry the best chicken in eastern Ohio. My yo-yo rugs are the prettiest anywhere. And I don't miss much. That's why I seen a face in town, lately. The boy from Cleveland who was paying so much attention to Willow is back. Nice and mannerly as he was, good as he treated Willow, I knew something wasn't right, even if what was wrong was just the timing. Wasn't entirely his fault. Something got left out of that Anderson boy's upbringing. And wasn't so much left out as, well, like when I do laundry, and I use too much bleach.

I see it in some children. They look colored, but their insides is just whey. Maybe their parents is afraid that if that stuff gets the slightest Negro-ness, they'll be ruined. That bleaching shows in how the children pronounce things. How they walk and wear their clothes and maybe, sometimes, how they scratch. I knew one day, that Anderson boy would wake up. When the insides is just whey, pain must not be noticed as quick, 'cause he sure took long enough. Even though the flowers and the necklace he sent for Willow's birthday was nice, it couldn't top what Clement got from May Belle. A little emerald ring. Willow said it was like the one her mother used to have. Well, it does match her earrings. That was a nice party, too. Got me to feeling more like myself. Grand. But then it is that time of year. I feel myself getting ready to shake things up, turn things over. When the cake is baked and it's time for frosting, it's hard to keep from letting loose and hollering . . .

I am!

That's how I feel. Especially when I'm coming into my own.

I am!

And the am-ness that I am made it a point to be out there pulling dead leaves from my flower boxes this morning. Glad I was. When Willow stood on that stoop all happy about her grandma coming and fretting about that sweet boy across the street, my girl looked more beautiful than I'd seen her in years.

I told Willow, maybe that job was wearing poor Clement out. Don't · you know, Willow blew one of those blasted gum bubbles and ran up to me whispering that it wasn't his job, it was her. What could I do after that but say everything would be okay? I knew it would. Like I said way at the start, some things is just inevitable.

After Willow left, I was sweeping and singing up a storm. A confounded weirdness has been hanging around. Folks jumping at their shadows. Locking windows. I suspect there's guns under pillows.

Knives being sharpened. Everyone thinks the wind from the coke ovens's been blowing our way too long. I had to do something to stir the air and freshen things. Especially with this odd hot spell. Something's brewing weather-wise, too. Well, I'd get that cooled off soon enough. So now it's already after eleven. I smile, thinking about my sweet Clement coming over for lunch. Then he's going to help with my garden. Pulling some lettuce from the refrigerator, I get dizzy. Can't quite catch my breath. But I don't fret. I don't pay no mind to the little jabbing in my chest. I just close my eyes and roll my head around, then try some massage to ease the ache in my shoulder and arm.

Sparklers fizz in front of my eyes. Takes me back to my girlhood. Feels like a parade's starting. Like trumpets and drums are booming. Like magnificent flags are flapping around me. I hear the majorettes' boots clacking, and reckon it's time to go.

# 29

# Jimmy

## Thursday, September 20, 1979

## Moon: Balsamic

*But the essence of being human is that, in the*
*brief moment we exist on this spinning planet,*
*we can love some persons and some things.*
                                        —*Rollo May*

I know that. I've always known.

Two years ago. Standing on the basketball court. Abe squints at the setting sun. Says, "Rosh ha-Shanah's starting, my man. High Holy Days. It's supposed to be a time of happiness." Abe bounces the ball. Squints. Asks, "Ever wonder how I come to be Jewish?"

Two years ago, I'm thinking, Hell no. Why should I? Didn't I tell you my divorce decree just came?

"It's through my mother." Abe beams. "I'm Jewish without even trying. Amazing, isn't it?"

Light streaks what's left of Abe's curly hair. He rubs thick hands as though warming them. Says, "With this Rosh ha-Shanah thing, my mother said debts must be paid. The observant must right their wrongs. Heal wounds. There is no lip service for them. They know the names of the righteous are being written. Then the Book's going to close. THE Book, James. There's a lot of praying going on right now. Even the dead have to help."

Abe wipes sweat from his forehead. "Maybe I'll do it one year. Maybe I'll observe it for Mom. Maybe for those who came before her. Maybe for when I'm old. 'Cause after that comes Yom Kippur. The penitent Days of Awe. A lifetime ends." Abe shrugs. "Then what's a person do?" He shoves the ball into my chest. "They pick up the pieces, James. They try again."

Then and now, all I want is a goat to carry my sins into the wilderness.

I watch a cardinal fly low. As though it will land. I think, Maybe this settling of accounts must be honored. This calling to the ancestors is a rite. Perhaps after all dusks, dawn comes. No matter how dark and long the night.

I call Willow. Hope she likes the birthday gift. A necklace with small indigo sapphire. I tell Willow, it's for prosperity. It's for happiness and faithfulness. That's what I offer.

Willow says, "I can't take this, Jimmy. I have to give it back."

I say, "Enjoy it, Willow. Hold on to it a few days. I'm going south. It's a family thing. When I get back, I'll prove I'm the man for you."

I catch a plane. Drive into the country. Find shotgun and saddlebag houses. Tomatoes still ripening on vines. Sugarcane. Spanish moss draping molasses evenings. Smiles that welcome. Eyes wondering why I came.

Alone, I walk out into the Mississippi night. The tiny dancing woman and the man with a walking branch come from the woods. She playfully swings his hand.

When close, she says, "My grandmomma told me it was because the first town wasn't planned right. They started making another one after they realized their mistakes."

"That may be." He chews a piece of grass. Shoves big hands deep into frayed pockets. His smile doesn't quite brighten sad eyes. "What Uncle Gerald said was his people thought something better was down the road. But the well dried up. The crops didn't prosper. They come on back." He spits.

She spins. Pulls her yellow pinafore and long skirt wide. Pink slips rustle. Measuring spoons jingle. She says, "Well, sometimes it's hard to know—"

"Who are you?"

They stare. After a moment, she relaxes. Draws a heart in the air. Coyly covers her smile until all that's left are cicadas' songs and heat.

In Louisiana, the big woman juts her handsome jaw. Stamps her red umbrella. Is glorious in old but royal blue. Deep in the smoldering, lonely night, she says, "This is a righteous place!"

The young man rubs his muscled abdomen. Tilts his Panama hat. The cross on his chest glistens. He nods. Calmly says, "Great-Aunt Ada told me, in the beginning, it was God's Side. Don't that sound better. That the people here were kept by God's side?"

Her great smile sours. Her dark eyes glare. "Aunt Ada had lost more than a few of her marbles by the time you came along."

I shout, "What do you people want!"

The woman lifts her head. Regally, she stares me down. Nods proudly, as though her presence should mean something, then frowns. Looking suspiciously at the man, she says, "He don't know us?"

The man holds out his hands. He shrugs. The fringe on his buckskin vest flutters.

Her eyes dart between us. She stamps her umbrella. Scowling, she mutters, "No wonder otherwise intelligent people can't get where they need to be." She leaves.

He peeks at me from under that Panama hat. Shakes his head slowly, then smiles. Sly. Studies me a while. As he disappears, says, "You're getting there, boy. You're just about ready."

I stare until dawn, then drive to the airport.

*Your body is the harp of your soul.*
   *And it is yours to bring forth sweet music from it or*
*confused sounds.*

                                              —*Kahlil Gibran,* The Prophet

I know that. I've always known.

After lunch, Dad asks, "Where are you off to, Son?"

"I'm going to Good Sky."

Mom's hand rests on mine. I feel the warmth. The iron. She says, "James, all your father and I ever wanted was the best for you. We want you to be successful and happy."

I kiss her. I say, "I know." I smile. "Thanks, Mom."

Past mill smoke and fire. Past whitecaps. Past distant freighters and gulls. Sunshine falls like swords. The light slices through years until I again walk barefoot through Willow's Creame, Ohio. Through her Blue Meadow where the elm and locust, the crab apple and cottonwood vanish. All that survives is her cherished reading tree. The willow that regrows willows.

In hopes whispered above an orchard. Through laughter shared in fields of young grass. Beyond kisses in water scented like roses, like lavender, I try not to feel the disintegrating weave of what Willow's life with me could have been.

I hope for nothing except that Willow will listen. That she won't laugh. Call me crazy. That she'll consider. I hold these hopes until I pass the coke ovens, MileMaster, May Belle's and Mrs. Singer's and stare at the popcorn factory.

I get out of the car. Cross the parking lot. Climb the steps. Reach for the door as Willow rushes out. I call Willow's name, twice. She's down the steps. I call again. Willow turns. Gasps, "Jimmy! My God! I've got to get home! It's Ruby!"

When we reach Mrs. Graham's, that man Clement embraces her. They rock gently.

Clement and I study each other. Mr. Akkadian has a ruddy-faced man with white mutton chops explain. As he speaks, Mr. Akkadian eyes me, then looks at Clement warily.

The way Clement moves. His height. The long, coarse hair. The energy he projects. His lips, even if they are not as chiseled. His black eyes. Even if they are not like a cat half sleeping, Clement's presence disturbs me.

Suddenly, Willow says, "The bus! It's time. Lucille must be here!"

I offer to drive. I'm glad to get away. To see Lucille's spunky stroll. Her peacock-blue jersey and golden-brown skirt wrap like skin. Her earrings, necklaces and bracelets shine. I'm glad to be held in her wide, sexy grin as she says, "Boy, I thought I seen the last of you years ago."

At Mrs. Graham's, Lucille marches straight to Willow. Reaching to hug, she starts. Stares up at that man Clement. Stumbles backward whispering. "Oh! Sweet Jesus. No!"

Late that night. When all is quiet. I know.

*"Ain't Nothing Like the Real Thing"*

*—Ashford and Simpson*

I've always known.

# 30

## Clement

### Friday, September 21, 1979

### Moon: New

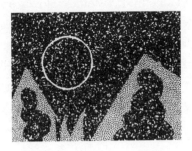

The foreknowing that Mrs. G would go intensified the agony. Afterward, trying to ease Willow's grief was worse. Then her grandmother arrived.

I thought Lucille would recognize my difference right away. Instead, she came close enough to touch. Then her gaze jerked from Willow to me. After Lucille's eyes popped wide, her pupils snapped into pinpoints. She gasped. Her eyes rolled up, and she collapsed.

We put Lucille in Willow's bed. For the rest of the evening, the best I managed was breathing. By handling that, I could keep down the shakes and put up a solid front, as much for that man James as for Willow.

As I worried about what Lucille would say, I could feel The Afreete. It vibrated like rain tapping a still pond. Gazing out my window, I thought of Antares, the red supergiant at Scorpio's heart. It could be reached by nonstop jet in a half billion years. Traveling at light's speed would take seven human lifetimes. But because time, therefore space, was elastic, Father could get there in seconds.

I'd worked hard, goodness knows, to approach Father's abilities. When I tried to stand proudly and be discerning, all those efforts just reminded me that I missed Father desperately. Compared to Father, I felt like the Moon. Like dull dust.

Perhaps those thoughts brought the nightmare more often. The one about dancers. People of many colors gathered in pink, turquoise, topaz, dandelion, ochre and amethyst costumes. Slowly and quietly, they approached me on a wide plain filled with larkspur, Canterbury bells and fairy's toad flax. Colors, music and sweet fragrances intensified as they danced. The rhythm built until their drums and bells, their hands and feet music made me so happy that as dusk deepened, I did not notice them slipping away. My mind so whirled with the singing that I did not feel the drying heat. I did not taste the dust blowing or see the flowers wither.

The flat land crunched up into darkening hills, then rose into night-black canyons. Cold, rough rocks pinned me tight. Stones pressed so hard my face imprinted in the rock. Struggling against the relentless pressure, bones snapped. Blood vessels ruptured. I bled into a hole with no edges. Realizing that my hemorrhaging could not stop until the chasm filled, I woke with cold sweats. I'd staggered to my window. I cursed the challenge created by Father's leaving.

For thousands of . . . well, a very long time, I thought home was a place to skin one's knee and be kissed, learn to say "thank you" and "please" and keep treasured, even if outgrown, toys under the bed. When Father died, everything that I wanted home to be changed. Unnerved, I ran so far and tested so many limits that even I wondered how I had survived.

I sighed and leaned against my window. Somewhere far beyond the stars that were blinking, I saw a fat-cheeked child, still too young to stand on his own. The child's froth of curly, rust-red hair framed his pink and milky face. His black eyes sparkled. A pearly pair of teeth peeked through his gums. He mouthed them contentedly. Drool glistened like liquid crystal.

He had a marvelous skill. Freshly nursed and propped on his mother's lap, he searched for his father and smiled. Actually, the baby glowed when the old man was near. One time, the child was given a luminous globe. When the child tried to return the ball, the old man would not accept it. The baby's small brow crinkled. His plump hands flexed. He wasn't sure if he'd got the facial muscles and the look quite right. But when the magnificent old man nodded and smiled back, the baby gurgled and beamed and clutched the ball close while wondering why, in the old man's shining eyes, above the happy mouth, tears gathered.

A sparrow landed on a thin sycamore branch. Bubbles formed at the bottom of my pot. I smelled seaweed, sulfur and decaying flowers. My tongue tasted like soured paste. Beyond the blood pounding in my ears, I heard the screaming millions that The Afreete had destroyed. Then, The Afreete whispered over my steps. I knocked my cup off the counter and stared into It's yellow eyes. Just like the first time, I could not move, and there was no other to run.

"At last!" It growled, hot juices dripping from its teeth.

The Afreete's body snaked higher. In the mirrored scales forming on It's breast, I saw It's plans for me, for Willow, for Good Sky and my world.

"Fear me!" The Afreete demanded. My knees buckled. My veins dissolved into the ooze that had been my blood. I fell backward as The Afreete sprouted webbed arms. The tips became talons. The Afreete's awful head waggled. It's hideous mouth opened. Steaming breath poached my face. The Afreete snarled, "You are pathetic."

When The Afreete called me by It's name, which was mine, a tiny voice, all that I had left, cried, "Father, help me."

The Afreete laughed. Curling It's body around mine, It's stare became cold and hard. "He won't, you fool. He can't."

# Oull

*Moonlight fractures and shimmies through indigo water. I am a leopard seal. When my shadowy form appears, penguins shoot upward and stampede onto the ice. Mine flutters and flails. He is almost too pitiful, palsied and meager to be worth my effort. But I grab. I maneuver his head between my canines and back teeth. I crush and . . .*

*It is dark. Deep. My skin is like sandpaper. I admire this agile body. Rows of barbed teeth lean back toward my throat. I like how they snag, rip and replace themselves. Such an aggressive creature that the young attack one another in the womb. Mine drifts just ahead. I snatch and gouge, but . . .*

*I wait just below a pond's surface. It is night. My forelegs are hinged like a clasped knife. They grab and hold. My beak pierces Mine's flesh. I insert a juice that paralyzes and digests. I enjoy the death awareness of dissolving Mine's insides until . . .*

*The rain forest canopy dims this river. I am a thin fish with red belly and gold flecking the dark brown. I and others sense Mine's weakness. Razor-sharp teeth slash. They tear him. Then . . .*

*Stop! I will not tolerate these dreams. Over. Finished. Be gone! I am ready for this thing's end. Too much plunder awaits.*

*I grow, tower, undulating, eruciform. The air heaves around this blue-green and ever-increasing bulk. My shadow drowns him. Bursting up from vegetation with round, red fruit, hundreds of legs stretch and claw. I glare down. Yes! Hah! How profane that I should come from such paltry impotence.*

*I open my mouth. Lengthening teeth tingle. I bend to annihilate. But Mine's flesh becomes opalescent membranes. Mirror-bright talons break through. Hundreds of silvered scimitars slice and tear with a viciousness that is my own. That only I in all the universe can produce. Bloated and luminous flesh rises toward me. A foaming mouth with teeth like rabid wolves.*

*I fight. Even as I am cracked open. Even as my intestines drip from the daggers that have become his mouth. Even admidst Mine's frenzied feast, even as the breath is sucked from me, I roar: You know me now. I cannot be destroyed. You cannot leave me. Not again. Not ever!*

Terrified, I awaited The Afreete's bite. The gnaw of It's digestive juices. Suddenly, the beast's form clung to me. As It's flesh dissolved through mine, my lips drew back. Teeth like daggers tingled through a death grin.

I could have crossed ten galaxies. Twelve thousand human generations could have passed in the time it took to slash and gouge, then lap and lick up The Afreete's cartilage, sinew and flesh. Overcome by tidal waves, the great floods that had washed away what I was, I flopped to the floor huge as a beached whale.

The beast within, I felt it growl. The Afreete's incendiary hunger burned. It's cravings overpowered and thrilled me. It's needs became my structure. The monster's drive was merciless. It's vision acute. It's decisiveness sharp. Strive as I might, I could not make it die.

I wished that if death could not come, that at least I would not think. Remembering what I could never be again hurt too much. By the time hot tears fell from eyes of stone, the first bubble for my tea broke the surface, the branch bent under the sparrow and my cup shattered. I snapped and swallowed a fly buzzing around my body.

# 31

## Willow/Clement

## Friday, September 21, 1979

## Moon: New

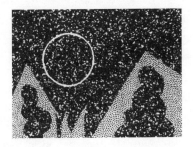

*You've got to walk that lonesome valley.*
*You've got to go there by yourself.*
*There's no one here can go there with you.*
*You've got to walk it by yourself.*

When Momma sang "Lonesome Valley," I tried picturing if there were trees. I wondered if the valley was deep and dark. Was the ground rocky or desert? What if someone got lost or died in there? And when they got across, what would they find?

From Daddy, I learned how things could be bright, like with the billiard balls, even though they had no light of their own. I found out that when people gambled, once, maybe twice, in a lifetime, they might win big. And Frau Edda taught me that there was a special guide deep inside that I had to hear.

I had missed the school bus the morning of a big, statewide test. By the time Otto's dad drove me, I thought I could catch up, but I'd forgotten my pencils. Daddy was real sick and Momma was away taking care of Mariah. Worrying about them made the questions on that blue paper dissolve.

When I got off the school bus that afternoon and went to thank Otto's dad for helping me, I also wanted to see if there was word from Momma 'cause we didn't have a phone. Frau Edda, she said, "We check on your papa. He ate soup and will be fine like fiddle. Your Momma will be home Saturday. Now it is for you, *mein Herz,* that I worry. It was an important test today. You look unhappy."

"I really wanted to show that I could be as good as anybody."

"And are you not?"

I couldn't answer her.

Frau Edda blinked, then smiled and said, "I think now of a great and handsome angel who came to answer a girl's prayer. Else was beautiful outside, but even more inside." Frau Edda tapped her heart. "That is why the angel loved her. But her eyes were up so much that she couldn't know the mud on the ground. And Lohengrin, all he wanted was that Else not ask his name or where he came from. If she made him tell, he would have to leave. Jealous and mean people, they raised the doubts. Then Else, *Die Unschuldige,* the innocent, *Die Einfältige,* the simple," Frau Edda sighed and shrugged, "*Die Naive.* She did not trust enough what she knew. She was good and sweet and forgiving. But in life there must also be strength. Strength to be sure of what we want and what it takes to keep it." Frau Edda patted my hand, "Even of the many voices that speak inside us, there is only one that will matter. It is very tiny. You must learn to hear."

———

# Clement

As an intensely pink line sliced the black horizon, I no longer wondered what it must be like when new land formed. By the time dawn bled into my eyes, I understood how lava pushing up thousands of feet from the ocean floor found air and light and loneliness until at some point a seed landed. When all but one star blinked and was gone, I no longer wondered what it must be like to be an Antarctic spruce growing one hundred miles from anything alive and green.

I was my Self again. At least the outward semblance. Somehow, if I was going to remain, I had to fight all that the night had done. I knew too much. History, future, the present, I heard and understood profoundly. Color, light, tastes overwhelmed me. The one clear thought I managed was, How could Father stand it all?

I knew while Willow lay in the dark listening to Lucille's mumblings that she would struggle against believing Mrs. G's death. Willow would keep hearing Mrs. G's pots and seeing Mrs. G smoothing back a curl. Over and over, Willow would ask how Mrs. G could go with no warning.

After a conversation over coffee and a day too full of visitors and chores, Willow would check for plenty of daylight and make sure that Lucille watched before crossing Evergreen. Peering through my windows and doorway, seeing that the downstairs looked ordinary enough, Willow would step into my house's cold light.

The building's peeling and pale decrepitness would cause Willow's stomach to draw tight. The air's heaviness would dampen her skin. Trembling, Willow would climb the groaning stairs that made no sound.

"Clement," she would call. "Clement, are you here?" Willow's voice would shiver against the brittle walls where loosening paper hung like little hands. Willow would jump at the plaster and dust dangling from cobwebs.

Just as her courage failed, Willow would catch a whiff of lilac incense and place one small, lovely foot higher and more carefully above the other. The intensity of her presence would nearly drown me.

When Willow reached the top step, she would note that sheets, towels and bedspreads had been tacked over the windows. Through the dark, Willow would see the glowing incense and its curl of smoke that couldn't quite hide the death smell.

"You're very brave," I'd say, my voice so husky, Willow would barely recognize me. "I could hear you when you opened the door, Willow. I wish you hadn't come."

When Willow fumbled for a light switch, I'd mumble, "Don't bother." Knowing that Willow wanted to run, I would whisper. I would infuse her name with all the meaning she had for me. I would cleanse and adorn each phoneme.

Testing her courage and my intent, Willow would fuss about the gloom. Willow would hear the sofa groan, papers swish, dishes clatter and a match scrape. Blinking at her in that feeble light, I would say, "You look like an ostrich trying to find a place to hide."

When I grimaced and leaned over, holding my stomach, she'd say, "Clement, you look awful." I'd sense enough concern in her statement that it would be hard to restrain grateful tears. With difficulty, I'd rasp, "Last night was hell."

That's when Willow would say, "Clement, my grandmother says that . . . remember how I told you Lucille could see things."

I would lift a glass. I would stare at the shaking water and say, "Your lovely and very perceptive Lucille has told you that I'm strange and different. Sounds familiar, doesn't it, Willow?"

"Yeah, but she means something way beyond what I ever talked about."

In the water, I would see Willow get heavier, wrinkle, become gray and hunched. And as though we would have had those years together, I would love Willow even more. Reluctant, I would force my reddened eyes level with Willow's. I would remember how the snowflakes sparkled into her face and her determination as she braved the harsh wind. I would remember Willow sampling my first baked bread, her mouth weighted as though she chewed lead. I would feel the dress Willow wore dancing and the honest way her body touched mine.

I would say, "Your grandmother, she said that I'm not what I seem. I'm not a person. At least, not a person as you and she think of one."

"That's right." Willow's teeth would set hard.

# Willow

It took a minute before I realized Clement was telling me everything word for word. As he talked, I knew Clement had seen Lucille pour hot water into her cup of coffee crystals, suck her teeth, tap the table with a fingernail and nod for me to sit down. He'd seen Lucille pull hard on her cigarette and knock the ashes into a square of tinfoil. He knew how she'd settled herself real careful. How she spit smoke toward the ceiling while studying me. How she looked out the kitchen window before saying, "Honey, listen good. You and me, we're getting out of here."

"What do you mean? Ruby's funeral isn't—"

With her smoking cigarette dangling between two fingers, Lucille turned and stared through my white curtains again. Dawn barely lit the trees and Clement's windows. Shaking her head, Lucille squinted and said, "Chile, while I was riding up here, I thought about that place. The man with the long hair, he lives there, don't he?"

"Yes."

"Now, as you know, I always felt good about you being in Good Sky and especially living here on Evergreen. And Mrs. Graham was an exceptional fine woman. But hasn't that house always seemed weird to you?"

Nervous, I answered, "Yes ma'am."

Lucille shook her head. "Chile, chile, child, the man ain't what he seem."

"What do you mean?"

Lucille leaned over and whispered, "I mean he ain't a person. Honey lamb, this situation here, it's beyond serious."

I said, "I don't think I heard you right."

That's when Lucille stood up, propped her fists on her hips and paced. "Tell me," she said, "that man from over there, he's the reason you been so happy. I seen it in your letters. I heard it on the phone."

I nodded.

Then Lucille leaned her face right into mine and said, "Willow, this flesh-and-blood world that you and I be living in, honey, it ain't the only world there is."

About then, my stomach felt queasy. Holding it, I said, "I don't believe it, Lucille. Are you saying Clement's not a flesh-and-blood human being?"

"He ain't."

"Is he what we're supposed to pack up and run from? Are you saying he's dangerous?"

"He ain't a natural person. He looks like one 'cause he wants to. But he ain't human. That's for damn sure. And honey, you don't have to believe me. Ain't a fact of life out there you got to accept. You don't have to swallow the notion that gravy's good on grits or fish swim or shit stinks. But a fact is still an actuality."

Lucille's words echoed around my kitchen a long time before I asked, "What did you see?"

"Frankly, I don't know what it was except, well, shit honey, there's a power in him, and it's growing. That's why we got to go."

"Lucille!"

"Baby, whatever he is, he ain't dangerous yet. This is what kept me from running out of here as soon as I woke up. And this is the thing that gets me. He, whatever he is, he does love you. Even in that brief little time I had, I could see it. It's just that he's like a child with matches and dynamite. Whatever's working on that boy, it ain't done yet, and he hasn't figured out what to do with it. So, honey, like I said, it's time to ship out."

I hated how small my voice sounded when I said, "I can't, Lucille."

"What do you mean, you can't? Honey, you *better*!"

That's when I took a deep breath. I concentrated on my two fists as I said, "Lucille, I'm not going anywhere. Not now. And if you really believe what you're saying, and he's not dangerous yet, I need you here. At least for one more day. Then maybe I'll go with you. But I'm not running from him. Not without an explanation. I deserve that."

# Clement

I would want to hold and comfort Willow so desperately. Even when she would steel herself to ask, "What are you?"

I wouldn't speak for a long time. I would let Willow study me, then say, "I'm essentially nothing, Willow. Nothing at all. I'm energy that can take form. I'm the ocean wave. I'm moonlight. I'm nothing, Willow. It's just that I can be anything. I wish with everything in me that you could accept what you see. Accept the heart of me that I've tried to share. To hear my truth, you will have to be strong. If you really want to know, I will tell you."

Quiet and firm, Willow would say, "Tell me."

I'd rub my face with hands that Willow would study hard. The shoulders I drew in as though cold, she'd decide they were like what she remembered. She would accept my saying, "But I can't do that here."

Willow would look at me as though I'd dissolve in daylight. She'd go down the steps behind me, avoiding my touch. When we got to the Calliope, I would look into the water wishing I could drown there. The clouds were pale rose and platinum. Across the wide Calliope, lights from homes, streetlights, cars and trucks blinked. The coke ovens, their flames and steam columns billowing, all of that would shimmer on the golden ribbon that turned iridescent gray, becoming brown, then navy. An early star would shine. I would breathe slower. Finally, I would say, "I'm sorry, Willow. If I could have told you without scaring you, without risking someone else knowing . . . At first, I was just delighted by the chance to be with you. In time, this lying by omission became hell for me. It hasn't just been the last few weeks and knowing that your grandmother was coming and, if everything you said was true, she'd know. Willow, I may have been selfish in pursuing my feelings for you, but was wanting to know you so wrong?"

"You lied to me."

"I came to love you."

Straining to hold back tears, Willow would shake her head and hold up her hand for silence. When she was ready, I would say, "Remember I once said that if anything ever troubles you, go to the river? The river enjoys sound and will try to help? Well, rivers aren't the only places where those powers exist. Your Lucille may not understand why, but she knows."

Willow would back away, crying, "Clement, how am I supposed to believe this?"

"You don't have to, but I'm telling the truth. So know this if nothing else. I need you, Willow."

"How could you?"

"Willow, I'm fighting two battles now. One is inside. I'm wrestling for my soul. The other is out, Mother and her demands. You see, Mother musters ships a thousand times bigger than those Great Lakes freighters. She summons armadas hundreds of miles long that churn through the air, sucking moisture up from Earth, growing bigger and more powerful . . . more charged. She commands violent storms, Willow. That's what my mother does. She makes tornadoes.

"Do you remember the petite woman with the long fingernails and blue scarves? You noticed her fragrance of juniper and honeysuckle in my hallways. She had dark eyes just like mine, Willow. She was waiting for you as you left for work one morning. Remember how you were afraid to meet my mother? The point is moot. She's met you."

Slowly, recognition would fill Willow's face. She would whisper, "That makes her very cruel. She kills people."

"Willow, at best, my kind are merely Life's agents. We are born and die. Father was a little stern, a little rigid. He was old, and I loved Father very much. As a child, my daily challenge was making Father smile. When he and then Grandmother Beah were gone, I ran away. But there are times when change is needed. Mother does that. When she's finished, the air is cleared. Life can begin anew."

Willow would close her eyes and shake her head, saying, "It's horrible."

"No, dear one. It's natural."

"You say that because your kind, they've got the power."

I cover my face a moment, then say, "To some extent, every one of us has the power. Look at the tremendous poverty here and the pain and suffering it causes. Yet others have the wealth and capacity to ease so much of that. They could take a little less so that others could have much more. But do they? At some point it's every man for himself, survival of the fittest, and let nature take its course. And nature will."

"Is that you, Clement? Is that what you're becoming?"

"This is what I am of, Willow. This is the monster that your Lucille wants you to run from. Look at me."

Remembering my own crisis after Mother's devastation of my apartment. Remembering how Willow grabbed me and pulled me back, I would want to hold Willow's hands, caress her strained face, protect her. After some time, I would say, "Father was the most magnificent being I have ever known. He shepherded the lights that are awaiting their next life's opportunity. How could I do something like that? Just thinking that the expectation would come was overwhelming. It's becoming less so. Willow, I don't want to leave here. I don't want to leave you. To stay, I have to be strong. I have to plan.

"I love you, Willow. I can do that. Love was with our beginning. I could not hurt you. I could not hurt anyone here. Even with the power your Lucille talked about. You know, Willow, power is a scary thing . . . even in the right hands if it's the wrong time. Willow, things are happening to me. You may not know exactly what I am. Hopefully, you now understand that, and please listen carefully, although I'm not what you thought, what you thought I was, I am."

Without ever looking at me, Willow would back away.

Like prayer, I would whisper, "Please, Willow. Please don't leave me."

# 32

## Willow

### Friday and Saturday,

### September 21 and 22, 1979

### Moon: New

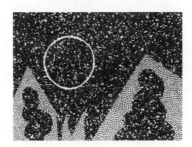

I ran around the corner so Clement couldn't see me struggling. I had so much stuffed into me, I couldn't breathe. When I could finally get in some air, I got back to Ruby's, but never knew how.

Jimmy'd been helping all day. But family sent him on so many errands, we never spoke. When I saw Jimmy's car still in front of the Svenson's, my nerves got even shakier. Walking into that crowded house didn't help. Ruby had a big family, and they ate and drank and laughed a lot. In Ruby's living room, kitchen, even her bedroom, I heard all kinds of stories.

"Hey, Joe. Remember your birthday last year when Aunt Ruby showed us she could still dance the Twist and the Mashed Potatoes?"

"How about that giant collard Cousin Ruby grew? Who'd she feed that thing to?"

"I think the best thing about Grandma Ruby was the cookies she baked for our Christmas trees."

"If you told the truth, you'd say it was her visiting. While she was there, you never got whoppings."

I had just found a corner to sit in and felt ready to start wailing when Lucille shoved a glass in my hand and said, "Drink that. All of it. And go on up and get some rest. Tomorrow ain't gonna be no better. There's hard and bitter truth we got to deal with sometimes. You've had enough for one day."

I thought I'd never sleep again. Next thing I knew, Lucille was shaking me and saying, "Come on, doll. You don't want to miss your landlady's funeral."

I was still groggy and had a headache when I squeezed into the back of Mrs. Faraday's car. With Amos in the front seat and me between Lucille and one of Ruby's cousins, a tall, exotic-looking woman named Faye, we drove up to Corinthian Baptist Church. From that little hilltop, I could find Ruby's house by Clement's sycamore. I could see beyond the coke works and the Calliope River winding like a blue ribbon. As Mrs. Faraday turned onto the blacktop road that cut through wildflower fields, she said, "Mr. Akkadian, do you remember the special candy my husband used to make?"

"I sure do. Ruby loved that stuff. So did I."

"I will see if I can find his recipe. It was a bittersweet candy. Difficult to make because it was soft and hard. Old-timers still ask for it. My husband would be happy. It is nice to be remembered for sweet things."

Amos said, "It was like a Sugar Baby, only bigger and had different flavors. Almost like a jelly bean, but better. Yes, why don't you make some more, Mei-Yeh. For old time's sake. For Ruby."

Mei-Yeh said, "I guess I was thinking of that candy because sometimes it's hard to understand how special things are, even little sweets. It was an expensive candy. Many just knew that the cost was dear. They sampled but never bought."

"Well I got dad-blamed lots of it. Ruby and I like to got sick from eating so much."

Mei-Yeh giggled. "Yes, you surely must have."

Amos snorted. "That's 'cause life done taught me to get my goodies when I can."

"As we see," Mei-Yeh sighed, "very little lasts forever."

"Amen!" Faye and Lucille said that together.

Most of Good Sky, even Jimmy, was in Ruby's church. I was still too dull, too much like a robot to feel anything except a deep, wasting sadness. After Ruby's service, helping carry flowers energized me. As we stood above Ruby's grave and the preacher said how we began as nothing and returned to nothing, I wanted to shout, What about the life we've got to live in between?

Clement came then. He looked like he always did, yet with an air that made everyone quietly draw back. Everyone except Lucille. She actually strode up to Clement. In fact, Lucille set her shoulders, braced her legs and stared up at Clement hard. And Clement, he just stood there and accepted it.

Finally, Lucille backed away a step, tilted her head and studied him some more. When Lucille strode back to me, I saw Clement bow his head a bit, as though humbled.

Holding my hand, Lucille whispered, "I said to him, 'Thank you. For my grandchile's sake and mine, I'm glad I met you proper.' He understood, and I never opened my mouth."

The wind lifted Clement's long, coarse hair. Odd shadows played across him as he stared at Ruby's casket. His face was so hard with grief, it hurt to watch him. Clement put down his bouquet of black-eyed Susans, bleeding hearts, sage and thyme like a lost child. But when Clement glanced at me, his eyes seemed a century older. Then he turned back toward Cabrilla. In the mad sensations tearing at me, the main thing I understood was that Clement knew Lucille would see him for what he was, and he hadn't run when he knew I'd need him. My lungs wouldn't let me breathe in or give out until my mind admitted that I wanted him. That I needed to comfort, kiss and be loved by him. That's when Lucille gripped my hand tight.

I saw Marla and remembered when she asked if I learned anything more about Clement. I told her that he was just a nice guy having problems. I again heard Mei-Yeh Faraday telling me that we could only get great popcorn if the skin could take the heat and pressure exactly long enough. I thought of Frau Edda giving Terry and me chocolates and licorices and saying how, even when our best parts seem *kaputt*, maybe they're only a little crushed and waiting to grow again. "Lord help me," I whispered. I pulled my hand away.

Although his back was to us, Clement paused. He raised his head and squared his shoulders. When I reached for him, Clement found my hand and held it. Then Clement whispered, "Thank you, Willow. I need you."

A repast was being served in the church. As folks headed back, the air got colder. High up, the wind whistled. Leaves torn from treetops flickered and whirled. The grass stiffened. My throat and nostrils dried. Dark clouds rushed over Good Sky spitting lightning. Then a brilliant blue stroke split into blinding blades and crackled into the town. Puffs of dust rose, then settled. After that, as fast as the clouds came, they went away.

Silence gripped the hilltop until Amos said, "Damnedest thing I ever saw."

Mia Svenson asked, "Can anyone tell what got hit?"

Clement held my hand tighter. I saw Lucille roll her eyes toward him as she pulled out a cigarette and said, "Reckon we'll find out soon enough."

Clement's intensity as we drove back to Good Sky was like the day he took me to the old cabin after the fight with his mother. But he radiated a kind of power that, though I wasn't scared, froze me in my seat.

Except for Clement's sycamore, Good Sky looked okay. Charred twigs covered curbs and sidewalks. One fallen limb, big as a regular tree, jabbed through Clement's second-floor window. Another leaned against the Valdezes' house. But the sycamore trunk and its other two main branches were unharmed.

"I can't see any more of this," Clement said. "I'm afraid of what I might do." He walked toward Hibiscus. In the block after Maple, Clement stopped at a redbrick house where most of the mortar was gone. The house was big and had a garden space in front where ragged rose and peony bushes grew. Small yards on both sides were overgrown. Parts of the wrought-iron fence sagged. Ivy climbed over the fancy carvings around the windows and doorsills. Most of the window glass was missing. Wallpaper with faded pink and yellow flower patterns could be seen inside. Surrounded by other buildings, the house looked awfully alone.

Softly, Clement said, "This is an amazing place."

"It's just a house, Clement. An abandoned old place that used to be nicer than anything else around here."

Clement went on, "You know, I think this home once had a lot of land and then parcels were sold until neighbors crunched up right beside it. Look at the windows. You could say that they're hollow. Or, now that the glass is broken, you might think that, for the first time, they're really open. Sometimes our existences are like that. Our lives can get pretty defined and confining, like the walls of this house. Even when we can see what's out and what's out can see in, the glass distorts reality and keeps the inner and outer worlds from interacting. Well, I wanted to feel fresh, unrefracted light, Willow. I wanted to splash in rain that fell like liquid amethyst. I wanted to taste real salt beneath frozen oceans. I wanted to hear avalanches fall off mountains so big they made a mole hill of Chomolungma. Willow, you just cannot grasp how restrained my life could be."

"You sound like you're going back."

Real quiet, Clement said, "I'm not giving up. I'm just facing reality. Like the rooms inside those windows, I'm thankful I no longer have to stare in awe at this world as though it were beyond a glass partition. The window went up. I jumped out and let wonder pour into my life. It's been fun, scary, up, down, hot, cold and sometimes I've been more dead than alive. But at least I was alive."

"Clement, why do you compare your life to that run-down house?"

"It is pitiful, isn't it?"

"Very few people seal their windows. We can lift them to catch a cool breeze or let out smoke or bring in outside noise when the four walls get too quiet. Most windows work that way."

Clement smiled, but he wasn't happy. "You're right, Willow. But keep in mind that the pivotal word here is 'most.' "

Clement breathed in, then out, seeming to release a lot that troubled him. He stood taller. He took my hand. We walked in silence all the way to the Calliope. As he looked out over the water, Clement said, "People have all kinds of stories about how the world began. Some believe that many things started at once, and they give the beginning to what they know.

"Some think that first there was only one being. One wholeness. One energy. Out of silence and nothingness, a first awareness emerged that learned It could have an impact. It could create vibrations, send out It's voice and hear, feel, touch. When It realized that It's energy could manifest, it was like understanding one's shadow for the first time. The First One began learning. And with learning, there were needs. The first was a way to recognize It's Self. First One would dream and then companions came whose existences were bright lights in a darkness that was never understood as night. What satisfied most was the aural, the best being heartbeats, river currents, tides ebbing and flowing."

A blue wisp veiled the sun. I got a feeling like when, in the country, from far off, I could hear storms coming. The sky overhead might have been clear, but the crickets chirped songs into air so quiet and treetops so still that leaves twirled straight down.

I shivered and said, "Clement . . ." But he kept on, "Once there was no this and that, Willow. There was no before and after. There was no other. Whatever there was, was the First One. That is why, even now, in the differences that have been made, we seek pieces of First One's light and warmth and music in another. That is where love is. That's what happened to me, Willow. That's what I found in you."

# 33

## Jimmy

### Friday, September 21, to

### Tuesday, September 25, 1979

### Moon: New to Crescent

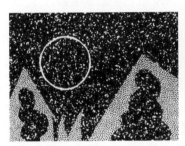

All of Friday, I can't get near Willow. When I try, someone arrives with a month's worth of luggage. Mrs. Graham's people talk a lot. Tell stories of faraway places and far-out folks. I enjoy them. Relax. Smile. Listen until Lucille sends me to the bakery. For groceries. To May Belle's for dishes. Back again for silverware. May Belle takes her time. Chats about the weather. Flowers. The beauty in glassware. The artistry in porcelains.

Saturday morning, I stand on a rise that's more air than earth. Where I watch Willow go to Clement. Where I ask: Why a man like him? No meaningful job. No decent home. Sullen. Sad. But who am I to protest? To say that Willow deserves better? Who would be better? He opens doors. Haven't I always closed them? And so I understand. Even with nothing, he has more.

Lucille swaggers up to me. Sucks her teeth. Says, "I told you, don't go breaking my grandchile's heart."

All day, there's no sign of Willow. No Clement. I spend the weekend running for French vanilla, strawberry and peppermint ice creams. To Mrs. Faraday's for warm pans of gingerbread, apple cake, paper plates and napkins. To the Applegate Mall for detergent, fabric softener and herbal teas. Then Mr. Akkadian wants help moving furniture. Jump-starting a battery.

Sunday evening, I look across Evergreen before driving home. Under the amputated sycamore, through the deepening dusk, I see how Willow leans. How her tenderness brightens his haggard face. They never notice me. Not when I slam the door. Start the engine. Blast the radio. Hear the forecaster say, ". . . partly sunny in the morning. Becoming mostly cloudy in the afternoon with a chance of thunderstorms. Warm and humid with high in the eighties. Wind from the southeast increasing to twenty to thirty miles per hour and gusting."

It's hard to drive for wondering, Will I have a chance to create a world where Willow can wrap her universe around me? Take me to the fields? Scratch the earth and plant me? Let sun and rain fall? Let me grow? Bear fruit? Be harvested? Dried? Heated? Explode into the life that should have kept going nine years ago?

I get home. Go straight to bed. Hours later, someone shouts, "Jimmy!" I rush to the dark hallway. No one stirs. I hear whispers upstairs. Despite the moonless night, everything is gilded. My easels, frames, boxes of paints, cans of turpentine, linseed oil, my palettes, the brushes, fine woven canvases, everything looks like half-formed ghosts under the sheets. I wipe the dust off old photo albums. I lift a volume. Open. See them all. Even in black and white, Josephine Daniels' brass-handled umbrella shines red. The royal-blue dress glows. Grandfather Virgil, when he was young, grins slyly in that Panama hat. The cross shines on his bare chest. I see the knife sheath. I turn other pages. There's Great-grandmother Arnethea. She holds a ladle and copper measuring spoons. Great-grandfather Caleb stands with that walking branch. Chickens and hounds in the background. His hat and Arnethea's hair sparkle. Puddles at their feet shine. Quiet laughter lights their eyes. The girl who would one day adopt Dad stands between them.

I close the album. I look around the attic. In a corner. In a hazy gold oval. I hear the berimbau. A Black man in old sailing clothes spins. Cartwheels. Lonnie stoops. Balances on hands. They sway. They twirl like maple seeds. They fly.

A drummer beats: da-da-da-da-da-da-da-da-Dah!-Dah!

I hear: CLAP!-CLAP!

Hundreds sing of Kwanzaa. Middle Passage. Odunde. I find Lonnie's djembe. I sit through the night. Fingers and then palm. For the souls who are God's Eye and Hindsight, Tha-Thump.

For Willow, Tha-Thump.

For clouds moving like sheep. For the rails. For rock and hemlock. For frigid wind, crushed bones and blood dripped on snow-crusted pine. Tha-Thump. Tha-Thump.

I yank the sheets off my easels. I open the boxes of brushes. The trays of paints. I write Mom and Dad a note. Shower. Don't shave. Notice my eyes become gray. My hair thickens. I'm taller and paler as I walk to my Lincoln. That's where I hear, ". . . rush hour still an hour away. Expect a day that's partly sunny becoming mostly cloudy by later afternoon. Thunderstorms likely. Some possibly severe. High seventy-five to eighty degrees. Winds twenty to thirty miles per hour from the southeast and gusting."

Trees are summer olive, goldfinch, honey and Titian red. By a small white church, a stenciled sign reads, CHRISTMAS BAZAAR, SAT., NOVEMBER 3, 9–4. The only paint left on countless weather-beaten, turned-to-charcoal barns says, CHEW MAIL POUCH TOBACCO. TREAT YOURSELF TO THE BEST. On cardboard outside a long wooden shed, orange and black letters offer, APPLES, CORTLAND, MCINTOSH. APPLE BUTTER. CIDER. BLUE GRAPES.

I see signs for taxidermy. Another says, DEER PROCESSING, 5 MI. Points down a gravel road that vanishes into forest. In a town I could drive through in three heartbeats, I refill the tank. Newspaper headline includes photo of vandal bear pillaging garbage bins. Cashier boasts that there are no traffic lights in entire county. Houses are miles apart. Every doorstep has pumpkins. Some yards have bundled cornstalks. Little ghosts made of tissue and torn sheets hang from porches, bushes and trees whose leaves shimmer.

I drive until the road becomes dirt. I need no map to find the small field with junked cars. Rusting buggy wheels. Ancient tractors. The woods lay long blue shadows across dry grasses. Pheasants rise suddenly. Their wings thrash. Bristling earth plummets to a silver cord called Angel River. Down there, evergreens jab as though on rumpled beds of nails.

A rusting sign warns, DANGER. KEEP OFF BRIDGE. It's a dark steel web stitching earth and sky. Not named for its color but the coal mine and its train. The Yellow Butterfly.

Looking across Adoria Gorge, I think of a woman on her back, knees raised and wide. The tracks across Yellow Bridge are dull, oxidizing. I gaze with eyes that feel like mechanical lenses. I hear them whir in and out as focus shifts. Steel replaces my flesh. Crossing the bridge, I stumble. Sometimes my foot breaks through weak timber. I creak. Come crashing down. Struggle up stiff and awkward.

I am halfway across when I feel Lonnie's warmth. Feel his heartbeat within my chest. Share his vision of steam pulsing above distant trees. Hear the train hoot and whistle.

The bright sun cools. The sky is pearl gray with stark white and pewter clouds scudding below. Sharp smoke stings my tongue, nostrils and eyes. I blink. Marvel at the brilliant red and golden leaves. At flickering shadows. Lonnie's breath brushes my neck. I smell swamp mud and Spanish moss on slow and luscious evenings. I taste barbecue smoke, gumbo and fried chicken feet dripping gravy. I hear pots clatter, mosquitoes and folks talking low.

The Yellow Butterfly rumbles onto the bridge. It's bigger than any engine I've ever seen. The light from its Cyclops eye drills through me. I feel nothing but air and these ties shimmying. I hear nothing but wind and pines grunting harmony as the engine huffs, "Death, chah-chah-chah. Death, chah-chah-chah. Death."

When I wonder why the bridge doesn't collapse, I see four-year-old Melinda giggling at my hand shadows. Mom reading *Snow White*. Dad's old truck. My daughter's first Christmas tree. Abebi laughing, dancing as Lonnie drums. Lonnie putting pennies on the tracks until dark iron obliterates my sky. Until all that's left are their faces. Josephine. Virgil. Caleb. Arnethea.

The engine crashes through me. Iron and steel disintegrate into glittering sprays of hollyberry, tiger lily, yellow radiance, sunlit forests, blazing turquoise, dark plum, wisteria and more. Hues I cannot name. So vivid they hurt. With face against splintered lumber, long, green leaves cover my newly exposed flesh. Encased and in darkness, I feel them wither and husk. Hours later, I watch my chrysalis crumble, its dust and ashes flaking into Adoria Gorge.

When strong enough, I rise. Drag to my car. Drive into a bitch's brew. Turbulence that jars and rocks. Shuddering thunder that swallows my high beams. Lightning lighting my way. The radio is static. In slashes, I hear: "Severe weather." "Mansfield, Ohio. Cleveland." "Parkersburg, West Virginia." "Monster tornadoes strike." "East central Ohio." "The Calliope River." "Good Sky."

I hunch. Cling to the steering wheel. My wheels hydroplane. I stare through torrents swamping my windshield. Another car slides into my trunk. I sideswipe the guardrail. Bang my head. Bite into my lip.

Phone lines are down. The winds shove. Rip away a wiper. I can't wait. I fight an hour for each ten miles. I plow the car through water that swirls past the bumper. The engine quits. After it dries, I creep along murky roads littered with broken trees, fallen telephone poles, sheet metal, animal carcasses and wrecked cars. It's dawn when the coke ovens top the horizon. Ahead, rows of red car lights and state trooper beacons end at shattered buildings rising midhighway.

I stumble, wade and stagger through debris. My hands are fists so long, they can't be anything else.

Good Sky is bent. Battered. Fire trucks clutter Evergreen Way.

I ask for Willow. Neighbors stare like I'm a ghost. Point.

At the river, I've never known such a sky. Never seen water glitter this way. Never felt mists rise so dazzling.

# 34

## Clement

## Monday, September 24, 1979

## Moon: New

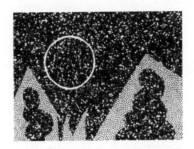

After Mother's assistants moved the Yukon's storms south into Oregon, that snow became a rain system big enough to shove the desert storms east. Then they sank a sea of cold air with a narrow band of snow into the Dakotas, Nebraska and Iowa, letting high winds push storms and warm air from southwest Kansas into Mississippi, Tennessee and Kentucky. Thunderstorms raged from Louisiana to southern Illinois.

Mother's first phalanx then blasted across the Midwest and continued toward Milwaukee, dying. As the main polar jet stream recharged and with the ground still warm east of St. Louis, her next storm systems ignited.

Meanwhile, a cold front colliding with warm air drawn from Mexico over Texas, Louisiana and into South Carolina detonated thunderstorms that raged from central Ohio to the Carolinas. Mother's emissaries then forced the polar jet stream hurtling from southern California to South

Dakota, south to Missouri, stirring up the violence that they would drive our way.

Overnight, Mother's stewards had eased warm air toward Lake Erie, delivering it an hour before daybreak. When that air crept north of the polar jet, the secondary surface low in northwestern Ohio deepened so fast that balmy air stalled over east Ohio and northwest Pennsylvania, flaring into storms near Toledo.

A pearl-gray veil of low clouds lightened but never revealed dawn at Good Sky. By eleven, as the cold front approached from western Ohio, our air pressure fell and the dew point kept climbing. Winds building higher up broke the stratus into soft gray stratocumulus.

By early afternoon, the west was overcast. Surface winds had built to thirty-five miles per hour from the southeast. To the north and west, sunlight glittered through the miles-high thunderheads capped with icy cirrus fingers. A low-level jet one mile up pumped in moisture from the Gulf of Mexico. As Mother's supercells rocked nearby Mansfield, Good Sky's temperature reached eighty-two degrees. The dew point registered sixty-nine. Her assistants were still building the warm moisture feed.

Three-thirty P.M.

Thunder, lightning and hail battered Cleveland and the area between Parkersburg, West Virginia, and Cambridge, Ohio. Mother's agents then backed surface winds to the southeast and increased vertical wind shear through the atmosphere. The first cumulonimbus cappitiallus, the supercell thunderstorms, formed west of Good Sky while cumulus capped by dense cirrus from distant western storms gathered. Our eastern horizon was still blue.

Four-fifteen P.M.

Funnels were dropped at New Philadelphia and Barberton, Ohio. Just south of Cleveland and near Canton, tennis ball–size hail fell. More funnels formed. Downdrafts from thunderstorms north of Youngstown and from the lead section of the supercell south of Canton converged on the moist air channel between Akron and Good Sky. Within ten minutes, a tornado landed twenty miles west of Alliance. Cumulonimbus darkened Good Sky's southwestern horizon. Distant lightning flared like a fireworks finale. The wind slowed.

Four-forty P.M.

Although still light to the east, the sky was like coal on Good Sky's northwestern horizon. From a new mesocyclone forming near the main storm updraft's core, a second tornado struck fifteen miles to our west-southwest. Continuing to draw the moisture-rich warmth that had been developed days before, Mother drove that thunderstorm east along the prior storm's outflow boundaries. Cumulonimbus mamatus approached Good Sky. Their lightning sizzled.

Mother's assistants kept the upper atmospheric winds moving from the southwest while intermediaries veered the surface air eastward. Others choked off the energy flowing into the supercell south of Cleveland as the new supercell near Canton moved east-southeast to maintain its moisture feed.

Four-fifty P.M.

Mother's agents retracted the first tornado back into its thunderstorm while she personally widened the second tornado to nearly half a mile. As the supercell main updraft core moved over Alliance, winds from the east dropped to five miles per hour.

Mamatus clouds converged above Good Sky. West-southwest, the distant cloud base lowered, rotating fiercely. Continuous lightning ripped the sky. Ice chunks big as baseballs fell.

Four-fifty-five P.M.

Mother's tornado widened to three-quarters of a mile. The sky was curdled, swirling and ultra-blue-black. With Good Sky's western horizon brightening, then came that eerie calm. Mother's powerful updraft core, nearly stifling in its warm and moist stillness, moved overhead. Rain and hail stopped. Nothing moved until, on the far south side of the hill miles across the Calliope, her vortex breached the horizon ringed in lightning. By then, Mother had built rotational speeds to nearly three hundred miles per hour. The funnel was almost one mile wide and barreling toward the river at over fifty miles per hour.

I knew without having to see how deliberately the silver and electric-blue cylinder splintered trees, gouged buildings, tossed trucks, rutted the landscape and sucked up what Mother pleased. Miles away, shredded cornfields, forests, homes, schools, concrete and trailers were discarded. For all the destruction, not one person had been killed. Mother was meticulous. When Mother cared, she could do that. She could.

By the time I got to the embankment, rain heavy as manganese pounded me. Rock-size hail blasted everything. The wind cut like razors as the funnel drew the Calliope down so low the bottom showed. I was about to holler, to rant into the winds, to threaten and roar when I was wrapped in light. I felt nothing except a sunbright quiet spread over tall, bowing grasses. People dressed as colorfully as stars chanted softly, but grew quiet when Mother said, *"Hijo mio."*

Standing straight, shoulders back, head high and calm, I answered, "Mother."

*"Se te acabó el tiempo."*

Time. It was elastic and yet went nowhere. She was wrong. Time could never be up.

Calmed as the storm whirled around me, I wondered why I'd been so upset. After all, coolness broke thunderstorms, therefore their tornadoes, just like a lack of heat shut down stars. A storm's own rain could collapse its updraft. I also knew that confrontation, that friction energized and transformed. It created tension, a stress that could strengthen. It was necessary in the same way that power was maintained only by the upward flow of warm energy.

In that moment, I felt—I knew—that if I would fill that space with some minuscule part of my will, I could make everything Mother was doing stop.

# 35

# Willow

## Sunday, September 23,

## to Tuesday, September, 25, 1979

## Moon: New to Crescent

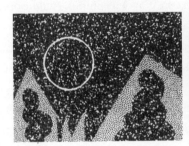

Sunday morning, I asked Clement if it was hard being human. He looked at me with his marvelous black eyes and said, "With one exception, there's nothing in this universe that is hard for me to be. When I was running away, I always avoided worlds where life developed beyond the natural systems. It seemed that just living was complicated enough."

I massaged Clement's chest and asked, "Is that one exception being human?"

Clement smiled. "No. That's not so bad. After all, my kind was human once. As with Mother, some occasionally return. The really tough one is being myself."

Finally, I asked, "Why'd you do it, Clement?"

Clement smiled. He looked pleased and contented when he said, "I did it to know you, Willow."

"That can't be all."

Clement moved over me and kissed me. I loved feeling his body cover mine. I got misty eyed a little as Clement said, "You give me so much, Willow. In your anger and your laughter. In your guarded moments and your openness. In your courage."

I enjoyed his admiration and other things for a while. Then I crossed Evergreen, set the tables and served food at the big lunch for Ruby's family. While helping them pack, I realized their mood about Ruby was so much like a celebration, it was hard for me to stay sad. Jimmy was around, but Lucille, Mrs. Faraday, Amos and May Belle kept him busy. There was so much to do. Lucille would leave in the morning. Everyone else was gone by sunset, and Evergreen Way was empty. Neighbors had parked elsewhere. Only Cabrilla had returned.

By the time I got back to Clement, he wore silence as heavy as a soaked winter coat. I thought I should leave and got up when he grabbed me and said, "Don't!"

Clement held me tight and whispered, "Don't be afraid." I heard a sound like crinkling cellophane, then lightning and thunder blasted so fierce, I got dizzy. The building jumped. A whole section of Clement's tree dropped past the window. Lights went out, then came on real dim. Frightened, I grabbed Clement.

"Trust me, Willow. Nothing will hurt you."

He looked quickly toward his front window and was on his way when a vicious sizzling followed by a blast like an atomic bomb blew Clement backward. Silver-blue torched my eyes. I was thrown to the floor. Through the ringing in my ears, I dimly heard glass shattering, metal groaning and hubcaps rolling on cobblestones. All the air felt breathed up.

When Clement lifted me, he felt stronger than I remembered. Kissing my face and eyes, he whispered, "You'll be okay, Willow. I won't let you be hurt." Clement spoke in fits like he thought I was dying.

Thankful that I wasn't deaf, I waited for the blank brightness that was breaking into dancing balls to finish dissolving so I could see. I heard nothing but stone silence until I recovered enough to get to the window. One huge tree section lay up the middle of Evergreen Way. Its leafy branches blocked the entrance to Cedar. The other part was sunk into Cabrilla. Clement's eyes were black fire. His jaw twitched. I never saw such hardness. Then his anger slid into exhaustion. While one hand gripped the window ledge, Clement rubbed his face with the other and said, "Please, Mother. No more."

Neighbors gathered below. Looking down, Clement asked, "Willow, what does our love mean?"

"It means everything to me, Clement."

"Can it break? What could destroy it?"

The only thing I could answer was, "Nothing."

"By nothing, Willow, do you mean space? That no distance, no amount of time can change what we have?"

"Clement, what I mean is something could come along and fold up the sun and pack it like laundry. The stars could crumble. The mountains could flop down flat as that street. The oceans could roll like boiling potatoes. It's nothing compared to what's in my heart because this love is like a flower garden. And each flower is stronger than steel around what I hold for you. My garden was always there. But it wasn't until you that the seeds had the water and the sunlight and the temperature to grow. I like this garden, Clement. I want it forever."

"Please remember, Willow, because it's not tidal waves and earthquakes that destroy what's great. What we can see, we can deal with. It's the small and invisible things like whispers. Like mosquitoes that numb and draw blood before we've noticed. Like doubt. It's tragic when little things bring low what is good and beautiful."


Monday morning, passengers were boarding Lucille's bus when she turned to me and said, "Willow, there's some things I figure your momma and Mariah didn't tell you, and you weren't in Homestead long enough. Frankly, there didn't seem much need. Especially after that Anderson boy moved on. But he appears to want you back, and if you let him come sniffing around, make him pay. That boy's got plenty, and you ain't going to be young forever."

Lucille leaned closer, "You should have noticed by now that there's a breed of man that actually wants to be worked. The more stuff he hauls home, the more like a man he feels. So don't go being backward this second time. As for our friend across the street, if it wasn't for his being, well, you know, I do believe I could like him even more. Despite his troubles, we could have a real good time. He moves like my Boston. Honey, I do declare there's things like slim hips, firm backsides and a certain way of walking that smart women develop an eye for."

Lucille sighed, then shrugged. "Oh well, he's going through a lot to be with you. Your heart's leaning his way so all I got to say is, pray. I'm rooting for him. Even if he isn't, you know, one of us, he cares. He's trying like no man I've ever known. Be sure and tell him I'm sorry about his car. But by now, from what I see, he can just—"

A tall and handsome, Hershey's Kiss–colored bus driver said, "Ladies, we've got to get going." Lucille crushed her cigarette and slipped a mint in her mouth.

"Just what, Lucille?"

"Here chile," Lucille handed me an envelope. "Take this money, and be nice to yourself. And don't pay no attention to what I was starting to say. I'm trying to think of too much at once. But remember, if you need a place to stay or just want to talk, pick up the phone. I know your landlady's people said they wasn't going to sell the place, but sooner or later, you'll want another home. You're too young to be holding up in this little town and as far as Homestead goes, I'm about ready for a change myself."

I sat in the MileMaster Train and Bus Depot and looked at people waiting on benches and the pictures of the old-fashioned buses and trains and, in the center of the station, the big mirror ball that had a few more scratches than when I'd first come. I looked at the ladders for men working on the skylight.

After the Amtrak came and left, I found Clement outside the

MileMaster. Sunlight glinted red and gold in his hair, across his shoulders and down his arms. I hadn't seen Clement since I passed him helping the neighbors move the tree. I looked for any trace of worry or anger or trouble, and Clement smiled. I felt like I couldn't keep seeing him stand there like that. I'd have to either die or run into his arms.

I extended one hand. In Clement's skin, real faint, there were lights that made me think of his candles. As Clement walked me to Faraday's, I thought how his struggles were chipping him down to something beautiful. I wasn't the only one who noticed. Folks we passed greeted Clement with a solemn regard.

Mrs. Faraday was talking to May Belle in front of the bank. When she saw us, she said, "Willow, you don't have to come back to work today or even tomorrow."

"I'm ready," I said.

Mei-Yeh shrugged, then, with eyes sparkling, licked her finger and held it to the wind, saying, "Looks like we might get some rough weather today. My toes," playfully she limped a bit, "they're talking to me real loud."

Mei-Yeh saw Clement tense and smiled at him, saying, "But what's a little rain? We could use a change, don't you think? Besides, as with trees, every storm survived strengthens the roots."

When we reached the loading-dock door, Clement said, "I love you, Willow. For always. Remember that."

I said, "I love you, too. For always."

When Clement kissed me, I felt like a hundred lifetimes rushed through me.


In the country, I could sense the temperature dropping or rising by the degree. I could see the clouds changing miles away. I could feel the grass bending and watch trees sweeping their branches in new directions. I could smell the earth releasing what was locked inside way before rain crossed the horizon.

Town was different. Even in a small place like Good Sky, nature was muted. Monday afternoon, the weather stayed so muggy, everyone complained. Walking home, it didn't take long to see that we were in for more than an ordinary storm. The winds shoved in thick, dark clouds that seeped blue-silver down through our air. High up, shrieking winds bullied across the leaden sky. Rain and then hail fell like little bombs. Lightning and thunder crashed and blasted. The world held its breath. Then, no doubt about it, I saw her face hovering high but clear in the clouds.

Wider than life, the tornado writhed, hypnotizing, a monster dance whirling toward the Calliope River. As it got closer, the wind was like giant hands shoving trees and buildings. I was cut and wasn't sure what little things slashed me. Tree trunks and huge limbs, plywood and aluminum siding tumbled into cars and houses. Dirt and leaves and paper, curtains still on the rod, awnings ripped from porches and shops, a suitcase, even a tea kettle and chest of drawers flew past and crashed into walls.

Lights flashing in the vortex hurt my eyes. Lightning crackled so fierce and fast, I thought a giant machine gun was firing. The tornado's roar, the rumbling and groan of trees and buildings trying to hold their foundations, all that deafened me. Then I was back in Blue Meadow. I was being yanked into Mr. Allister's truck. I was tumbling into the Melkpaths' storm cellar. I was staring past the lantern at Frau Edda's jars of rhubarb, string beans and peaches. That's when, with crystal clarity, as though we were still in his mirror room, I heard Clement naming the candles. I remembered his face reflecting the glow. I saw his eyes loving that space.

I went very cold. Not knowing where Clement was, I screamed his name. I wailed as though somehow Clement might hear. Even though the thunder felt like a giant paw that kept shaking me, I hollered until I couldn't anymore.

Right when I was sure there'd be no Good Sky left, the tornado turned. It stormed off like a nightmare bride in a long, midnight and electric gown. I saw the tornado veer and waggle until it drew back up like the last of chocolate milk rising through a clear straw.

Good Sky was left cool, stark and strange. Trees, power lines and telephone poles lay every which way. Streets were lakes floating broken glass, pots, clothing, window frames, tires and chairs. I wandered between Clement's house and the one he'd shown me on Hibiscus. I went down to the Calliope and over to the MileMaster. Other folks were out collecting stuff and cleaning up. Everything looked ghostly. When it got too dark, I found my way back to Ruby's and listened for Clement. The wind bumping the windows made we weepy thinking of how it lifted Clement's hair. Trying not to notice dogs howling through the dreary night, I lit some candles and stared into them as long as I could.

I woke up just before sunrise. The lights had come back on, and the house throbbed. I smelled smoke and struggled out of bed, snatching some clothes. My kitchen was filled with biting grayness. Spinning red lights made an eerie bright-dark rhythm. Outside, spotlights lit fuming smoke like day. In snatches, a creamy orange scorched the walls inside Clement's house. Blue flames leaped from his third floor.

When I got downstairs, I tripped over hoses, bumped into the fire truck and splashed through water. Coughing, I stumbled toward Clement's door until Emilio Valdez pulled me back, saying, "The place is falling apart, Willow. No one can get in or out. We got to wait."

Carbon smeared everyone's faces. I grabbed neighbors, asking, "Did you see Clement?"

They shrugged. Then Renee Carpenter tapped my hand timidly. "Miss Willow, I was getting the newspapers to do my route. I saw Mr. Clement. He even tipped his head when he saw me. You know how he does."

"Did he . . . was he okay, Renee? Did he look all right?"

Real careful, Renee said, "He looked like he did the first time, Miss Willow."

"The first time?"

"Yes ma'am. Back at Christmas. One morning, I looked up and Mr.

Clement was there. But then again, he really wasn't." Renee frowned and twisted her lips. "I couldn't tell no one else that. Just thought I was imagining a part-invisible person, until there he was this morning. He was the same way, kinda there and kinda not. But maybe it was the mists and the smoke. Maybe I wasn't full awake. I know it sounds crazy."

"Where was he going, Renee?"

"Toward the river, Miss Willow."

I climbed over the hoses and edged past spray that made pale rainbows under the searchlights. From the river wall, I couldn't see the Calliope. I couldn't even see beyond my hands for the fog mixing with the smoke. Cracks and rust spots and peeling paint on the wrought-iron railing nicked my fingers. Finally, in a cone of lamp light, a man's figure appeared. I ran and grabbed him. Realizing he wasn't Clement, I said, "Oh, I'm sorry. I was looking for . . ."

"I know," the stranger said. "In this fog, seeing anything's going to be tough. It's a mess around here, isn't it? But the sun will break through soon. Things will get better, child."

As his footsteps faded, a boat hooted. It's light pressed through the fog like a key trying locks. That's when I remembered. I fumbled through my pockets and found my keys, then clanged the railing. I stopped, listened and heard startled ducks and geese. I tried again, banging harder. Nothing but the river.

"Clement!" I called. My mind snatched after forms in the fog. "Clement, please don't leave."

A bit of mist thinned. Through it, a small patch of river sparkled. I smelled peppermints, licorices, nonpareils. I tasted great big pancakes soaked in Karo syrup. Frau Edda's music and Momma's songs warmed my heart. I relaxed, and Clement held me, saying, "That's the joy of it, sweet Willow."

I breathed Clement's name between our kisses. When my heart stopped racing and my tears slowed, Clement said, "I couldn't just go."

Inside, I felt tiny and cold. I said, "So your mother won. She had her way."

"It seems that family will prevail." Clement smiled. "And, as I've learned, by any means necessary. But Mother has no power over me. At first, I couldn't figure out what was happening. I was changing and my efforts to stop it were as useless as trying to stop life. It hurts to admit, but I don't have to go, Willow. It's just that I cannot stay." Clement shrugged. "Who I am becoming begins to feel natural. I am finding my way. And it will be my way."

I looked up into Clement's wonderful eyes. His skin was again too pale. His hair floated free. He held my hands and said, "There are things that I feel and things that I will do that I am beginning to accept. And yet," Clement smiled, "I need not do things as they were before. As I now understand, fight and run and struggle as I did, there was no other way for me."

Clement moved his hand up my arm. He touched my hair. He pressed my lips.

I cried, "I'll never see you again."

Clement rocked backward as though my words stabbed him. After a second, he said, "Listen carefully, Willow. There's a song that grew in me. From light-years distant, it drew me to you and holds me still. That hold will never break. Not from my doing. It will keep me always."

Clement held me close. His arms were warm and strong. I needed them. I needed the way he lifted my face, kissed me, then whispered, "Please know and always remember that life lived here is a vivid dream, an illusion that flits before the eyes just before dawn. If you can hold a small place in your heart for what we have created, when you wake, I'll be there. What I fear is how time, for me, can be extruded. Moments without you will feel like eons. But worse, Willow, will be that the difficulties and joys of your life will make you forget."

I touched Clement's heart and said, "I'll remember."

He smiled and whispered, "I'll await you."

The fog drifted up the Calliope. It rose like pale dancers and faded into a purple and pink dawn. Clement stood away from me and said, "Don't say anything now, Willow. Let me see you looking this lovely, the morning light on your face, in your eyes and hair, on your lips. Let me hold this."

As the last wisps of fog lifted, Clement was gone. Geese flew over. A misting rain fell until the whole world shone golden and silver. Inside the Calliope were purple mountains. Castles shimmered down there. Gold glinted. I heard singing. Voices chanted my song in new and wonderful ways. The hands of my mother and father, Mariah and Cleopatra, and all who came before, they helped me stand.

In the days after Jimmy helped me get home, I sat alone and marveled at all the memories that came back. I heard Frau Edda's rocker on the porch rugs, the way catkins rustled and the noises that filled a carnival. I thought about how, a long time ago, I stole that candy apple. There was the quick happiness of getting something for nothing, but I paid a price and, for me, candy apples were never sweet again. That wasn't the worst of my thieving though. Turned out, I'd been so good at stealing me from myself that I didn't know I was missing. As I pieced myself back together, I realized the green I'd been looking for wasn't on Mr. Porky's pool table. My green was like kale, young corn and clover. The kind I could water and tend and keep growing.

I understood Momma singing,
*This little light of mine*
As she pulled weeds
*I'm gonna let it shine*
As string beans and sweet peas plinked into her pots
*All through the night*
'Cause Daddy bought Momma flowers
*I'm gonna let it shine*
*Everywhere I go*
As Momma finished one of her quilts
*I'm gonna let it shine*
*All over this world*
*I'm gonna let it shine*

As Momma put me to bed

*This little light of mine*

I used to think the light was a candle. And if I had that light, its heat would glow right under my heart. Now, especially on really good days, days like this one, I feel like I'm the light.

*I'm gonna let it shine.*

# 36

## Grandmother Beah

After all my darling grandson said, you probably thought I'd gone to the "Great Beyond." Well, nothing ever lasts as long or is over as quick as we think. And I do believe some of us have earned a round of applause.

First, my daughter May Belle had some trees and a bathtub fall in her shop. What little bit wasn't destroyed by the ceiling collapsing and the rain coming in, she gave away. James helped her and got that fancy chess set. Nice touch. So May Belle's packed up and gone.

The flooding, hail and winds ruined Amos' junkyard and little office. Couldn't have thought of a better ending myself. Makes a mother proud. And I really admire how Ruby handled things. After all, she had to leave. The sun crossed the equator that Sunday.

Months before, I let folks know I was ready to retire. I'm glad Frank Singer could take over the popcorn factory. Makes me feel good giving the business to nice people.

None of us like interfering . . . much. And it's hard for me to admit, but my oldest son's wife does have her good points. She's real meticulous. It's just some of us believed that she was too tough on the boy. Knowing he hadn't come into his full powers and my daughter-in-law had lost all patience, we had to do something. We all know what her temper's like, and if that sweet child's mother stayed steamed too long, well . . . But then I always did believe she should have had more children. That would have settled her down some and taken the focus off of my heart, my Clement.

The boy was bound to come around. And time, since it only affects those paying attention, means whenever he was ready was soon and good enough. But could we explain that to his mother? It really is beyond me why my son chose her. Especially at that stage in his life. Still, I do admire that girl's tenacity and, like I said, her attention to detail.

Ruby, May Belle, Amos and I, we're all pleased with how we disguised ourselves. But then we're old hands at that. That's why my Willow child's grandmother couldn't see us, and she's good. In fact, she's so talented, I had to work a little special stuff when some of the more unusual family members came for Ruby's finale. My sweet Clement, he never suspected a thing. Not until the very end. By then, of course, he was on his way.

And my dear Willow child, *Mein süsse Schokoladenpüppchen,* my sweet little chocolate doll. I made sure she had the book she'd loved so. The one with Siegfried and Brunnhilde and Parsifal and the Flying Dutchman and all the other heroes that I painted brown. It was on her counter when she and Jimmy returned. Thought that crooked table leg getting fixed would give her a smile, too. Just like James will in the years to come.

But there'll be mornings when she'll watch a freighter glimmering far out. The lake near their home will still be blushing pink. *Mein kleines lakritzkätzchen,* my little licorice kitten, she'll imagine the engines thumping. She'll feel the rhythm and remember the dancers. She'll think of morning light on heart-shaped pumpkin leaves and the tall and beautiful cottonwoods and elm and locust trees as dawn and the green reappeared.

Yes, I know quite well how like the sea, like the winds dewed and playing at dawn, young bodies rise and fall together. Willow will lean back, warmed as when my precious grandson once held her. Then the night's last star will flicker. She'll take a deep quivering breath, smiling as one tear drops. It'll seem to take years, maybe a thousand, to cool and slip from her chin. All in all, *Mein Kind der Sonne,* my child of the sun, she'll have a good life. After that, well, my darling grandson did make a promise.

Thank goodness this work is done. My strawberries, tomatoes and sweet peas need tending. Time to say, *"Zài jiàn."* Farewell, children.

# Acknowledgments

First, I gratefully and lovingly thank my daughters, Cassandra and Candace, and grandson Aaron Malik for their patience, support and endurance.

I thank Carl Richardson Gould and Margaret Kimball Blakely for this life, therefore opportunity.

Also:

David Blakely for his help in so many ways and for being the father my own could not.

Readers, troubleshooters and editorial guidance:

David Bradley• Casey Cox • Barbara Hausman Romella Kitchens • Cindy Lollar • Sophia Mah • Reginald McKnight• Gilbert Moses • Libby Reuter • Sherie Schmauder.

Victor J. Nouhan, meteorologist.

For his help with the German and insights on Hamburg, thanks to Thorsten Grigat.

For their help with the Spanish, much appreciation to Francisco En Elba Gonzalez and Catherine Gammon.

Also helpful with languages: Li-Hua Lan, University of Pittsburgh Department of Asian Languages and German.

For their inspiration, H. Jackson-Lowman and U. H. Wall.

For information on corn and its popping, thanks to Ken Boyle, Ernie and Carol of Refreshment Services, Inc. in Pittsburgh, Ken Ziegler of Iowa University, the Popcorn Institute in Chicago, Vogel Popcorn Co., Weaver Popcorn Co., Jolly Time/American Pop Corn Company and Orville Redenbacher Gourmet Popping Corn.


ARTS ORGANIZATIONS:

Centrum • Cottages at Hedgebrook • Delaware Center for Contemporary Arts • Djerassi Resident Art Colony • Dorland Mountain Arts Colony • Dow Creativity Center • Kalani Honua • Millay Resident Art Colony • Pennsylvania Council on the Arts, Artist in Education Program • Ragdale Foundation • Ucross Foundation • University of Pittsburgh English Program • Vermont Studio Center • Yaddo


MUSIC

Music was an indispensable part of creating and maintaining *Popcorn* energy. I'd like to acknowledge the following for providing mood and emotional range:

Earth, Wind and Fire's "That's the Way of the World" • Dean Evenson's *Ocean Dreams* • *The Universe* (a CD distributed by Distributions Madacy, Inc.) • Tony O'Connor's *Mariner* • Herb Ernst's *Dreamflight I, II* and *III* • Vangelis' "To the Unknown Man" and *Invisible Connections* • Steven Halpern's *Inner Peace* and *Higher Ground* • "Oh Happy Day" by the Edwin Hawkin Singers.


I'd also like to thank the following newspapers for providing information on tornadoes that struck in their areas during 1979: *The Hartford*

*Courant, The Lawton Constitution,* Lakeland Florida's *The Ledger, Kossuth County Advance, The Rosholt Review* of Roberts County, South Dakota, *The Worcester Telegram* and *The Sidney Argus-Herald* of Sidney, Fremont County, Iowa.

Special thanks to Harriet Wasserman, my agent, and to my editor, Michael Denneny, for their faith and guidance.

As a resource and inspiration, *Joseph Campbell and The Power of Myth with Bill Moyers* must be acknowledged.

Thank you to the Ungraded English Program pioneered at Westinghouse High School so many years ago.

There are so many who've helped *Faraday's Popcorn Factory* in very important ways. Thank you, all, including Oscar Hijuelos, Dorothy Randall Gray, Leonard Tolbert, Rik Sanjour, the Carnegie Libraries of Pittsburgh, the National Geophysical Data Center, Guy Ottewell and the Universal Workshop, Carnegie Mellon University Physics Department, the Pittsburgh Zoo and the public libraries in Lake Forest, Illinois, and Midland, Michigan. Much joy, and I hope all are pleased with our efforts.

SANDRA LEE GOULD worked in a steel mill while raising two daughters and earning her college degree. She holds a Bachelor of Arts in Media Communications and a Master of Fine Arts in English, both from the University of Pittsburgh, and an Associate Degree in Specialized Technology, Photography/Multimedia from the Art Institute of Pittsburgh.

Ms. Gould presented her first one-woman quilt exhibition at Pittsburgh's Manchester Craftmen's Guild. Her textile work has also been featured in regional and national spaces, including Wilberforce, Ohio's National Afro-American Museum and Cultural Center, New York City's American Craft Museum, Atlanta's Apex Museum, and the Smithsonian's Renwick Museum. She has presented two one-woman shows in photography (for Studio Z and at the Westinghouse Corporation's corporate headquarters) and is currently producing a book of photo essays about Pittsburgh's last steelmaking facility.